The Dule Tree

Bruce Adam

PAGE PUBLISHING
Conneaut Lake, PA

First originally published by Page Publishing 2024

ISBN 979-8-89157-027-6 (pbk)
ISBN 979-8-89157-046-7 (digital)

Printed in the United States of America

CHAPTER 1

The Crossroads

The darkness seemed to press in on her after she left the lights of the inn. Part of her wished she had taken up Darren's offer of a lift, but he had been drinking, and she felt sure he might be over the limit. Besides he had no doubt had a smoke before he met them in the Cross. He always had the sickly sweet smell of weed about him as if it was coming out of his pores.

Whose idea had it been to go out drinking on a Tuesday anyway? It had become one of their regular nights. This part of Lower Law was dimly lit, but as she made her way to Upper Law, she knew that the streetlights would soon peter out. Despite the blaze of Edinburgh across the Forth reflected in the still waters of the river, the path to the farm would be lit only by the moon that peeped coyly on occasion from behind the scudding clouds. There was a random scattering of houses after the crossroads, but they, too, would provide little illumination.

The crossroads.

She wished that Jennifer hadn't told them about all the superstitions that had been associated with crossroads since the middle ages. Since getting her history degree from St Andrews University, she was always anxious to show off her superior education to everyone. She had always liked Jennifer less than the other members of the usual gang that met a couple of times a week in the Cross Inn.

Perhaps it was the way she always called her Letitia when she was Letty to everyone else. She did it without apparent irony, but Letty detected a subtle sneer behind it nonetheless, as if she was emphasizing that a lowly farm girl had no right to such an apparently posh name. Perhaps she was just being oversensitive. Anyway, she liked her name. Her late mum had told her that it had been the name of a great aunt and that it meant "joy" or "gladness."

She suspected that Jennifer had always thought herself a cut above her and the other three members of the Law Society, as they had called themselves since school. Come to think of it, hadn't it been Jen who came up with the name? Perhaps, Letty reflected, she was entitled to consider herself as being in a different social class from her contemporaries.

Jen lived in the Big Hoose that sat brooding on the hill above Upper and Lower Law in the middle of a large estate. Letty's father had said, somewhat resentfully, she thought, that it stretched over around 1,300 acres. Jen's father was the local Nationalist MSP who undoubtedly could have afforded to send his daughters to private school, but that would have dented the man of the people, "We're all Jock Tamson's bairns" image he projected. Jen and her older sister had been to uni though whereas Letty still worked on her dad's pig farm. Angus was a mechanic, Beth looked after her ailing mother, and Darren…was Darren. Nobody really knew how he got by on unemployment benefit, but she knew he had a few less than legal enterprises on the go, one of which included a little dealing.

Jen hadn't found employment after uni and had to be content with doing some clerking for her dad—not that she needed the money. So really, she had no right to play the lady of the manor looking down on her serfs.

She could just make out the gothic shape of the Big Hoose up on the hill above the woods, and the sight only increased her nervousness. She was conscious of the hair on her arms beginning to stand up.

On the numerous occasions Jen had invited them all round to her house, Letty couldn't help being rather overawed by the sheer size of the place. Her whole house could have fitted into the reception hall. She always felt ashamed when any of the others came round to hers and was self-conscious of the stone floor in the kitchen where sat the oak table scored and gouged by the farmers and farm hands who had eaten there over the years. And then there was the smell of the pigs. Letty only really noticed it when the others came round, and she was sure Jen's nose visibly curled up, and she affected a little dry cough as if she was struggling with the fumes.

The shabby old-style armchairs and sagging sofa in the living room at the farm were a vivid contrast to the opulent furnishings and the expensive-looking artwork that adorned the walls of the Auld Hoose. They even had a game room in the basement with a full-size pool table and a sixty-inch TV screen.

Nevertheless, it wasn't the thought of the difference between Jen's home and her own that made her feel perpetually ill at ease when she visited the former. It wasn't Jen's dad either though Campbell Lake could be distinctly creepy, always making apparently innocent physical contact with her and the other girls—a hand on a shoulder or a light pat on the bum.

No, it was the house itself. There was something *off* about it. You felt it as soon as you got to the ugly black ironwork of the main gate. Then when you walked up to the house, the poplar-lined drive always felt dank and gloomy even in the summer with the woodland brooding in the background.

This impression was reinforced by the building itself. It faced south and never seemed to be lit by the sun. The facade had been restored using stone quarried locally, but to Letty's eyes, there was an ugliness to the outside of the house. Its sloping roof—a mansard roof Jen's dad had boringly informed them—with its jutting bay windows made it look as if the house was staring blindly into the distance while the turret on the west side looked as if it had been an architect's afterthought designed to somehow make it seem more baronial.

She never quite settled when she went inside the house either. Okay, the entrance hall was impressive with its polished wooden floors, its great stone fireplace, and the decorative woodwork of the banister on the staircase that stretched up to the upper floors. But for Letty, the staircase seemed out of line somehow; the first turn at the top looked off-centre and too sharply angled.

And the stained-glass window at the turn of the stairs was disturbing. It depicted a naked woman emerging from a pool, reaching for a quiver of arrows. Nearby, a pack of dogs were attacking a deer. Jen's dad explained it depicted the myth of the hunting goddess Diana or Artemis, who, spied upon while bathing by Actaeon, had transformed him into a deer, and he had been torn apart by his own dogs.

Darren had made a joke about it: "Bit harsh for a bit of innocent voyeurism, Mr. L." But it had done nothing to dispel Letty's unease. Besides, she frequently felt that someone was watching her when she was in the house. She would glance round abruptly to find no one there. Once she thought she felt the ghostly touch of a hand on her shoulder.

That was one of the reasons she never ventured upstairs. They were told it was out of bounds anyway because Mr. Lake had a study and office on the first level presumably containing lots of confidential political stuff, but she never felt curious enough to explore up there.

She had once caught Darren sneaking back down the stairs, so he had clearly had no such qualms. He had just smiled casually and placed a finger to his lips, and no more was said about it. She wondered if he was looking for something to pilfer, but he had always had a barely concealed crush on Jennifer, so he was probably looking for her bedroom, perhaps for a surreptitious rummage through her underwear drawer.

Distracted by her thoughts, she suddenly realized she was nearing the crossroads. The ancient sycamore loomed out of the night, a light wind stirring its leaves.

Again, that mine of local historical information Jen had informed them that it had stood for generations. It was known as the Dule tree because it probably had been the local gallows for years— Dule meant *grief*, History Brain informed them. It was situated at the crossroads because that was where they had buried criminals and suicides in the past—a ritual, she had said, that had been abolished only in the early nineteenth century. She said it in that affected voice she had put on since university, no doubt an embarrassment to her dad who, if anything, exaggerated his broad local dialect to emphasize that he was Scottish and one of them.

4

Jen had added that the crossroads was associated traditionally with evil. People said you could summon demons there or even Auld Nick himself. The night air was mild, but she shivered as she got nearer to the cross, and she felt a nagging urge to pee. She should have gone before she left the pub, but she knew her sudden discomfort sprang more from the fact that Jen's stories had got her spooked than the drinks she had consumed.

She tried to scold herself, *Come on, Letty, get a grip. You've done this walk a hundred times at night.* But wait, wasn't there something under the tree? A black shape that her eyes could only just discern in the layers of darkness created by the night and the overhanging branches. Was there someone standing there?

She stopped, almost resolved to retrace her steps back to the inn. She could get a taxi from there even though she couldn't really afford it. She peered into the gloom.

The figure she thought she had seen had blended back into the shadows. Was it still there? Had she just conjured the shape out of her fevered imaginings? She gave herself a mental shake and switched on her phone's torch function and pointed it toward the tree. When she moved it around, it seemed to her only to create more shadowy areas. As she edged closer to the tree, an owl suddenly flew up from it in an explosion of fluttering wings.

She stifled the scream that rose in her throat. For a moment, she simply stood gulping in air while her heart hammered in her chest. For fuck's sake, she was going to give herself a coronary at this rate. What was she, five years old? Afraid of the dark and nearly wetting her knickers?

Speaking of which, she would have to go. She couldn't hold out till she got home. Squaring her shoulders, she strode out with more conviction than she felt toward the tree, shining the phone around her as she approached.

When she reached the tree, she walked tentatively all the way round it, expecting someone to jump out at her at any moment. There was nothing. She looked around at the crossroads but as far as she could discern, the roads leading off in all four directions were deserted and there was no traffic. Admittedly, she couldn't see that far because the roads were quickly consumed by the darkness though down to the south, she thought she could discern the outline of a vehicle pulled up on the grass.

If there had been anyone standing under the tree, perhaps they had gone there. She realized that she had been holding her breath. She was conscious that her sudden exhalation sounded loud in the surrounding silence. Even the leaves of the tree had stopped moving.

With a last glance around her, she switched off her phone, quickly slid down her jeans and underwear, and squatted under the tree. The splash of her urine on the ground was exaggerated once again by the quiet around her. She had an absurd thought that if people were buried here in the past, perhaps she was desecrating their graves or maybe she was unconsciously enacting some kind of ritual for raising evil spirits.

For fuck's sake, I ought to be worrying about getting piss all over my shoes or some random passerby coming across me with my pants down, she thought, *instead of being concerned about conjuring up the dead*. The wind began to pick up once more, rustling the branches of the tree. It made her look up. Something was hanging there.

She hurriedly pulled up her clothes even though she hadn't quite finished, and she felt instantly the dampness in her knickers. She shone her phone's torch upward. At first, she couldn't quite decipher what she was looking at. As realization struck, she blindly stumbled backward, dropping her phone. Its light flickered and died.

But there was no mistaking what she had seen before the darkness enveloped her once more. It was a noose. It was hanging from a branch of the sycamore as if awaiting its next execution or suicide. Was this somebody's idea of a joke? If so, she was finding it as funny as a funeral.

She knelt and began groping wildly around the ground for her phone. Just as her fingers found it, she had the overwhelming feeling she wasn't alone. The torch function on her phone refused to work.

And then she saw a dark shape. A figure appeared to be standing perfectly still on the road that led toward the farm. It was as if it had been formed from the darkness or had risen out of the ground.

"Hello. Who's there?" Her voice trembled, and she knew she must sound like a frightened child. She tried again, willing herself to sound more confident and assertive but failing miserably. "Hello. Can I help you?"

Then the figure began to move toward her, imperceptibly at first but gathering speed as it approached. Letty took a few steps backward and then turned and began to run stumblingly back toward the inn. She had always been good at athletics at school, and her manual labour on the farm had given her a sturdy strength that she used to power her legs, attempting to put as much distance as she could between her and whatever was at her back. One thing was for sure, she had no desire to confront them or it.

She wasn't really religious, but she came from generations of country people who had a healthy respect not just for the turning of the land and the seasons but also for the old rituals and superstitions that had been attached to them. There might not be a devil with cloven hooves and a forked tail, but she wasn't prepared to bet on it, and she was well aware that evil did exist in various guises and manifestations.

A primitive dread clutched at her, filling her veins with ice. She felt she was running on the spot, the road beneath her trying to bear her back toward her pursuer. At any moment, she expected to feel hands grabbing her from behind, dragging her down to drown in a sea of ink.

She risked a quick glance behind her, seeing nothing in the murk. As she turned, she ran at full speed into a shape that came out of the night. She fell to the ground, winded. As she lay there writhing and gasping for breath, a figure leaned toward her. She felt as helpless as an insect about to be crushed by a giant boot.

CHAPTER 2

The Law Society

C olin Sark dashed round collecting glasses before customers started clamoring to be served at the bar again. Saturday night was always a busy one at the Cross. There were the usual regulars but trade picked up at weekends. The inn offered reasonably priced bar meals till 8:00 p.m. on Thursdays to Sundays. As if on cue, his mother appeared looking hot and harassed, balancing three steaming plates on a tray. Her traditional cooking drew in the punters, but tonight they were shorthanded.

Where the fuck was Janine? This was the fourth night in a row the barmaid-cum-waitress had failed to turn up for her shift with no explanation. His dad had tried calling her mobile several times, but it had gone to voice mail. The last thing he wanted was to drag his old man downstairs to help behind the bar. He always took Saturday afternoons off, and Colin was loath to bring him down to help serving before he was ready. It was one of the few respites he had from the long hours he put in.

Ever since they had bought and renovated the Cross Inn almost ten years before, his parents had been consumed by the business. They opened at eleven in the morning and closed the bar at eleven at night, but they rarely finished before one after all the clearing up and especially if they had guests staying. Then it was up early in the morning to take deliveries, supervise cleaning, go to the cash and carry, or any of the endless chores that went with being innkeepers.

His dad always put that down as his profession rather than hotelier or publican out of respect, he said, for the old ways.

Although Lower Law was a small village, the inn had provided them with a very decent income in the past partly because of its popularity with locals—the only other pub nearby, the Queen of the Forth, had a reputation for being a bit rough—and partly because it had a decent passing trade with tourists keen to explore the beauties of the Fife coast. The inn's four guest bedrooms used to be heavily booked in summer.

His parents even took separate holidays one week each per year: his mother to lie on the beach for a week on the continent and his father to go fishing up north. They wouldn't dream of closing up for a week. And Colin knew that lately business had been bad. It was the weekend trade that was keeping them afloat, and Colin had heard his parents arguing more frequently, usually about money. What his parents had thought a blessing on their move here was steadily becoming a curse. The inn had given them a living, but it now sucked at their souls.

He was determined that he wouldn't be like them. He had left school after his Standard Grades to help with the family business, and everyone assumed that when his folks became too old to run the inn, he would be there to step up though recent financial problems made that increasingly unlikely. Anyway, he was going to take the police entry exams later that year. He made no secret of his ambitions.

His mum had been supportive. Her own sacrifices were writ large on the lines that appeared more frequently each year on her face. And his dad was a borderline alcoholic, sinking two doubles swiftly from the whiskey optics as soon as his shift was over and drinking after hours with the usual hangers-on long after the bar had been closed.

His mother realized perhaps how easy it would be for her son to become shackled by the daily routine of the inn and the struggle to keep up footfall and how rapidly his youth and vitality could be poured down the drain like the slops from the beer trays if he accepted that this was his fate. His dad was more cynical: "It's no' like you'll become Endeavour Morse, son."

A couple of the punters at the bar rattled their empty glasses on the bar to get his attention. He hated that. It was as if they thought he was a dog, conditioned to react to a particular noise command. In a small act of rebellion, he took his time taking the empties back to behind the bar and loading them in the washer.

As he served them, he ignored what they fondly imagined was their witty repartee: "Could you no' see we're dyin' of thirst here?"

"Maybe thought if he was any longer, your hand would be shakin' too much to get your pint to your mooth, Billy."

That was another thing: he was becoming increasingly intolerant of the customers and their demands. If he didn't escape, he envisioned a moment when he would lose it over some crass comment and start smashing glasses into their smug faces. Right, that would do wonders for his future police career.

The door to the bar opened, bringing a brief draught of cold air into the overheated bar. It was Darren Boyd and Jennifer Lake. Not for the first time he wondered why they hung out together. It seemed to him as if they were chalk and cheese. She lived in the Big Hoose on the hill, and he had a caravan on the inappropriately named Nirvana caravan site, which was really a glorified field with a shower block and toilets situated to the west of the village.

Jennifer was as head-turning as ever in an expensive-looking suede jacket and designer jeans, her long dark hair looking as if she had just stepped out of the hairdressers. He thought she must notice the lecherous glances of the men at the bar, but she always looked too cool to be perturbed by them.

Darren, on the other hand, was his usual unkempt self. He always wore the same black jeans and T-shirt with a scuffed and old-looking leather jacket over it. His dirty blond hair looked as if he had been caught out in a storm. Colin acknowledged he wasn't bad looking and had a certain rough and ready charm but still. Jennifer's father, the big shot MSP, must have serious reservations about his daughter's choice of friends. No doubt the others would be in soon.

"All right, Sarky? How're they hangin'? I'll have a pint of Brewers Droop and a G and T for the lady."

Jennifer flashed Colin an apologetic look from her green eyes that hit him in the solar plexus as he began pouring a pint of Brewers marque. "Hi, Clipper. Busy tonight."

Everyone called him Sarky, which pretty much summed him up, but she always called him Clipper. It was no doubt some historical private joke, but he had never had the courage to ask.

Darren was unembarrassed as she handed him a twenty to pay for the drinks. "The delectable Janine no' in the night again? I miss her cheery wee smile."

"You miss her décolletage, you mean."

"Speak English, woman. I never did French at school."

"You miss ogling at her tits."

"You know I only have eyes for you, doll."

Colin couldn't stop the blush that suffused his cheeks at Jennifer's cavalier crudeness. Janine was not in her class as far as looks were concerned. She was the stereotypical buxom wench compared to Jennifer's sylphlike lady of the manor, but Janine made the most of her rounded femininity by wearing dresses that were just a bit too tight and very low-cut. She enjoyed the way the male customers' gazes would linger on her breasts as she leaned over the bar.

He had enjoyed the odd fumble with her after hours himself. She was a straightforward lass with no inhibitions about sex though he had never gone that far with her. He recalled with a twinge of lust and shame his gasping and hurried orgasms as he stood in the darkened car park of the inn, his trousers and pants round his ankles. Her breasts had been white in the half light as she moved her hand vigorously up and down his cock; his fingers were damp inside her knickers.

Jennifer, unlike Janine, appeared unaware or uncaring about the effect she had on men. "Those people are just leaving. I'll grab the table before the others arrive. Bring the drinks over."

"Aye, aye, milady."

He couldn't help glancing at Jennifer's firm buttocks in her tight jeans as she walked over to a table by the window. Darren caught his eye and regarded him with amused understanding. Colin felt his blush deepen.

"Seriously, where is our bouncing barmaid tonight?"

"Don't know. This is the fourth night in a row she hasn't been in. Not answering her phone."

"Perhaps she's bouncing some lucky guy's brains out as we speak," said Darren. He seemed unaware of the young barman's discomfort as he took his drinks. He asked quietly, "Need any merchandise?"

Colin had scored some weed from him on a few occasions, but he was trying to avoid doing anything that might jeopardize his ambitions. "I'm fine, ta. The others coming in tonight?"

"Aye, usual shoot-the-shit Saturday. Fuck all else to dae around here."

As Darren sauntered over to join Jennifer, Angus McKissock appeared. He was wearing a crisp white shirt and Lee Cooper jeans but still managed somehow to look as if he had just stepped out of his mechanic's overalls with his greasy-looking hair and wispy beard and his permanently oil-stained fingernails. He ordered a pint and went over to join the others.

Colin realized with a sudden pang that he was envious of the close-knit group that met regularly at the inn. He had been a year ahead of them at school, but he had been aware of their closeness even then.

He lacked friends near his own age mainly because of the anti-social hours he worked. He would have liked to be included in their circle. Darren was a bit of a waster, but he was likeable. He had known Angus for years since his dad socialized on occasion with Angus's dad and other local business owners and always had his car and van serviced at McKissocks' garage.

His acquaintance with Angus unfortunately had not provided him with an entrée to the group. Apart from his unrequited desire for Jennifer Lake, he found the other girls in the group attractive too, perhaps even girlfriend material if they were prepared to tolerate only seeing him when his shifts allowed.

Letty Vane had a certain robust athleticism to her that he liked, and he had found her occasionally regarding him appraisingly with her large brown eyes. Beth March always looked rather melancholy and downtrodden, but there was no denying her elfin prettiness.

Colin thought if she put more effort into her appearance—perhaps got her hair cut into a fashionable style, applied a little bit of makeup now and then, and even smiled a bit more often—she could easily emerge from the shadows cast by her friends.

He knew her mother suffered from motor neuron disease, and Beth was her main carer. The gossip was that the prospect of watching his wife succumb to the relentless progress of that horrible illness had driven Beth's father into the arms of another woman with what everyone judged was obscene haste. He was the groundsman-cum-gamekeeper at Jennifer's folks' estate, and Colin suspected he was less than tolerant about the weaknesses and infirmities of others.

So Beth no doubt had other priorities than paying attention to her own appearance. She used to bring her mother into the Cross after she was first wheelchair-bound for an afternoon drink, but she hadn't done so for a while.

As he thought of Beth, she appeared at the door. She glanced quickly once round the room to ascertain where her friends were then cast her eyes down as she headed to the bar. "Jack and Coke please, Colin." She never called him Sarky.

As he fetched her drink, he said, "How's your mum, Beth? I was just thinking it's been a while since we saw her."

Still not meeting his eye, she said, "Oh, you know, not great. She seems to have more bad days than good at the moment." Colin thought, *End of conversation then*, but she surprised him by looking briefly up at him and adding, "I feel a bit guilty about leaving her at night, but she has the television in her bedroom so she can watch the game shows and talent contests and that."

"You need some time to yourself."

"And what about you, Colin?"

"The only time I seem to get to myself is when I'm in bed." He laughed weakly at his own joke.

As she took her drink, a ghost of a smile crossed her face. It seemed to contain more sadness than humor. Then, not looking to right or left, she made her way across to her friends' table. Colin reflected that these were the longest conversations he had with her. He wondered when Letty would appear. She was the first to arrive usually.

*****

"Letty no' here yet?" Angus asked.

"Aye, she's invisible, and you're sitting in her lap." Darren's wit often amused himself more than others. "Seems to be catching these lassies disappearing. Sarky was just saying the pneumatic Janine's no' been at her work for the last couple of days." He began to sing the theme tune from *The Twilight Zone*.

"*Pneumatic*, that's a big word for you, Darren," Jennifer said playfully.

"Pulchritudinous then. How about that?" Darren replied with a smirk.

"It's not funny though. Did you no' see all the police activity up at the crossroads on Wednesday and Thursday?" They all turned to Beth, surprised at her interjection. She usually sat quietly till one of them made a point of bringing her into the discussion. "The rumor is they've found th-the remains of Carol Chalmers. You mind, she disappeared when we were at school. Mum wouldn't let me go out for weeks at the time."

"Christ, aye. Not be much left of her if it is her. What was that, seven, eight years ago? She was in sixth year when we were in fourth." Angus added, "Most of the guys had the hots for her and no' just the pupils."

"Sixteen goin' on 36-22-34," said Darren.

"Get your brain above your belt buckle, Darren."

"Just sayin', Jen, probably raped, murdered, dismembered, and buried in a shallow grave."

"Darren!" Beth took a quick gulp of her drink.

"Actually though, when you think of it, there have been a few unexplained disappearances over the years from these parts. You must have heard the stories."

"Before you commence the history lesson, Jen, whose round is it?"

"Fuck's sake, Darren, you sank that pint fast," said Angus.

"Thirsty."

"About time you put your fucking hand in your pocket. Anyway, I've still got half my pint."

"I'm havin' a few cash flow problems."

"It's all right, Angus, I'll get them." The others exchanged glances as Beth threw back the remains of her drink and rose. "Anyone else?"

"Well, I could have another G and T if you're sure you can—"

Eyes downcast, Beth headed for the bar. When she was out of earshot, Angus said, "I can't believe you were about to ask her if she could afford it. For fuck's sake, Jen."

"Sorry, it's just they can't have much of an income given her and her mother's…situation."

"She's come out of her shell tonight though, eh?" Darren tried to lighten the mood. There was an uncomfortable silence. Darren looked toward the bar. "Fuck, Beth, you were in front of those two wankers. I'd better go and help her, or she'll never get served."

"Get me another as well then. I'll be finished by the time you get your second."

As Darren went to the bar, Angus said, "You gettin' a bit anxious about Let? With the polis bein' up at the cross and that. Think we should phone her mobile?"

"Won't do any harm to check where she is." Jennifer retrieved her phone from her bag and was holding it to her ear when the others came back with the drinks.

"Letty," explained Angus.

"Good idea," said Beth and then looked worried as Jen indicated that there was no answer. "Wish we'd never started talking about missing girls now." As she sat, she looked behind her, her frown vanishing. The others turned to see Letty entering the bar.

"There you are, nothing to worry about. No sign of dismemberment."

"You shouldn't joke about things like that," Beth admonished him, but Darren gave her his cheeky daft laddie grin that he fondly believed charmed everyone into accepting even his most outrageous remarks.

As Letty stood at the bar, Len Sark appeared from the back to help his son serve. He exchanged a few words with Letty, looking concerned. She seemed embarrassed before coming over to join them. Angus asked a couple at a table for four if he could take one of their chairs, and they rearranged their seats to make room.

"Nice of you to join us at last, Let. Thought we'd have to trawl the Forth for your body," said Darren.

"Darren!"

"Sorry, I'm late. Women's Indoor Athletics Championship was on the box. Wanted to see the end of the heats."

"I remember you were pretty good at the two hundred meters at school, Letitia," said Jennifer. "And you were great at gymnastics, Beth."

"Till I buggered up my ankle," Beth replied stoically.

There was a moment when the others were transported back to Law High School before Angus said, "I like watching athletics."

"You mean you like watching girls running and jumping in those tiny wee pants they wear."

"Fuck off, Darren."

"What was Lechy Len wanting then?" Darren asked.

"Nothing." She looked discomfited and spilled some of her Blue WKD as she brought the bottle to her mouth.

"We were beginning to think you had joined the ranks of the mysterious missing girls of Law," said Angus.

"What do you mean?"

Jen explained, "He's joking. Apparently, the barmaid here's gone AWOL, and it reminded us of Carol Chalmers. Remember her, Letitia? And then there was all the police activity up the road. Don't suppose you've heard what that's all about?"

Letty began to choke, and Beth pounded her back vigorously. When she had recovered, Letty said, "I hadn't thought of her for ages."

Ever the diplomat, Darren said, "Christ, Let, you look as if someone's shat in your drink. What's up?"

Letty squirmed under the attention of the others and began peeling the label from her bottle. Finally, she blurted out, "Actually, I had a bit of a scary experience a few nights ago after I left here."

She told them of her walk home in the dark from the inn on Tuesday night and the dark figure she thought she had seen. When she told them about the noose hanging from the tree, Beth gasped and put her hand to her mouth.

"Then I…thought I saw someone watching me from the road, and he-she-it came after me. I was running back to the inn. I ran straight into someone and fell. I don't mind admitting I was terrified. Then I recognized Mr. Sark. He asked if I was all right. He could see I was upset, and he walked back here with me. He said he would have given me a lift home, but he'd had a couple of drinks."

"Couple of buckets," Angus murmured.

Ignoring him, Letty went on, "Anyway, he was really kind. Ordered me a taxi and gave me the money to pay for it. That's what we were talking about when I came in."

The others waited in a subdued silence for her to continue. Even Darren refrained from making a facetious comment. "The thing is I don't know how much of it I imagined. Jennifer had been telling us these stories about gallows and evil spirits that congregated at crossroads, and all of that was in my head."

"It's just history after all," said Jen with an awkward smile, looking around the table for support.

"You couldn't have imagined the noose, surely," said Beth.

"Who knows? I went past the tree the next day with Dad in his truck, and there was no sign of it. In daylight, it just looked like any other tree. I just wonder how much of it was just me conjuring up spooky shapes in the dark like when you're a kid and you're convinced there's a monster in your wardrobe or lurking under your bed."

She looked at them shamefacedly as she finished, expecting them to scoff at her, but Beth put a hand on her arm and said, "Sounds like a horrible experience. I'd have been really scared too."

They all sat quietly for a moment, but finally Darren couldn't resist. "I'm surprised the driver let you in the taxi."

"What do you mean?"

"After you'd messed your pants."

The girls began to condemn him roundly though Angus suppressed a snort of laughter and immediately apologized.

"I knew you'd think I was being stupid. That's why I was reluctant to tell you."

Jen, indicating Darren, said, "Ignore this idiot. We don't think you're being stupid at all. There are more things in heaven and earth, Horatio, than are dreamt of in your philosophy."

Everyone recognized the reference to *Hamlet*. They had studied the play in Higher English. Jen went on, "Ghouls and ghosties aside, don't you think it's odd that Law has had more than its fair share of people—girls mainly—vanishing? I mean there are stories about the Big Hoose in the past."

Beth said, "I don't think we should talk about that just now given Letty's—"

"It's okay, Beth. I managed to walk down here tonight as it was getting dark without having a meltdown. I didn't see any police, so whatever they were doing, they must have packed up. And Dad said he would pick me up later if I didn't stay too late."

"As I was saying, you only have to go back to the nineteenth century and the tales that surrounded the American owner of the house."

"Here we go, Local History Module 5."

"No, go on, Jen, we're interested," said Letty. She ignored Darren's exaggerated sigh and raised eyebrows.

"Well, you might have heard about the guy who bought the house from the local laird in 1866. His name was Gaylord Latimer."

"Gaylord, a name like that would get him drummed out of the flower-arranging club, eh?"

Darren looked round for appreciation, but Jen continued, "He had been a major on the Confederate side in the American Civil War. His family had owned a big cotton plantation in Arkansas. The story went that he couldn't accept the South's defeat in 1865, and he led a pretty unsavory and ruthless group of ex-Confederacy soldiers for a while after the war was over who marauded around the more or less lawless states robbing and *worse*.

"It's said that the readmission of Tennessee to the Union was the last straw for Latimer, and anyway he realized it was only a matter of time before he was hunted down. Somehow he'd managed to salt away a fair proportion of his family's wealth, and he got passage on a ship across to Leith."

"Why Scotland?" Beth asked.

"A bolt-hole as far away as possible from his pursuers? Though he might have been attracted here because it was the birthplace of Sir Walter Scott. The Southern aristocracy had all sorts of childish romantic notions about the chivalric past that they got mainly from reading the novels of Scott, books like *Ivanhoe*."

"Seen the old movie." Darren indicated his empty glass, and Jen distractedly handed him a ten-pound note.

"Slow down, pal," said Angus, but Darren went to the bar.

"In fact, the writer Mark Twain more or less blamed Scott for the Civil war. A society based on wealth, privilege, and, of course, the ownership of slaves was always going to come into conflict with the more liberal values of the North and President Lincoln.

"Latimer must have stood out like a cactus in a field of turnips when he arrived at Law and moved into the Auld Hoose with his gentrified manners, clothes, and alien accent. Plus, he was accompanied by a tall striking-looking Negro woman—you'd say African American now, of course. She completely mute. Rumors were that she'd been one of his slaves and he'd cut her tongue out for talking out of turn."

"This Gayboy sounds like a ray of sunshine. Must have fitted right in with the God-fearing Presbyterian farmers and fishermen here," said Darren who'd returned with his drink. "I hate to piss on your chips, Jen, but what has this to do with missing girls?"

"I'm getting to that. By all accounts, the locals were scared of the new lord of the manor and his sullen, silent companion, and the few of them that he employed as servants didn't last long in their work there.

"They came back with stories about strange goings-on at the house—debauched parties with whores that Latimer brought over from Edinburgh and strange rituals, séances, and the like. Some of the townsfolk saw the *dark-skinned* woman frequently at the crossroads at night. Naturally, there was talk of her communing with evil spirits and summoning the dead. Then local girls started disappearing."

Beth gave an involuntary sharp intake of breath.

"There was talk of them being held against their will in the basement of the house so the evil Latimer could have his way with them. Some people even whispered about rituals involving human sacrifice.

"According to local legend, Latimer held a séance one night in the turret room with four others present: a couple of the local-landed gentry, an Edinburgh prostitute, and the local minister's son, who by all accounts was very far from being as pious as his father.

"The next day, the servants found the girl lying dead at the foot of the stairs. When they went into the room, they found the son of the manse was also dead, frozen in his chair with his face contorted into what looked like an expression of horror. Latimer himself and one of his companions were unconscious, and James Montgomery, whose family owned a large estate near Leven, was gibbering and shaking in a corner of the room.

"When the two men came round, they refused to talk about what had happened. Officially, the girl's death was recorded as an accident and the minister's son was said to have died of a stroke. Montgomery never recovered though and was admitted to an asylum."

The others were all rapt as Jennifer went on, "Then one night, the daughter of the landlord of this place vanished, and all hell broke loose. Mein host made no bones about his suspicions that the master of the Big Hoose was behind it, and he and a few of his pissed-up customers decided to pay Latimer a visit.

"When there was no answer at the house, they went on a bit of a rampage, breaking windows, smashing some of the statues in the grounds, and so on. Apparently, two of the men managed to get into the house itself.

"It all becomes a bit vague after that, but it seems that the would-be vigilantes returned in a state of panic. A couple of what passed for police in those days—burgh constables or whatever—were called in and went up to the house to investigate. They found one of the villagers in the entrance hall. He had been killed by a single shot to the head. A trail of blood led them to another room where another man lay half dead. He had been shot in both knees and his…groin."

"Ouch." Angus and Darren crossed their legs instinctively.

"He didn't survive his wounds apparently. Of Latimer they could find no trace. But early the next morning, a local woman walking near the crossroads saw a body—sorry, Letitia—hanging from the tree there. It was Latimer's Black servant. Latimer seems to have disappeared into thin air. The house stood empty for years afterward."

Letty shivered as if someone had walked over her grave. Everyone was quiet. Even Darren seemed lost for some humorous observation. They didn't notice at first that Colin was standing at their table and were startled out of their reverie when he said, "Any empties here?" Jen handed him three empty glasses. "What's up, guys? Somebody steal your scone?" The girls smiled at him weakly, and feeling awkward, he moved on to the next table.

"Well, thank you for that cheerful wee story, Jennifer. I'm sure it has made Letty feel a lot better," said Darren sardonically.

"It's just—"

"I know, just history."

"You're not seriously suggesting that what Letty saw is connected to this, that what she saw was the spirit or something of the servant who died?" asked Beth uncertainly.

"Or maybe of Gaylord himself. You said there was a whiff of brimstone about him. I have come for your soul, Letitia, ma'am." Darren attempted to sound like a cross between a gentleman from the Deep South and the man who does voice-overs for horror film trailers.

"Stop it, Darren."

Angus piped up, "It's obvious what happened." The others looked at him skeptically. "This bunch of drunken vandals obviously went further than they intended. Latimer caught them in his house and shot a couple of them before he was overpowered by the rest. He was killed by the mob, and then they probably disposed his body in the sea. The servant saw it all, and they had to get rid of her too, so they lynched her to stop her from talking."

"Jen said she couldn't talk," Letty said absently.

"You know what I mean. And then everyone closed ranks so none of them could be accused."

"But why make the woman's death so public if they were trying to cover up their actions?" asked Beth.

Jen added, "And they must have been pretty cold to leave one of their own lying in the house grievously injured. And isn't there something strange about the shooting? Latimer was obviously used to handling firearms. One man with one bullet to the head and the other shot in such a way as to insure maximum pain? Second one smacks of sadism to me."

"Has anyone ever come across any other ways in or out of your house, Jen? Secret tunnels or priest holes or whatever?"

"Come on, Letty. Priest holes? Tunnels? This isnae an Enid Blyton book," scoffed Darren.

"I hate to say this, Jen, but I dinnae know how you can stay in that house, knowing what you do about its history," said Beth.

Jennifer suppressed the urge to say that it was preferable than to live in a characterless semidetached with dilapidated sheds in the garden on an estate full of similarly beige housing and said instead, "I've always been fascinated by the occult, but if there are ghosts in the Big Hoose, they're probably reluctant to show themselves. The place goes like a fair with people coming in and out to see Dad. Maybe we should hold a séance up there ourselves."

"Really, Jen. Haven't you given us the creeps enough for one night?"

"Beth's right. Can we change the subject?" There was a note of entreaty in Letty's voice. Jennifer shrugged, but it was evident from her thin smile and the way she immediately started looking around the room that she felt she had been unfairly reprimanded.

Darren broke the awkward hiatus that followed. "Any chance you could give the car a look over this weekend, Angus? The engine's missing a bit when I accelerate."

"Aren't you getting a bit old to be a boy racer?" Jennifer asked icily.

Darren drove a Citroën Saxo to which had been added alloy wheels, spoilers, and a body kit. Everyone knew that it was Angus who kept it on the road, working on it when his old man wasn't around and never charging Darren for parts or for his time.

"Bring it round tae the garage tomorrow afternoon."

"Thanks, neebs. I owe you."

"Ain't that the fucking truth."

"I'm going to give my dad a call and tell him to pick me up in half an hour."

"It's still early, Let," complained Darren.

"I said I wouldn't be late."

Just as she was about to phone, a man and a woman entered and made their way to the bar. The man was tall with gray hair and carried himself with an air of authority. His companion was an attractive woman with long red hair tied up in a chignon who looked to be in her late thirties. She walked with a marked limp and appeared to have difficulty raising her left arm as they both showed Len Sark their IDs.

Several of the punters subtly edged away from the bar, giving them a wide berth, and a few of them suddenly found the contents of their glasses to be very fascinating.

"Fuck. It's the police."

"What's the matter, Darren? You wouldn't have any illegal substances concealed on your person, would you?"

"It's not like you never indulge yourself, Jen."

The female officer spoke quietly but urgently to Len Sark, and he ushered them through the back.

"Wonder what that's all about? Think they've caught up with Lennie at last for his illegal shut-ins?" offered Angus.

"Your dad would be fucked then, Angus. He's always in here after hours."

"I wouldnae say always, Darren." There was an edge to Angus's voice that clearly made Darren decide not to pursue the subject.

"I've got a horrible feeling this isn't about licensing laws," murmured Beth. "This is about whatever was happening at the crossroads."

As if to confirm her fears, the publican emerged and spoke urgently to his son before going over to his wife. She looked so shocked at what he told her that he had to grab the tray of empty plates she was carrying before they fell to the floor. They both made a hurried exit to the back of the bar.

"Sarky, gonnae get your finger out," shouted one of the men at the bar, rattling his glass so violently it seemed it might crack. The young barman seemed not to hear, standing rooted to the same spot at the bar, staring at the beer taps as if he had never seen them before. His face was ashen.

Finally, he heard the man and glared at him angrily before wrestling his expression back into professional mode and serving him. The five friends at the table observed it all with a growing feeling of disquiet.

"When he's not serving, Beth, why don't you go over and try to find out what's going on?" said Jennifer.

"Why me?"

"Clipper likes you."

"He likes you too."

"He'd like to get into her pants—that's a different thing."

"Honestly, Darren, you can be so fucking crude at times."

"All right, I'll go." Beth went to the bar and hovered there till she caught Colin's eye. The others watched, fascinated, as he held up a hand as if to ward off her inquiry. Then he looked furtively around and drew closer to her. She took a step back as if she had been struck. Colin looked around, fearful of being overheard, before clutching Beth's hand and clearly issuing some urgent instruction.

Beth nodded and made her way back to the table as if she was wading through treacle. She stood there looking bewildered before Darren said with a weak laugh, "You look like he asked you to give him a blow job, Beth."

"It's not fucking funny, Darren." Everyone was startled by her vehemence. Beth rarely swore.

"What is it?" stuttered Letty as if she half feared to hear the reply.

"Colin asked me not to say."

"It's us, remember, Beth?" urged Jennifer. "Is this about Carol Chalmers?"

After a moment, Beth leaned in toward them and whispered reluctantly, "No. It's...they've found...they've found a body. They think it's Janine."

They sat as if they had been petrified suddenly. The sounds of the bar around them faded into the distance, and they were conscious only of Letty's low moan as she clutched at her chest.

CHAPTER 3

Lost Girls

Detective Sergeant Agnes (Nan) Wilson listened as DI Malcolm Bruce took the lead in questioning the landlord of the inn and his wife. She couldn't help but notice the inn owner's hands shaking as he listened to the news about the death of his employee. His wife seemed to shrink into her chair beside him as she twisted a tissue she had produced from her pocket though her eyes remained dry.

Nan shivered inwardly as she recalled the events of the last few days. She had huddled in her coat under a sinister-looking tree at a crossroads on Wednesday night as a biting wind drove in from the Forth. She had watched as SOCOS in white suits swarmed over a mound of earth. For some reason, they reminded her of maggots crawling over a piece of blackened fruit.

Not so inappropriate, she thought, as her memory shifted to that morning's briefing at the station. A photograph of the dead girl had been blown up and placed on the board: Janine Gunning, aged twenty-four. She'd been identified easily because her driving license and passport had been found in her handbag that had been buried with her.

So young, Nan had thought, as the DI took the assembled officers through the findings at the Cross. Janine had lived with her single-parent mother in a terraced house in the Upper Law. She was—had been—a barmaid at the Cross Inn. Her mother had said it wasn't unusual for Janine to stay out for nights at a time without explanation.

Nan reflected she had at least been spared the dreaded death knock though she had attended the postmortem with Bruce. Watching what had been a living, breathing body being expertly dissected sickened the stomach and the soul, but it was easier in her book than facing the reactions of next of kin to the news of a loved one's death: shock, disbelief, denial, then a crumbling to dust. She had witnessed more than her fair share of that.

Looking even rougher than he usually did—unshaven, pale, gray hair sticking up in all directions, and his crumpled suit looking as if he had slept for several nights in it—Bruce had managed at least to appear dispassionate as he talked about the girl. A female dog walker had discovered the body when her spaniel started digging at the crossroads. Bruce explained that the body was partially clothed—the top of the victim's blouse had been torn open, her bra pulled down, and her skirt pulled up to her waist. He had faltered briefly when he told them her *underwear* had not been found as if by saying panties or knickers, it would somehow remove another layer of dignity from the girl. Nan had liked him for that.

He didn't, however, spare them from the PM details. There had been a great deal of blood around the body, but the pathologist said it mostly came from the fact that the victim had been penetrated both vaginally and anally by a large blunt object. There was no trace of semen.

The perpetrator had carved some crude-looking symbols on one of her breasts and her upper thigh using a sharp small bladed knife. These were being investigated, and the details were not to be made public. But the cause of death was asphyxiation. There were clear marks and bruising on her throat consistent with strangulation.

Even the more hardened cops in the room were silent after Bruce had finished, but this was quickly broken as they were galvanized when teams were assigned various duties: door-to-door inquiries (though, Nan thought, there were few houses in the vicinity of where the girl had been discovered), trying to trace Janine's movements over the past few days, and interviewing friends, boyfriends, employers, colleagues, and customers at her place of work.

So here they were. Nan had been so wrapped up in her musings that she failed to realize that the DI was addressing her.

"Sorry, sir."

"I was asking if there were any questions you would like to add."

"Was Janine a good worker?"

The Sarks looked at each other, puzzled.

"I've just asked that, Sergeant."

"Right, how popular was she with the customers?" Nan crossed her fingers that she hadn't missed the answer to this too. She had to focus, but her brain was fogged with fatigue.

"Very," answered the man. "She's always...she was always... havin' a bit o' a laugh and joke wi' them, like."

"The men liked her especially." It was the first thing his wife— Margaret was it?—had said.

Nan didn't think she had imagined an element of barbed disapproval, malice even, in her tone. "To your knowledge, was there anyone she was particularly close to or perhaps someone who didn't like her or perhaps someone who paid her a lot of unwanted attention?"

The inn owners looked confused as well they might, thought Nan. Bruce ought to have known not to ask a complex series of questions like that. He seemed to have forgotten the basic rules of interrogation.

Mind you, he looked as tired as she felt. His eyes were glassy with dark circles underneath them. He probably hadn't slept much that week. She knew how hard this must be for him—a dead girl on his patch. When she had joined the Fife force from Edinburgh, she had heard the stories of the teenager who had gone missing a few years before on his watch.

Even those officers most loyal to the DI admitted that he had been so obsessed with finding her that it had cost him his marriage and almost his career. She was pretty certain that he still worked the case clandestinely in his own time. She forced herself to pay attention to the couple's answers. Her notebook was in her hand, but she had yet to write anything in it.

"No' really. She didnae have a steady boyfriend or that."

"Plenty of casual men friends though," his wife chipped in. Her critical tone was more marked this time.

Sark gave her a sharp look before going on, "As I said, everyone seemed to like her. She was full of nonsense, and that appealed to the regulars. As for anyone givin' her unwanted attention, well, Janine lapped up attention, and she knew how to deal wi' men that overstepped the mark. She wasnae a shrinkin' violet if you ken what I mean."

"Thank you, Mr. and Mrs. Sark. We may need to talk to you again. And we'll need to have a word with some of your customers, especially the regulars. Could you give DS Wilson a list?" The DI rose as if to conclude the interview.

"Aye, we'll try."

Margaret Sark said unexpectedly, "Had she been...interfered with?"

"I'm afraid we're not at liberty to discuss details of the case at this stage."

"So she was," Mrs. Sark concluded grimly, giving her husband an ambiguous look, partly triumphant as if to say, "See, I always knew she'd come to a bad end," and partly accusatory. Nan grimaced as she got up, her knee stiff with pain from sitting on the hard kitchen chair the Sarks had provided.

So much for the quieter life she had envisaged when she had transferred to the Fife Constabulary four years before from Edinburgh. She had seen more than her fair share of rapes and murders there, and now here was one right on her doorstep.

She had moved here because she knew it would be just a matter of time before the relentless current of crime in the capital sucked her under. Even before the incident with Chris Angel—shit, never had anyone been so misnamed—she had been suffering already under the weight of stress caused by her constant dealings with the sub-life forms that proliferated in Edinburgh's dark underbelly.

She knew her thinking was wrong—to view the gang members and junkies and pushers and dealers and prostitutes and their violent pimps as less than human—but her well of compassion had run dry quickly. Her original idealism when she joined the police and her pride in making detective had long been dampened by too many dead junkies in stinking squats with needles still in their arms, too many bodies in alleyways carved up for a bag of skag, too many blank-faced young girls shivering in thin clothes under bridges while they waited to rent out their cunts to the next fat drunk in the queue, and too many men trying to justify having sex with girls who clearly were underage: "She told me she was sixteen."

So she had suffered the insomnia, the IBS, and the embarrassed lies to her doctor about how many units of alcohol she consumed in a week. But Chris Angel had been the last straw. Perhaps she and DC Rab Lewis had been lulled into a false sense of security that day by the fact that the sun was making a rare appearance above the buildings of Great Junction Street in Leith. Everyone knew Angel was a prolific dealer who had already done time, but they were acting on a tip-off that he had somehow acquired a bumper load of coke that was stashed currently in his squalid third-floor flat.

They had knocked repeatedly at his door. There had been no answer, but she was convinced somebody was in because she had heard the sounds of a radio or TV being hurriedly muted when they arrived. She tentatively turned the handle. When the door opened, he came at them instantly like a bull, barging her aside and knocking Lewis halfway down the narrow stairs that led up to the flat.

She recovered quickly and took off after him, both of them leaping over a disoriented-looking Lewis on the stairs. On the next landing, he had turned abruptly with a look on his face that was both demented and somehow euphoric.

An excruciating pain in her left knee made her crumple onto the landing. It was then she saw the claw hammer in his hand. He raised it above his head, and she could only throw up her arm instinctively as he brought it down.

She had heard an audible crack, and the agony that traveled up her arm seemed to loosen all of her muscles. She could only watch helplessly—a puppet with its strings cut—as he raised the hammer again. Before he could strike, a body came barreling into him from the stairs, and suddenly Lewis was struggling to restrain him on the ground.

The hammer had been knocked from his grip, but whatever cocktail of substances he was on appeared to have given him an unnatural strength, and he managed to throw Lewis's not inconsiderable bulk off him and reach for his makeshift weapon again. She tried to find the strength to rise, but she was consumed by pain, and her head swam as soon as she tried to move.

Both men had now risen to their knees. As Angel brandished the hammer, Lewis locked a hand around his wrist and smashed his forehead into the other man's nose with a shocking sound of breaking bone and gristle. Angel instantly dropped the hammer and fell back onto the filthy landing, his hands clutching his face but failing to stem the stream of blood and snot that poured down it.

Lewis raised the hammer, his own expression a mask of rage.

She remembered shouting, "Rab, don't. The little shit's not worth it." Lewis appeared to come to his senses. He flipped Angel roughly onto his back and handcuffed him.

Every time she moved, every time she tried to lift her left arm, and every time she was aware of others noticing her limp but being too polite to ask what had caused it, she thought of that day. The aftermath of her surgery, the painful sessions of physiotherapy, the extended sick leave, and the frequent appointments with a counselor had all made her question whether she really wanted to return to her police career. Even when she had been cleared to resume light duties, she suspected that she had lost her nerve. How useful would she be on the street now?

She had talked it over with Rab Lewis. He knew she had saved his career that day. Nevertheless, he had been disciplined for using excessive force to bring in a suspect despite Nan's impassioned testimony in his favor. That wee scrotum Angel had won damages as well after suing the police, so it had probably cost Rab any prospects of promotion for the foreseeable future. She knew his advice to quit was driven partly by his bitterness.

The move to Fife then had been something of a compromise with herself. Her four years there had gradually brought her some kind of peace though she still woke up at nights, drenched in sweat from the terrors that still haunted her dreams.

The worst things she had faced in her time here had been domestic assaults or assaults after the football or after the pubs closed. There had been some minor sexual assaults though she questioned the use of the word *minor*. Yes, there were ongoing problems with drugs and some incidences of prostitution, but it was hardly on the scale of the capital and rarely involved organized criminal gangs.

And now this: rape and murder and a year's old unsolved disappearance that she feared was about to rise up from wherever it had been buried like a rotting corpse in a horror movie.

When they returned to the bar, Bruce went over to a group of men standing there. When he showed them his warrant card, they looked at him as if he had just produced a turd from his pocket. Nan looked swiftly around the room. Most of the customers caught her eye and quickly turned away. There was a group of five twenty-somethings at a table who continued to scrutinize her with frank curiosity and interest as she limped over for a word with the landlord's son.

"Hi. Colin, isn't it? I'm DS Wilson." He barely glanced at her warrant card as he took a tray of glasses from the washer. "Got a minute?"

"Well, we're really busy so—"

"Won't keep you. Must have been a shock to hear about Janine." His anguished eyes met hers briefly, and he gave an almost imperceptible nod. "Were you friends?"

"I wouldnae say friends exactly, but we worked together and got on all right."

"You never went out with her?" The question seemed to shake him.

"No, no. No' really." His face flushed.

"Not really?"

"I mean we never…not in a boyfriend/girlfriend kind of way."

"What kind of way did you go out with her then?"

He looked around frantically. "I'd better serve that—"

"In a minute. So your relationship with Janine." He was unable to meet her frank gaze.

"I mean, it was nothin'. We had the odd kiss and cuddle and that, usually when we'd both had a couple of drinks, but neither of us took it seriously." He had reddened so much that Nan thought his face might burst into flames.

"When was the last time you saw her?"

"Maybe about 7:00 p.m. on Tuesday after her shift? She'd been on since 11:00 a.m."

"Did she leave the inn with anyone?"

"No. Only…" Nan waited. "I noticed she'd got changed in the ladies' before she left. She'd taken off the dress she'd been wearing and put on a smart-looking blouse and skirt. Quite formal for Janine. And it was obvious she'd made a bit of an effort with her makeup and hair and that."

"You think she was meeting someone straight after work?"

Colin shrugged his shoulders.

"We'll talk again. Meanwhile, if you can think of anything else, contact me." She handed him her card.

He scurried away to serve a waiting customer. Nan turned to find a nervous-looking girl at her elbow. She was attractive with large brown eyes in a face whose complexion suggested she spent a lot of time outdoors.

"Excuse me, are you with the police?"

"Detective Sergeant Agnes Wilson."

"Only we heard about…about Janine, and my friends over there thought I should talk to you."

So much for trying to be discreet, Nan thought, as the girl indicated the group Nan had noticed earlier. Two of them were pretending only a nonchalant interest, but the pale girl in the group stared over like a startled deer, and the blond young man in the scuffed leather jacket seemed to baulk at her scrutiny as he hurriedly pulled out a packet of cigarettes and went outside.

"I'm Letitia Vane, and it's probably not relevant, but I thought— we thought—I should tell you about the strange experience I had the other night just in case."

The girl fidgeted from foot to foot as if she needed the loo as she recounted her experience at the crossroads on Tuesday night. As she spoke, Nan felt a jolt of electricity running up her spine that made her suddenly alert. Tuesday night, the crossroads where the body had been discovered, someone's presence there, the noose, and the girl's encounter with Len Sark shortly after fleeing from a potential attacker—each revelation lit up her instincts like flares.

CHAPTER 4

The Big Hoose

Campbell Lake breathed a sigh of relief as his last constituency interview of the day ended. A local pressure group had handed him a petition with a thousand signatures on it objecting to the proposed housing development on three sites in the area: the site of the recently demolished Pitlaw Primary School, the site where a large factory had been built with some generous funding from the Scottish government but never came into operation so that it sat there like a great white elephant, and a site along an area near the seashore.

They argued that there was insufficient infrastructure to sustain even more additional housing in the area. There would be far too much demand placed on GP and dental practices and, ironically, primary school provision. The conservation lobby in the group was angry at what they saw as the destruction of habitat for skuas and surf scoters. Lake had looked suitably concerned. He presumed they were some kind of seabirds, but he wouldn't know one if it flew in his window and perched on his desk.

He said he was impressed by their arguments and had assured them earnestly he would look into all the implications although he'd added they would have to understand that would also include consideration of the benefits to local trade.

What they didn't know was that he had spoken on Sunday to Paul Rand, the owner of Rand Properties. He knew Rand and some of his less-than-savory friends, but then a lot of people he'd dealt with during his time in office had dodgy acquaintances. He had guaranteed the property developer that he would use his influence with the council with its SNP majority to ensure the green light would be given for the project. Once Lake had smoothed over local difficulties, he expected the usual donation to his own secret bank account.

He knew he was taking a risk. Then there was that other matter with local businesses. If that came out, it could mean the end of his political career though knowing some of the people Rand was in bed with, that might be the least of his worries.

On paper, he didn't really need the money. His marriage to his late brother's wife had made him extremely well off. But he liked to prepare always for any eventuality, and a nice little nest egg of his own money would help that preparation if circumstances should change.

After all, he hadn't foreseen his first wife, Laura, walking out on him after that unfortunate business with his PA that had almost sunk his career—sexual harassment indeed, a drunken feel after a drinks reception. She had been as up for it as he was. No surprise when the bitch was persuaded to settle out of court.

His second wife, Eloise, was personable enough though she was not the beauty Laura had been. Campbell saw a lot of the latter's beauty in his younger daughter who had preferred to stay in close proximity to her friends and her chosen university rather than to move down south with her mother after the split. Her elder sister had moved to Grangemouth to work as soon as she had completed her degree in chemical engineering. He hardly saw her now. Her regular visits to the family home had stopped as soon after her mother departed.

Eloise had never taken to Jennifer perhaps partly because next to her, she became too aware of her own physical shortcomings: her rather too masculine bearing, mousy hair, and a mouth and nose that seemed too large for her face. But she came from old money, which was very attractive indeed. In Campbell's view, she had poured too much of it already into his brother Connor's ailing retail business before he had taken her aside and given her some sensible financial advice that effectively stopped the flow.

Before he drowned in a sea of bad debts, Connor did so literally, wading into the Forth one night, leaving his clothes neatly folded on the shore. He had no doubt that Eloise would have bailed him out once again if his brother had asked her, but Connor was a proud man who took failure very hard.

Campbell saw his brother's suicide as a pointless act of stupidity, but the field was clear for him to move in. His urgent courtship of Eloise was embellished with promises of a settled life and the social perks of being an MSP's wife. True, eyebrows had been raised at their marriage coming so soon after Eloise had been widowed, and he was conscious of the whispers about the boost that the match had given to his own depleted finances after his ruinous divorce.

But Campbell was as thick skinned as a rhinoceros, and like that beast, he had charged with single-minded purpose after what he wanted. He had always cast envious eyes on his brother lording it in the Big Hoose. A few knives pointed at his back were never going to deter him from his ambitions to replace Connor there.

He could survey his domain from the upper stories of the house and look back on his past as through the wrong end of a telescope. He had come a long way from his upbringing in Lochgelly though he played the humble working-class beginning's card at every opportunity with voters. His father had been a teacher, but to hear Campbell talk, it was coal dust from the many pits that used to proliferate there rather than chalk dust that was ingrained in his DNA.

His PA, Brenda, entered. Eloise had insisted on being in on the interview for her appointment, and he suspected it was because of what had happened with the last incumbent of the post. His second wife was many things, but she was no fool.

Thus, Brenda—fair, fat, and fifty with sensible cardigans, woolen skirts, thick tights, and unflattering glasses hanging on a chain around her neck. There was little danger of sexual scandal there. He did catch her often giving him a certain look. He knew he was far from being a handsome man, but some women were attracted to power, and he had no hesitation in exploiting her interest, being unfailingly charming and solicitous to her.

He needed to ensure her trust, loyalty, and discretion because she was inevitably party to much of his political dealings. Besides, she was by far the most efficient and hardworking PA he had ever employed. As she donned her glasses and bent to put papers on his desk for his signature, he entertained himself with a perverse fantasy of suddenly grabbing her and having her over his desk, sensible tights and Marks and Spencer's underwear round her ankles.

"Are you all right, Mr. Lake?"

"Sorry, Brenda, miles away."

"You work too hard. Did you hear about the barmaid from the Cross Inn?"

"Aye. My daughter told me about her on Saturday night when she got in. Apparently, the police were in the pub. Terrible business."

Despite the fact that they were the only two people in the room, Brenda lowered her voice and leaned in conspiratorially. "I heard that it was like a ritualistic killing. Unspeakable things had been done to the poor girl."

"We shouldnae listen to village gossip, Brenda."

"Her clothes had all been ripped off, and she had been sexually molested and mutilated." She shook her head and removed her spectacles as if that would stop her from envisaging the scene.

"Now, Brenda."

"We've been here before in this place. Remember that schoolgirl who disappeared? Maybe there's a serial killer on the loose."

"Let's not get carried away. I remember the case vaguely, but it was years ago, and we don't know she was murdered. She was never found."

"All the same. With the nights starting to draw in, I'm not walking down through the estate on my own when I finish work. You never know who might be lurking behind those trees. I'll get Steven to pick me up."

He had met Brenda's brother Steven once or twice. He was an unlikely sibling for the straitlaced Brenda, with his beer belly, shaven head and foul mouth.

"You know you don't have to walk home at night alone, Brenda. I'll get the car to take you."

"That's kind of you, Mr. Lake. I don't want to be any bother."

"You're not." He smiled at her, and she flushed with coy gratitude. "Do you think you could type up these notes from today's meetings for me?" Anything to get away from the doe-eyed teenager look she was giving him that was as incongruous on her as a miniskirt and crop top would have been.

When she left, a feeling of unease made him rise and stare out of the window. Another mystery surrounding a young lassie from the Law—that was the last thing he needed. By connecting the two cases, Brenda had done just what everyone in the area would do.

There was nothing vague about his memories of Carol Chalmers. Her father, Liam, had run a successful law firm and was one of his staunchest local political supporters. He had mentioned that his daughter was interested in studying political science at university if she got the grades in her Highers. When Liam asked him if she could shadow him during her Easter holidays to get some insights into how local and national politics worked, he had agreed immediately and not just to keep her father onside.

Not to put too fine a point on it, he had lapped up the attention of the striking girl. Carol was a schoolboy's wet dream with her tall willowy figure, long strawberry-blonde hair, and eyes that were almost sapphire. She was sixteen but looked older and behaved more maturely than her years. During his week with her, he had enjoyed the way she seemed to hang on his every word, those frank blue eyes on him.

Though she always dressed demurely in white blouses and dark-pleated skirts, her physical allure was undiminished. He knew she was aware of it too. Laura said charmingly that he puffed himself up like a gibbon when Carol was around and chided him that he couldn't stop his eyes drifting toward her every time she crossed her legs. His then fourteen-year-old daughter also made no secret of her displeasure at the attention he gave to this interloper from her school.

Toward the end of her placement though, she seemed to be nervous every time she entered the house, and then mysteriously a few days before her time there was supposed to end, she stopped coming. It led him to question his own conduct when she was in his presence. Had he been giving off unconscious signals about his sexual attraction to the girl?

When she vanished, the police had taken a great deal of interest in the time Carol had spent with him, both at the Big Hoose and in Edinburgh. He was very careful in the media to appear both appalled by her disappearance and outraged by the lack of progress made by the police.

He had even paid a sympathetic visit to Liam Chalmers and his wife, but they barely acknowledged him, wrapped up as they were in their own distress though Chalmers had given him a strange look that mixed suspicion with contempt as he had left. The lawyer had taken no further part in his political campaigns since then.

A persistent policeman investigating the case, a DI Bruce, had paid him several visits, not least after he had got wind of the sexual harassment business with his secretary. The fallout from zealous police scrutiny had threatened more than his reputation, and he had been forced to take steps to bury some of his less kosher dealings for a while.

Now he could see the fat worms wriggling out of the can he had taken such pains to reseal. There was a light tap on his door, and Brenda's head appeared round it.

"Mr. Lake, the police are here. They'd like a word with you and your daughter."

"Of course. Show them in, Brenda, and ask Jennifer to come up."

Shit, he thought. The police were here already. His heart sank further when he saw the familiar figure of DI Bruce entering his office. He looked as if he had aged ten years since the last time he had seen him. He was accompanied by an attractive redhead. As she crossed the room when he asked them to take a seat, he noticed she was limping. They declined his PA's offer of tea or coffee, and she left.

"You no doubt remember me. This is DS Wilson."

He smiled at the policewoman, but she only nodded and regarded him with a serious expression as she took out a notebook. She made him feel even more uncomfortable.

"Sorry to bother you, Mr. Lake. I know you're a busy man," Bruce said, not seeming apologetic in the least.

"Never seem to have a minute these days. Constituency business is never ending, and then there's the commute to Edinburgh to the parliament and so on. How can I help you?"

"You'll no doubt have heard of the murder of a local woman, Ms. Janine Gunning?"

"Well, the jungle drums and the rumor mill have been very active." His nervousness was making him mix his metaphors. "She was definitely murdered then?"

"Oh yes."

"That's hellish. I'd appreciate it if you'd not go into too much detail when my daughter gets here. Why do you want to speak to us anyway?"

The Wilson woman chipped in, "We're in the process of interviewing everyone who frequented the victim's place of work. I met your daughter and her friends briefly a couple of nights ago at the inn."

The DI added, "And we wondered if you had come across the young woman since you must know a great number of people in the area. Or if perhaps you had heard anything on the grapevine or the bush telegraph." Had Bruce noticed his linguistic faux pas and was taking the piss deliberately?

Just at that point, Jennifer entered. She looked animated and exclaimed, "Have you got him yet?" as she went to stand behind her father's chair.

"When we have him or her in custody, I'm sure you'll hear. Did you know Ms. Gunning personally, Mr. Lake?"

"No, I might have seen her on the rare occasions I went to the Cross Inn, but I can't even think what she looked like."

"Curvy, big knockers. You must have noticed her behind the bar, Dad. Sorry, Officers, that description seems a bit disrespectful, but Janine was the kind of girl men noticed. And she came here, remember?"

This last sentence caught the detectives' attention. They regarded Lake inquiringly.

"You see I do a bit of part-time office gofer work for Dad, but recently I thought it was distracting me too much from finding a real job, and I needed to focus. Janine happened to mention she was looking for a bit of extra income. Her shifts in the pub weren't paying enough, so I suggested she could maybe fit my duties here around her bar work. The general dogsbody stuff I do doesn't exactly require a master's degree in quantum physics, not that I thought Janine was thick or anything, so I suggested her name to Dad and Brenda."

"My god, that was her. The name didn't register. I'd forgotten all about her. She came here the other night for an informal interview."

The look that Wilson and Bruce exchanged suggested they had just encountered a large alien object on their radar.

"What night was that, sir?"

"I think it was Monday or maybe Tuesday."

"Tuesday," they both spoke at once.

"I mean, I only set eyes on her briefly. I was a bit miffed at Jennifer to tell you the truth, and I'd asked Brenda my PA to stay on a bit in the evening to talk to the girl."

"And how did that go?" asked Wilson.

"I never really asked. To tell the truth, it slipped my mind. But we can find out." He crossed to the door and pulled it open. Brenda almost fell into the room as if she had been standing just on the other side. *At least she has the grace to look embarrassed*, he thought.

"Ah, Brenda, you remember last week, I asked you to interview someone to replace Jennifer? The young woman you saw was the *murder victim* of the other night."

Brenda looked both shocked and tantalized by the news. "How dreadful. I had no idea it was that barmaid. She never mentioned to me that she worked in a bar. She said she was a student."

Jennifer interrupted, "I'm sorry, but I told her to say that. Thought it would go down better at an interview for clerical work."

DS Wilson said, "We have reason to believe she was killed soon after that. How did she seem at the interview?"

"She was well turned out, nice formal blouse and skirt, and she was quite cheerful and chatty. Only I felt there was something about her that convinced me that she wouldn't fit in here. I'm not a snob, you understand, but I thought she was quite, *well*, common."

Campbell Lake gave an exasperated sigh. Brenda's middle-class pretensions could hole his carefully cultivated working-class image beneath the water line if they became public.

"I'm sorry, Mr. Lake, but you must know what I mean. She would be meeting important people here and doing things like answering the phones. Her Fife accent was so strong I thought people would have trouble understanding her, and she was quite, I think the word some people would use is *gallus*."

Bruce spared the MSP further discomfiture by asking, "How did she seem when she left here? Was she disappointed that you weren't offering her the job?"

"Oh, I never told her that. I said we would have to take up her references, and then we'd be in touch. I suppose she did seem a bit put out by that, but we shook hands quite amicably, and she made a lot of enthusiastic noises about the house as she left. How great it must be to work here and so on. Of course, I had no intention of employing her."

"Well, nobody's going to be employing her now, Mrs.?"

"Ms. Evans, Brenda Evans." She glared at the DS as if she had reprimanded her unfairly while Wilson made a note of her name.

"Can you remember what time she left here?"

"Perhaps around 8:30 p.m., quarter to nine."

"And what did you do then?"

"My brother Steven picked me up and took me home. I was only just saying to Mr. Lake I don't like walking home in the dark on my own."

The fate of Janine Gunning, who had done just that, seemed to strike them all at the same time, and the silence was palpable.

"Did you see her leaving, Mr. Lake?"

"No, I don't think I did." He realized how weak his answer sounded, but he could hardly admit that he had been outside smoking a cigar when the girl came bouncing down the stairs from the front door, and he had watched her striding down the drive, admiring her firm calves and round behind. He tried not to fidget under their suspicious gaze.

"We'll need you all to make an statement. Are there a couple of rooms we could use so we can talk to you all individually? It would save time if DS Wilson spoke to your daughter and I interviewed you and your secretary, sir."

"You can use my office and the sergeant can use Brenda's."

Brenda looked as if she might object.

"And we'll need to take a DNA sample."

This time, the PA did begin to protest, "I already told you we shook hands so—"

"Is it really necessary to take samples from the ladies? I can understand you wanting one from me though I hasten to add, I would never *you know*. And I understood the young woman had been…raped." This last was almost a whisper, and he realized that he was blustering and stammering like a guilty fool.

"No details, sir, remember? I'd like to have a quick word with my colleague, and then we'll call you in." Bruce gave him a smile that failed to reach his eyes.

CHAPTER 5

Interviews

When they were alone, the DI said to Nan, "How did our respectable and upstanding MP seem to you, Nan?"

"I always think someone who says 'to tell you the truth' so often is either lying or about to lie. And his trousers were immaculate."

"His trousers?"

"He seemed to be having a problem removing lint or troublesome stains from them as we were questioning him."

"I've met our Mr. Lake before, and beneath his urbane professional appearance, I always get the impression he's squirming like a snake on a hot plate. You can almost hear the bones of the skeletons rattling away in his closet. If he has nothing to hide, I'll eat my tie. Besides, two girls encounter Lake under separate circumstances. One goes missing, and the other is murdered. I've never been a great believer in coincidence."

"How do you want me to play it with his daughter?"

"If you can, see how much she knows about Daddy and his dealings. And find out what she knows about her friends. We'll get round to interviewing them all, but I get the feeling that lot would alibi each other out of loyalty. Look for any tensions or discrepancies. We can't afford to cock this up, Nan. They're already planning to parachute in a DCI from Edinburgh to take over the case."

Immediately he'd left, there was a confident rap at the door, and Jennifer Lake entered. "Where do you want me?"

Nan sat in the chair recently vacated by the girl's father and pointed to the one opposite. Was it her imagination or had there been some flirtatious ambiguity in the remark? She had always been slightly in awe of women like Jennifer, women whose beauty, intelligence, poise, and background made them appear permanently at ease in their own skin. Nan had realized early on in her development that she was attracted to both women and men. Her first serious relationship had been with Julie, a tall self-assured cadet at police college.

She had later found herself engaged to Daniel, a male colleague at the Edinburgh station, but the relationship foundered on their too frequent clash of wills or, as Nan preferred to think of it, his unreconstructed macho bullshit. Certainly she was not oblivious to the charms of the young woman who now sat across from her regarding her with cool composure, but she knew when to adapt the persona of a professional interrogator.

"So, Jennifer—may I call you that?—why did you suggest to Janine Gunning that she might get work here if you didn't know her that well?"

"To be honest, I was desperate. The work I do for Dad is beyond tedious: filing, photocopying, answering the phone. I was never party to the interesting, important stuff: the political issues of the moment or Dad's wheeling and dealing. Oh, he did let me go with him to Holyrood once. Whoop-de-do."

"You and your father don't get on?"

"We're okay if we aren't in the same room together for too long. Mum was right to ditch him. He's always been a terrible old lecher, and that sleazy political charm he puts on makes me puke. He's like a used car salesman and just as dodgy. I think he only married poor old Eloise for her money. Not that I'm complaining."

"Really?"

"For Christ's sake, don't quote me on that. I need my allowance. I'm sure he only made me work for him to keep tabs on me and to punish me for not making the most of my four years at uni, which, he never tires of reminding me, he bankrolled. I overheard Janine moaning about her rubbish wages and never having enough money, so I thought she might be my get-out-of-jail free card."

"But you didn't know her well?"

"None of us did, I mean my friends and I. I think Darren might have had a one-night stand with her, but he didn't talk about it to us."

Nan consulted her notebook. "That would be Darren Boyd?"

Jennifer was instantly on the defensive. "Look, we all know he's been done for possession a couple of times, but just because he has a liking for a bit of odd wacky baccy doesn't make him a bad sort. He's harmless."

"You've been friends since school?"

"Yeah, we get on. And none of them give me too hard a time about my father or the fact that compared to them, I'm the original spoiled rich girl. Besides, that has its perks for them. They're always round here eating our food, drinking Dad's booze, playing pool, or watching movies on our big screen TV downstairs."

"Any serious relationships within the group?"

"Not in the way you mean. I know Darren has the hots for me, but he knows I see him as just a mate, so he doesn't push it. I think Angus and Beth had a thing once soon after we left school, but it just seemed to peter out, and they stayed friends afterward."

"That's Angus McKissock and Beth March?"

"Yes. And I always thought Letitia, Vane, might bat for the other side if you get my drift. Not that she ever came on to me or Beth or anything, and I have seen her giving Clipper the eye a couple of times, so I might be way wide of the mark. Or maybe she swings both ways." She gave Nan a look that was both knowing and coquettish.

"Clipper?"

"Colin Sark, the innkeepers' son. Sark? You know, *Cutty Sark?*" She must have seen the puzzled look on Nan's face. "It was the name of a famous nineteenth-century clipper ship. That was a fast merchant sailing ship. Clipper's a better nickname than Cutty with its connotations of Burns's witch in her short nightie, don't you think?"

Nan thought that the young woman was assuming a thick plod would have difficulty in identifying her cultural references. "Do you think he had a relationship with Janine?"

"Depends what you mean by a relationship. He might have shagged her, of course, but that would hardly put him in an exclusive club. Not that I'm suggesting she was a slut or anything. She was just *popular*."

Someone else suggesting the dead girl was rather generous with her favors, Nan thought. "Have you noticed anything else that you think might be relevant to our inquiries?"

"Just that it seems odd her body was buried at the crossroads." In an authoritative tone, Jennifer reiterated her knowledge of the folklore associated with such places.

When she had finished, Nan said, "I don't think our victim was killed by a ghost somehow."

"But maybe as part of a ritual. I hate to say this about my hometown, but there are plenty of mouth breathers here and folk who haven't evolved much since the feudal system."

"Thanks for your help, Ms. Lake. No doubt we'll speak again."

"Can't wait."

Soon after she left, DI Bruce entered. "Anything useful from the girl?"

"I suspect that Ms. Lake flirts with everyone, and between that and asserting her superior education, she didn't give me much. She did reveal that she's less than impressed with Daddy's behavior. She also thinks the victim was rather sexually incontinent and that she may have been killed as part of some black magic ritual."

"That's interesting. The markings found on the body haven't been made public."

"The rumors are out there though, sir."

"Still, might be worth taking a closer look at her and her mates."

"How did you get on with her father and his PA?"

"Brenda Evans is very protective of her employer. She insists he didn't even encounter Janine when she was up here last week. I got the impression she's carrying a bit of a torch for him. Some women's taste in men never ceases to amaze me. As for him, he's smoother than a silk mirror. But my gut tells me there's something off about him, and he knows where the bodies are buried, metaphorically speaking, of course."

"So what now?"

"You follow up with her friends. And we should have another word with Len Sark. Find out what he was doing wandering around outside the night the girl was murdered."

Nan said, "Might be worth speaking to his son too. Jennifer thinks that there was a sexual relationship between him and Janine. And I'll be asking Darren Boyd about Janine. Jennifer thinks that he knew her in the biblical sense as well."

"He's had his collar felt a couple of times in the past but just for minor drug and traffic offences. I can't see him as a murderer somehow. Truth is, I always felt a bit sorry for him. His dad spent more time in jail than with the family, and his mum died when Darren was still at school. Then the family home was repossessed, and Darren finished up living on his own in a caravan. The laddie never really stood a chance."

Nan knew that Bruce was an empathetic copper, which was one of the reasons his failure to resolve the Carol Chalmers case had hit him so hard.

As if by some weird telepathy, the DI went on, "I'd like to have another look through the records of the Carol Chalmers disappearance as well. I interviewed Lake at the time, but it's worth checking to see if any of the other current players were on our radar then. I know we interviewed a guy called March, who was the gamekeeper here, and I'm pretty sure his daughter is one of Jennifer's set."

Nan thought this was a connection however tenuous, but she also thought that Bruce's review of the missing girl's case files was unnecessary. He must have been through the details of the Chalmers disappearance so often that they were imprinted indelibly in his memory.

Reddening, he turned from her but not before she thought she glimpsed in his expression the guilt and pain that still pierced him, the spectre of a young girl dogging his footsteps, plaintively crying to him and making him look over his shoulder always to find nothing there.

Confessions 1

You know you're fucking stupid. Just when you thought all the fuss had died down about Carol Chalmers, you had to make the same mistake. When will you learn? Now the Law is swarming with police again, and at any minute, you expect a hand to lift the stone you're trying to hide under.

Apt comparison though actually you feel lower than an insect. How many times have you stood at the edge of the Forth but never had the guts to throw yourself in? Or maybe when you were up that tree rigging the noose, you should have slipped it round your own neck.

There's something wrong in your head. Maybe you're possessed by one of those evil spirits that are said to roam around the crossroads. Why else would you choose there to get rid of her? And those meaningless signs you forced yourself to carve on her body as your hand shook and you bubbled like a bairn. Where had they come from, and how long do you think they'll distract the cops?

You stands to lose everything because of those lassies and for what? None of them are worth it. You've always put them on a pedestal. You should have left them there, been content with your fantasies about them. Because the reality was always different, always dirtier somehow, always trouble.

Right from the start, right from Carol Chalmers when you approached her and she looked at you with an expression of embarrassed incredulity. Then you saw her laughing with her friends. But despite her disdain for you, afterward you treated her almost with reverence. Undressing her and washing that beautiful body—a woman yet still a young girl. That was before you had to…

And your first tentative relationships. Trying to move from friendship to something more. That night in your room when you were both half undressed and she seized your hand, telling you it was her period. And then she reached for you and you bolted as if the demons of hell were chasing you.

And the goddess. Waiting for her secreted in that enormous antique wardrobe in her room. Hardly daring to breathe as she came in and stripped for a shower. You thought her perfect. That was before she farted as she got into bed. Hardly goddess-like behavior. Why did they always have to spoil it? Make it sordid somehow? And then you were stuck there for ages, your legs beginning to cramp, until you thought she was sound asleep so you could sneak out.

You're pathetic. You're wired up wrong.

You just needs to look at the scrap of garish pink material in your hand, Janine's knickers. If they find them in your possession, you might as well walk down Lower Law High Street naked with "I did it" carved into your chest. They don't even have her smell on them anymore. You'll have to get rid of them. You might have known her underwear would be a tarty G-string.

What the fuck were you playing at that night? You'd drunk too much, but that's no excuse for the chances you took. Going up to the Cross. Why? And then she was there.

You don't know where you got the guts to approach her anyway. Sidling up to her like a tongue-tied kid asking for the first dance at the school disco. Maybe it was the drink…or maybe it was because she was looking positively demure as she walked down the road in contrast to her usual brash vulgarity. You should have known as soon as she opened her mouth, "What the fuck are you doin' sneakin' up on me like that? You nearly made me shit myself." Then when she recognized you, "Oh, it's you. What you after?"

You remember standing there blushing and stammering like the village idiot.

"Come on, spit it out. Havenae got all night. I'm gaspin' for a Bacardi. I might let you buy me one or more than one."

If only she hadn't touched you playfully. When you backed off as if you had been electrocuted, she had said, "It's okay. I'm hardly aboot tae rape you."

Then she had laughed. "Fuck, you should see the expression on your face." And she had laughed even more loudly. That was what had triggered it, what had switched the pressure gauge in your head into the red zone. The rest was a bit of a blur, but it keeps coming back to you in short bursts as if a bare light bulb were swinging from a ceiling, illuminating different parts of a darkened room.

Her face changing as she felt your hands around her throat, just as well your eczema had been playing up and you were wearing gloves. She was suddenly aware you were stronger than you looked. Then the frenzied tearing of her clothes; her white breasts, obscenely big and pendulous, spilling from her bra, and those ridiculous panties all leaving you shivering as your spine turned to ice. Digging at the soft earth with your bare hands, then the frantic dash to find tools, hoping no one would stumble on her. Using the shaft of the hammer to…

What the fuck had got into you?

All the time you were trying to cover her, you had the feeling someone else was out there in the gloom, watching. The rope in the van next to the tools gave you the idea. *Obfuscation*, that was the word. Use the old stories about the crossroads and the tree to lead the police up the garden path.

Carving those meaningless symbols into her skin made you nearly throw up. Then the tree was relatively easy to climb, but you heard something that made you shin down the tree in a panic, scraping your arms and legs…

Before you could run, she came strolling out of the darkness, switching on a torch for God's sake. You had to throw yourself face down in the dirt, wishing you could burrow under it, still with that horrible feeling there was another presence there. You were forced to watch her pissing for fuck's sake. No matter how desperate you were, you would never do that. You took the chance to rise tentatively then, hoping that she wouldn't spot you in the darkness but…

You might do it all again. Are you some kind of monster? You read that book that the goddess had recommended, *Metamorphosis*. This guy had woken up one morning and found he had turned into a giant cockroach. That's how you feel, and you know before long, everyone's going to see that's what you are. You have to do something more to protect yourself. You have to muddy the waters even more.

CHAPTER 6

Suspects

A quiet Tuesday night. The usual smattering of regulars. Colin was on his own tending the bar, but he thought that he might even be able to do a surreptitious bit of swotting for his exam if they didn't have a sudden influx of customers. He was confident enough in his reading comprehension and written skills, but he had always been weaker in math, and he needed to practice his arithmetic skills—these were largely untested in the bar with modern tills doing all the work—and he wanted to do some memory practice.

Though he knew he'd probably have difficulty concentrating after all the business with Janine, he still couldn't believe she was dead. The phrase "larger than life" might have been invented for her, and he expected still to hear her ribald laugh and feel her cheekily pinching his bum as she moved around him behind the bar. He simply couldn't envisage her as a pale silent corpse lying in a mortuary, all her animated spirit gone, leaked like air from a deflated party balloon.

The funeral was on Friday, and everyone was coming back here afterward for the aftermath. He thought his father might have offered out of respect for Janine, but he'd overheard him telling a couple of regulars that Janine's family accountant had approached him with a generous offer to cater for the funeral. Colin was surprised that Janine's mother had enough income to justify having an accountant.

He wasn't sure if he could bear having them all here. He had felt apprehensive and ill at ease since that good-looking police sergeant had interviewed him. He knew he must be a suspect like a hell of a lot of others in the Law.

The police would be digging into everyone's lives, unearthing all the dirty little secrets in the Law, perhaps putting them on display like the raw meat and fish on the stalls at the market that was held once a month on the riverfront. This place was cursed right enough. He had overheard Jennifer Lake pontificating about the superstitions connected to the Cross. Perhaps she was right.

He didn't think for a minute that Janine's death had supernatural origins however. Plenty of men had fancied her, including him. She exuded an almost animal sexuality. Maybe she'd given the wrong person the come-on and changed her mind and the perpetrator had lost it—taken what he wanted anyway and then killed her so she wouldn't identify them.

The police must be spoiled for suspects. He wouldn't put it past some of the punters in here who had leered at her constantly and made suggestive remarks. Wee Hughie Syme, for instance, who had lived on his own for years after his long-suffering wife had taken off after one too many fat lips and black eyes at his hands. The police here must know he was capable of violence against women.

Or Arthur Bauld, the local butcher, who always smelled faintly of blood. He had flirted with Janine all the time as if he would have the remotest chance with her with his big beef-stuffed gut and arms that were so hirsute they might have belonged to a gorilla. Janine had made no secret of her contempt and revulsion for him. Maybe his frustration had spilled over that night.

Then there was that fat cat bastard, Paul Rand. He occasionally came in with his arse-licking cronies. One evening, he had drunk too many brandies and pulled a protesting Janine onto his lap. The look he had given her after she had slapped his face in front of his laughing friends had chilled Colin's blood. It was obvious he was a man you shouldn't antagonize.

Could it have been one of the younger customers? Janine had certainly flirted with them—especially Darren and Angus—perhaps just to demonstrate to the girls in their circle that she had the power to distract the males in their set. He wouldn't be surprised if one of them had acted on her unspoken promise.

Though he was reluctant to admit it to himself, his own father must be in the frame. He had observed how frequently his old man accidentally on purpose brushed against Janine when they were both behind the bar. She would treat it as a joke and occasionally thrust her backside against him as she winked at Colin. Why had he been outside the night he encountered Letitia Vane on the road?

He wished that he was a qualified officer and that he could use his powers of interrogation and deduction to run down the murderer. His father's sarcastic voice echoed in his head: "It's no' like you'll become Endeavour Morse, son."

*****

The five of them came in together. Unusual, but it was a Tuesday, and he assumed they must have met up elsewhere before coming to their usual haunt. They were having an animated discussion as they headed for the bar, with Jennifer saying, "Come on, don't be such a bunch of pussies. We might learn something."

Darren responded, "A, I don't believe in that shite. B, It's not a brilliant idea with the police sniffing around."

Colin looked at them expectantly. Jennifer broke off to say, "G and T, Blue WKD, Jack and Coke pint, and an orange juice for Darren because he's driving please, Clipper."

"Oh, come on, I can have one."

"Half pint, instead of the orange juice." She took a twenty-pound note from her purse.

Angus looked around and said, "Christ, it's like the night of the living dead in here."

"Unfortunate comparison," said Letty, looking pointedly at Jennifer.

They took their drinks and headed to their favorite table. There was only a low murmur of conversation in the bar, so Colin moved to the end of the bar where he might be able to hear something of what they were discussing. He tried to conceal his eavesdropping by restocking the coolers there.

"Saturday night, we'll have the house to ourselves because Dad and Eloise are going to an opera at the Kings. She's basically dragging him there. His musical tastes run more to The Proclaimers and Simple Minds."

"But a séance, Jen? I'd be too scared." Beth took a sip of her drink as if to fortify her.

"Look, I've asked one of my old lecturers to come up, Sol Chapelle."

Darren scoffed, "And does he have a long beard and a cloak?"

"I think you might get a surprise when you meet *her*. She lectures in social psychology, and she's done a bit of research into séances. I've told her about the history of the Big Hoose, and she's fascinated."

"I don't know, Jen. I don't like it. I've had quite enough scares recently." Letty had both arms wrapped around herself as if she was chilled.

"It'll be interesting. Who knows how many spirits still walk the corridors of the Big Hoose? We might even get some clues about what happened to Janine."

Darren made no attempt to hide his scorn. "Seriously? Do you expect Janine to appear and tell us who murdered her?" He put on a ghostly voice, saying, "Hello, it's me, Janine. It's so lonely and cold in the hereafter. I've no one to fuck here. One of you should cross over and join me for some celestial rumpy pumpy."

"That's right disrespectful to her memory, Darren," said Beth, but he seemed unabashed.

Unexpectedly, Angus warned, "Isn't it supposed to be dangerous to meddle with things like that? What about that story Jen told us about the time that American guy tried to hold a séance there?"

"Aye, if we do it, two of us will die and one of us will go insane. I thought you were the practical one, Angus. Come on, put on your big boy pants and let's do it. Might be fun, and we can crack open a few of our local MSP's beers afterward and have a game of pool."

Angus looked aggrieved. "You've changed your tune, Darren."

"I'm no' expecting anything to happen, and I rarely miss an opportunity to hang out at Jen's place."

"That's true," said Jen. "And speaking of Gaylord Latimer's experience, I think we should hold the séance in the turret room."

"I thought your dad didn't like us going upstairs," said Letty.

"He won't be there, will he? Besides it would be more atmospheric."

"We wouldnae have to go through the house. Jen could let her hair down, and we could climb up it." Jennifer slapped Darren on the shoulder with the back of her hand.

"Well, you can count me out."

"Please, Beth. It would be so much better if we were all there. With Sol, it will mean there will be six of us around the table. Six is the perfect number."

"Can't wait to meet Madame Arcati. Does she have a crystal ball?"

"You'll have a black-and-blue ball in a minute, Darren."

"Love it when you talk dirty, Jen."

At that moment, DI Bruce and DS Wilson entered.

"Look out. It's the filth," Darren said.

The man made his way over to Colin, who showed him through to the back.

Darren said, "Bet they've come to arrest Len Sark. Knew there was something fishy about him. I think the good-looking redhead fancies me. She keeps looking over here."

Almost on cue, she made her way over to them. "May I join you?"

Darren's bravado disappeared instantly as he clumsily rose to offer her his seat, but she remained standing so that he was left dangling gormlessly.

"I've spoken earlier to Ms. Lake, but I just wanted to ask the rest of you a few questions."

"Fire away. We have nothing to hide. Can Jen get you a drink?" Nan caught the glare Jennifer gave Darren.

"No, thank you. You all know by now what happened to Janine Gunning. Can I ask where you all were last Tuesday night?"

"I thought we'd told you we were all in here," said Jennifer.
"And afterward?"

Letty piped up, "That was the night I told you about. After…
after it happened, I went home in a taxi."

"I dropped Angus off, and then I went straight home," Darren
said.

"Anyone see either of you?"

"I think the couple in the next caravan might have peered out
from behind their curtains. They're always moaning about the noise
my car makes."

Angus said, "When I got back, I went straight to bed. Doubt if
my old man knew I'd come in. He was snoring in front of the telly."

Beth said, "And I went home to see to Mum, but she was dead
to the world when I got in, so I didn't like to disturb her. She doesn't
sleep well normally, so—"

"I suppose that means none of us really had an alibi," said
Jennifer airily.

Angus looked nervous. "None of us are really suspects though,
are we?"

Nan merely pursed her lips. "I'll probably want to talk to some
of you again. Darren, might I have a private word with you?" She
moved to an empty table.

As he went to follow her, Darren said, sotto voce, "Told you, she
wants me." His cool swagger failed to disguise his obvious agitation.

"Typical," said Angus. "Round up the usual suspects just because
Darren has a record."

"No way he's a murderer," said Letty, but her words lacked
conviction.

"I suppose any of us could kill someone if we were driven to
it." The others looked at Beth with surprise, but her expression was
unreadable as she looked over at the sergeant and Darren.

Colin appeared and asked, "Any empties?"

Jen drained her drink and handed the empty glass to him.
"Refill that, will you, Clipper. I need it after another third degree
from the fuzz."

"It was hardly that, Jen," said Letty. "I thought she was quite nice."

With surprising vehemence, Angus said, "Don't be so naive, Letty. She must be hard as nails to do that job. She must deal with scum every day. It would hardly give you a sunny view of human nature."

Colin asked, "What's going on over there?" indicating with a slight nod at the table where Darren and the policewoman sat.

"We could ask you the same thing," said Jen. "Why is that tall policeman in the back with your dad again?"

"They're obviously going for the most likely suspects. It'll be you next, Sarky." Angus had just swigged the last of his pint as, looking thunderous, Colin peremptorily snatched the glass from his hand and returned to the bar.

"There was no need for that, Angus," Beth sulked.

"It was just a joke. Fuck, has everyone lost their sense of humor in this place?"

*****

"I understand you once had a relationship with Ms. Gunning."

Darren squirmed in his chair. "Who told you that?" Then after a moment, he said, "Did Jen tell you that?" He glanced across as if he couldn't believe her treachery. "Look, it wasn't a relationship as such. We went back to mine a couple of times. I got a half bottle of Bacardi to take out if I remember right, and she came back to the van for a nightcap."

"And that was as far as it went?"

"Listen, I won't kid you. Janine was hardly a vestal virgin, so… we gave the caravan springs a bit of a work out, if you get my drift." He tried to smile, but it was more sickly than cocksure. "As I said, it was just a couple of times."

"And you didn't see her on Tuesday night or early on Wednesday morning?"

"No, she wasnae working behind the bar on Tuesday when we were in."

At that moment, DI Bruce reemerged from the back of the pub, and with a curt nod to Darren, she went over to join him.

When Darren rejoined the others, Jen said, "I was expecting her to slap the cuffs on you and take you down to the station. That was short and sweet. What did she want?"

"She can handcuff me any time," he joked, but he looked pale and nervous. "I told her I hardly knew the lassie. We'd had a drink once or twice, and that was all."

"So you didn't tell her you fucked her then." Jen eyed him coldly. The others shuffled uncomfortably. Darren gave an alarmed glance across at the two police officers as if they might hear her. They had ordered what looked like soft drinks and were having an apparently casual chat with Colin Sark.

"Can we just drop it and change the subject? Whose round is it?" Darren piped up.

"Yours," said Angus.

After a performance of searching the pockets of his jacket, finding his wallet, and looking inside it, Darren said sheepishly, "It's just it's another week before I get my next giro, and I havenae been able to do much sellin' recently. I've had to keep a low profile wi' the police bein' about sae much." When he was put on the spot, his Fife accent was more marked. He usually tried to sound more sophisticated, mainly for Jennifer's benefit.

She tutted exasperatedly before saying, "I'll get them. But before I do, what about this séance? Show of hands. Who's up for it?"

Darren thrust his hand in the air immediately, then looked pointedly at Angus who glanced away and put up his hand. After a long pause, Letty raised her hand tentatively. Beth regarded her with a hurt look as if she had somehow betrayed the sisterhood.

"Sorry, Beth, it's just after the other night at the cross, I want to be sure there was nothing *otherworldly* about my experience."

Beth said angrily, "Get a grip, Letty. This is nuts. And it's disrespectful. Janine's funeral's on the Friday."

"We're trying to find out who did this to her, Beth. What's disrespectful about that?" Jen's voice was gently cajoling. "And what have we got to lose?"

"Just our sanity or our lives," Darren muttered.

"Do you want me to buy you another drink or not, Darren?"

As Darren held up his hands in a gesture of surrender, Beth said, "I can't on Saturday. Mum's not been so great and…" She broke off and stared down at the table.

Jennifer couldn't catch her eye to convey her disappointment at her reaction but just said okay quietly and made her way to the bar. Angus put a hand on Beth's shoulder but, after a moment, dropped it as Beth sat like stone.

*****

Later when the last of the stragglers had left the bar, Colin decided to shut up a few minutes early. To his relief, his dad hadn't been doing so much lock-in drinking with his cronies since Janine's death, but he had caught him a few times standing alone behind the bar after closing time, systematically refilling his glass from the whiskey optic and staring sightlessly into the room. His melancholy expression suggested that the stacked tables and chairs there were a mocking reminder of the orderliness and routine of a disappointing life—a life of confinement and servitude.

Colin reflected on the evening. He had overheard Jennifer Lake trying to persuade the others to hold a séance on Saturday. The only spirits he had encountered were the ones he served to the punters every night, but the familiar feeling of being left out nagged at him. He had never had an invitation to the Big Hoose.

As he lifted the rubber spill mats and wiped around the bar, he wondered what the police had been asking his dad. When they had come back into the bar and spoken to him afterward, he had sensed that there was a hostile subtext in their questions as if they were taking all his answers with a pinch of salt. He was so disconcerted and anxious they might just as well have taken him into a dark room and shone a desk lamp directly into his face.

He was certain the red-haired sergeant's searching look missed nothing. When they asked again about his relationship with Janine and whether she had ever confided in him, she must have noticed how he had reddened with shame at his memory of his sordid encounters outside the pub.

He was aware too of how she scrutinized him when Jennifer Lake came up to the bar. Despite trying so hard to appear nonchalant and businesslike, he knew he behaved like one of Pavlov's salivating dogs around her, unable to prevent his gaze from automatically traveling over her body. Christ, the police must have him pegged as some kind of sex maniac.

He switched off all the lights and dragged himself dejectedly upstairs. His parents' bedroom light was on still, and he could hear their voices raised in anger. As he stood on the landing, he heard his mother saying, "Why would they come back if they hadnae any suspicions? Did you admit you were aye sniffin' round that slutty lassie like all the other dirty buggers in here?"

"Shut your face. I'm no' like that bunch o' losers."

"You're happy enough to drink wi' them though instead of comin' to your bed. I cannae mind the last time you looked at me, far less touched me."

"That's rich. When was the last time you showed the slightest interest?"

"I wouldnae be surprised if the police think you did it. What happened, did she give you the come-on and you couldnae get it up so you lost your temper?"

There was a silence as if the room was holding its breath before his father replied, "Is that really what you think o' me?" Colin could hear the anguish and self-pity in his voice.

"Wouldnae put it past you. You've done some disgusting things before."

"Ten years and you still carry that around like a stick to beat me wi'. How many times? I was under stress. My head wasnae in the right place, or I would never have even thought of goin' to these lassies."

"I was that ashamed when the police arrested you, I could hardly even go to the shops. Then when they started askin' questions about where you were the night that lassie got—"

"Do you honestly think I could be capable of somethin' like that?"

Colin slunk away to his room when he heard the door of the en suite bathroom slamming. His thoughts were in turmoil. What had they been talking about? He was appalled. It was as if he had stumbled upon them engaged in some unspeakable sex act.

As he went to draw his curtains, he looked out into the dimly lit car park, fearful that he might see some monstrous deed from the distant or even recent past made flesh and watching him and his family with eyes that burned in the darkness.

CHAPTER 7

The Funeral

Janine Gunning's funeral took place in Lower Law Parish Church. Her body was to be buried in the small cemetery on the outskirts of the village. DI Bruce had decided that there was little to be gained from holding onto her remains.

Forensic examination had not unearthed any real useful clues to her attacker, who had been wearing gloves when they strangled and assaulted her. DNA had been unhelpful, and an extensive fingertip search of the area around where she was discovered had failed to turn up the object that had been used to violate her. Many vehicles used the road, mainly farm traffic, so finding useful tire tracks was another dead end.

The symbols that had been carved into her body had been researched extensively. So far, no connection had been found to any kind of linguistic context, religious imagery, or occult symbolism.

Nan stood outside the church with Bruce, watching a steady stream of mourners filing in after first making their way through a throng of reporters and photographers. Nan recognized a reporter from the local paper with his camera and notebook. He was a one-man band unlike the representatives from the nationals who had come mob handed with their recording equipment and sophisticated-looking cameras with enormous lenses. An STV van was parked across the road from the church, and a fresh-faced young woman was doing an earnest piece to camera.

The flurry of activity from the press as the hearse and a single funeral car arrived reminded Nan of a flock of greedy pigeons squabbling over scraps. The cars negotiated the group at the gate and pulled up at the entrance to the church. From the black car, a skinny birdlike woman in a faded black dress and a dark coat that might have been fashionable in the '80s was helped by an older-looking man. She looked startled and dazed.

Nan assumed this was the dead girl's mother and the man was a close relative or friend. As they entered the church behind the pallbearers, the woman leaned heavily on the man's arm, bent over so that she looked like a dark comma someone had inked on the bright morning.

When they had gone in, Nan and the DI went to stand at the back of the church. His eyes restlessly scanned the backs of the heads of the closely packed congregation as if he expected one of them suddenly to crumble at the sight of all this grief for the dead girl and throw themselves into the aisle to beg forgiveness from God.

Nan struggled to remember the last time she had been in a religious establishment, but she had a vivid memory of a long weekend break in Barcelona she had taken with Julie years before that had been spent intoxicated on the taste of tapas, rioja, and each other, but they had both stood in awe before Gaudi's magnificent facades at La Sagrada Familia.

Needless to say, Lower Law Parish church failed to compare, being more of a building that celebrated Protestant functionalism with its rows of uncomfortable-looking pews, the plain dark wood of its altar and pulpit, and its one rather poorly executed stained-glass window.

She noticed the familiar figures of the group from the pub sitting near the front. Len Sark slumped at the end of a row while his wife sat poker-straight beside him. She thought she recognized a few of the others who sat in their pew as customers who had been present on her visits to the inn. She was surprised that Colin Sark was not in attendance.

A few rows back from them, Jennifer Lake sat with her friends, looking immaculate in a tailored black dress, her hair gleaming in the light that came in through the church window. Darren Boyd sat next to her. In sharp contrast to Jennifer, he didn't look as if he had even bothered to wash his hair, and he sported his usual battered-looking leather jacket. Beside them, Letitia Vane wiped her eyes till Beth March handed her a bunch of tissues. There was no sign of Angus McKissock.

Jennifer clearly preferred to sit with them rather than her father whom Nan had seen earlier outside the church, pressing the flesh with a suitably somber expression on his face, no doubt ensuring that the assembled photographers got his good side. He sat alone near the front in a black suit that must have cost the equivalent of a month of Nan's wages.

She listened distractedly as the female minister talked of a young girl who had been born and raised in the Law; who had gone to school there and was remembered by her teachers as always being popular, cheerful, lively, and engaged; and who had grown up to be a lovely young woman, someone who had lit up any room she entered. She had been so cruelly deprived of a bright future by a person who would soon be called to justice but who must be walking around now weighed down by the leaden guilt in their heart.

Nan wasn't so sure. She had come across plenty of evil bastards who had committed appalling acts but remained untroubled by any feelings of contrition.

There were audible sobs from some of the mourners, and Nan felt her eyes pricking with unexpected angry tears. Though she hadn't known Janine, she had known too many others like her whose lives had been shortened or blighted by being in the wrong place when darkness came calling. She sympathized with the Reverend Sheila Gow, who must find it difficult to reconcile such a death with God's plan.

She herself had no real faith to lose, having been brought up by parents who were resolute atheists. Her pharmacist father was positively hostile to religion, blaming it for so many of society's ills. Her mother seemed to have faith in only the purity of numbers, teaching mathematic courses at Heriot-Watt University with such esoteric titles as deterministic and stochastic dynamics. She knew she would have preferred Nan to follow in her footsteps into academia rather than the police.

After her daughter's assault, she had urged her to quit and retrain in something safer, and her weekly phone calls, checking up on how Nan was, always carried an undertone of anxiety. Nan spared her from a lot of the grubby detail of her work but realized with dread that she would have to tell her that she was part of the investigation team for this case because it was so prominent in the news.

She became aware again of her surroundings, having effectively tuned the minister's voice out. She had been lulled by the singsong patterns of her speech, the unvaried falling cadences at the end of her sentences that spoke of finality and certainty. At least the hymns were cheerful, "All Things Bright and Beautiful" and "Onward Christian Soldiers," even if the singing of them by the congregation was muted and desultory.

During the second hymn, Bruce edged past her and left the church. They had prearranged that he would go to the graveside in the rather forlorn hope that the murderer couldn't resist observing from a distance. Nan thought that only happened in crime shows on TV, and the DI had the air of a man who might as well be clutching a handful of straws. She thought that his instruction to her to get to the inn early for the aftermath was equally futile.

She slunk out before the blessing and made her way to the side entrance to the church grounds as reporters barked questions in the distance. When she got to the inn, Colin Sark was filling trays of glasses with whiskey, sherry, orange juice, and water while two young girls in black skirts and white blouses were ferrying platters of cling-wrapped sandwiches and sausage rolls from the back and laying them along the bar.

He started as she appeared at his elbow, spilling some of the sherry he was pouring onto the tray. "Sorry, didn't mean to startle you." He smiled weakly as he mopped at the sticky liquid with a tea towel he had tucked at his waist.

"I was surprised you weren't at the funeral."

"We couldn't all go. Someone had to stay here to organize the catering, and we thought Mum and Dad should be there." He nodded over at the girls. "We had to call in a couple of the part-time staff especially as it was. I wanted to go *pay* my respects and that but, you know."

At that moment, one of the most striking-looking women Nan had ever seen entered the inn. She was at least six feet tall, and her skin was like polished ebony. Her hair was tied back in a bow, revealing features that looked almost sculpted: high cheekbones, full lips made up with a subtle pink shade of lipstick, and a long straight nose. Nan thought that she bore a resemblance to the beautiful American film actor Rosario Dawson. She carried an overnight bag, and her somber dark suit could not conceal the fullness of her femininity.

As she stood at the door, one of the girls who had been bringing out the food approached her and said, "Sorry, missus, but we're shut for a private function." The contrast between the wee, skinny, peely-wally Scottish lass and this exotic newcomer couldn't have been more marked.

The woman scarcely seemed to hear her as she strode to the bar. Nan's hand went to her hair subconsciously to check that it was still in place. She must have appeared as flustered as Colin who almost swept a couple of sherry glasses off the tray with his towel.

"I apologize for arriving when you're clearly busy, but I have a room reservation. Dr. Chapelle?" Her voice was smoky with an accent that mixed some of the local vowels with a hint of the Caribbean. She regarded the two of them boldly, a slight smile playing on her lips as if she had long since become accustomed to the reactions her appearance provoked in others.

Colin finally found his tongue. "We don't usually have check-in till two, but I think all the rooms are done, so if you give me a minute, I'll get you signed in and show you up." He called across to the skinny girl who continued to stare from the door, "Sharon, could you keep an eye on the drinks in case folk start arriving. I'll just be a minute."

The woman gave Nan a look of frank appraisal before following Colin out. She had to bend to negotiate the low beam above the door, and Nan couldn't help admiring the fullness of her unashamedly large buttocks in her tailored trousers. Inwardly, she admonished herself to behave like a fucking professional.

She took up position at the far corner of the bar where she could observe people arriving without being too conspicuous. She didn't have long to wait. The first of the mourners to arrive was a short ferret-faced man in a shiny suit. His companion was florid and corpulent. His own brown suit made him resemble a sausage that was about to burst its skin. Nan remembered both of them from her previous visits.

They made a beeline for the drinks trays, and before the girl Colin had addressed as Sharon had the chance to intervene, they grabbed two whiskeys each and went to sit on barstools that probably bore the permanent imprint of their arses from their frequent occupancy.

Sharon eyed them narrowly and lifted one of the trays in readiness. Slowly, the bar filled up with mourners, and she and the other girl circulated with the drinks. As more people assembled, their dark clothes seemed to suck any warmth from the sunshine that streamed through the bar's windows.

The Sarks arrived just as Colin was emerging from his duties in attending to the new guest. His mother went to him, and they appeared to exchange sharp words after which she disappeared through to the back and he hurried to remove the cling film from the trays of food and beckoned the girls to him. Sharon distributed them to the tables while the other girl went to the kitchen area and reemerged with two large pots of tea and coffee.

Len Sark went behind the bar, took off his jacket and black tie, rolled up his shirt sleeves, and began pulling pints for the punters whose one drink on the house was evidently not enough to quench their thirst.

The woman whom Nan had identified as Janine's mother and her escort sat at a table by the window, and a steady procession of sad faced people went to her, presumably to offer their sympathies and condolences. The man rose and shook hands as the woman sat there dry-eyed and impassive. She was a rock that the tide of people broke against and quickly dispersed.

When Nan had first been in uniform, she had been called in to a farm by the RSPCA on a serious animal cruelty case. The half-starved dogs that cowered behind the wire fences there had the same look as Mrs. Gunning: listless and apathetic, the light of hope and expectation long extinguished.

The group of friends had arrived together and, denied their usual table, milled around restlessly in pairs. Only Jennifer maintained her customary poise. The others looked like sheep who had become separated from the flock. At one point, Angus McKissock appeared standing out like a tramp at a society wedding in oil-stained overalls. He had a quick word with his friends and, giving everyone a wide berth lest he might sully their good clothes, made a hasty exit.

Nan felt that she was wasting her time here. What had Bruce expected her to uncover, and anyway where was he? It was conceivable that one of the people in this room was a murderer, but they were hardly going to furnish her with clues in this company. If one of them was at that moment heavy with the guilt that the minister had mentioned, they were unlikely to reveal it by skulking around the place giving furtive glances and shying away when someone tried to engage them like a bad actor in a silent movie.

Eventually, DI Bruce arrived in the company of Campbell Lake, who had the air of someone who had been buttonholed by one of his more annoying and persistent constituents. As the DI came over to join Nan, Lake visibly rearranged his features into a semblance of concerned sympathy and went over to Janine's mother's table. He greeted her companion warmly as if he knew him and then leaned over to Mrs. Gunning, lightly placing a hand on her shoulder. She regarded him blankly.

"Nice company you're keeping." Nan couldn't resist the jibe.

"Bumped into him outside. Anything?"

She shook her head. "What kept you?"

"After the graveyard, I swung by the station. The bad news is that a DCI Carpenter has landed with a couple of DSs from Edinburgh ostensibly to beef up our man power, but it's obvious the powers that be think we aren't making any progress."

"What's he like?"

"*She*, DCI Karen Carpenter."

"Karen Carpenter?" Nan asked incredulously.

"Maybe her mum was a music fan. She's young. Fast tracked through the ranks from university. So well-groomed she looked almost shiny. Anyway, before she takes over the investigation, I'd already asked Elsie and the team to do some digging into some of the local's records, paying particular attention to the denizens of the Cross Inn."

"And?"

He looked around to check if anyone might hear him and lowered his voice. "What a fucking den of thieves this place is. Don't look now, but you see the skinny guy and his fat friend at the end of the bar?"

Nan looked over casually at the two men she had clocked already, who looked as if they might be on their second round of beers.

"The thin one is Hugh Syme, who's been arrested in the past for domestic abuse. Apparently, his wife came to her senses and got out before he could do any more damage. Oliver Hardy, there is Arthur Bauld. His family have had a butcher shop in the Lower Law since forever. He was done a few years ago for seriously harassing a young teacher from the high school. She apparently stopped going into his shop when he kept asking her out. When she ignored his persistent phone texts and online messages, he took to hanging around outside the school playground and then her house.

"His messages got more *explicit* and then more threatening. The upshot of it was she took out a restraining order on him. He was taken to court and fined for ignoring it. The poor lass was so upset by his stalking, she got another teaching job in the west of Scotland and left the area."

Nan's interest was piqued—two men potentially with a grudge against women, one of them with a record of violence.

He nodded subtly over at the group of friends, who had managed to get their usual table together when some of the other mourners left. "Darren Boyd's record you know of already, and the other members of his friend circle are clean. But Angus McKissock's dad has previous minor stuff on the whole clocking motors, dodgy MOTs, and so on and a few drunk and disorderly charges. From what I've heard, his garage business has been struggling for some time so that might explain some of his behavior.

"However, when Elsie and the team asked around the station if any of them had encountered any attacks on women recently that hadn't resulted in official charges, a couple of the uniforms at the station remembered an apparent road rage incident a couple of months ago in which a middle-aged female motorist had come in claiming a man had been threatening and being abusive to her on the Lundin Links road. She had been afraid he was going to physically assault her. When they investigated, it turned out to be McKissock, but they couldn't prove anything, and no charges were brought."

"What a lovely bunch," Nan said bitterly. "They've obviously all qualified for their diplomas in misogyny."

"The guy with Janine's mum is Walter Dixon. He's some kind of relation to her, second cousin or something. He's an accountant. One of his clients is our old friend, Paul Rand. As you may know, the fraud team has had their eye on him for a while because of some of his dubious connections on the other side of the river. Haven't been able to prove anything. So far. And here's an interesting fact for you." He cast a glance over at Len Sark who was engaged in conversation with punters at the other end of the bar. "Our affable host, Len Sark, was done on two separate occasions for kerb crawling in Edinburgh around ten years ago."

"God, does everyone here have a dirty secret they'd rather lock in a box and bury deep underground?"

"And that's not all. One of the girls who plied her trade in the area where he was picked up disappeared around the same time. One of her friends and fellow workers went round to her flat when she didn't show up for a couple of nights. She raised the alarm when she found the door unlocked and the place looked as if someone had turned it over. She was never traced."

"Another of those coincidences you hate so much, boss. Should we pull him in? Interview him down the station?"

"Not yet. A ten-year-old case that he was never fingered for as far as I know? It's not enough. But we should keep an eye on him.

I'm not convinced by his story about going out the night Janine was killed so he could have a smoke because he didn't want his wife to know he had started again."

At that moment, the inn's latest guest appeared, ducking under the door's low beam again. Nan found that she had been unconsciously casting covert glances over to the door during her conversation with the DI in case the woman should come back. Along with nearly everyone else in the bar, Bruce's eyes were drawn toward her. "Now who is that?" He could scarcely keep the fascination out of his voice.

As if she was unaware of the scrutiny she had generated, the woman surveyed the room confidently and raised her hand when she spotted Jennifer Lake. The latter rose and crossed to her. They greeted one another warmly, Jennifer going on tiptoe to kiss her on both cheeks, before leading her over to her friends' table. As she introduced her to them, the girls were subdued in their welcome while Darren sprang to his feet and hovered awkwardly.

"I overheard her telling Colin Sark her name was Dr. Chapelle. Want me to find out why she's meeting Jennifer and her mates?"

"Not yet. I daresay we'll find out soon enough. She certainly stands out here."

Nan looked across at Len Sark's companions who were nakedly ogling her and obviously making salacious comments: "Aye, like an orchid on a dung heap."

Bruce gave her a curious look before saying, "Something certainly stinks here. Let's get back to the station. Best you should meet the new arrivals, and then we do some more digging. I have a feeling there's something nasty under the everyday life of this village that goes way back. We might have to go down into the sewers to find it. We'll pay some of the Cross Inn's inhabitants a wee visit later."

He looked jaded and disillusioned as he stared into the distance. Nan thought it was as if he was seeing into a past in which a young girl reached out her arms to him, beseeching him to find her justice and rest at last.

CHAPTER 8

Spirits

They watched the two police officers leaving. Darren clearly was feeling conspicuous and sat down again as Jennifer said, "Can I get you a drink, Dr. Chapelle?"

"Thank you, Jennifer. Scotch and ice. And please, call me Sol."

As Jen went to the bar, there was an uncomfortable silence. Everyone seemed overawed by the newcomer. Even Darren's customary brashness was subdued. Beth thought she could see the ghost of the immature schoolboy she had first encountered years before, gawky and shy in his frayed and ill-fitting blazer. Dr. Chapelle seemed unperturbed by the awkward atmosphere, sitting placidly with a faint smile playing on her impressive features.

Letty eventually said, "Sol, that's nice. What's it short for?"

"Solange."

"Like Beyonce's sister." Darren instantly looked as if he wished he hadn't spoken.

"I believe it means solemn or dignified, which you'd find difficult to believe if you saw me after a couple of drinks."

They laughed politely.

"So you're into spiritualism or the occult or whatever?" Beth asked, trying to avoid sounding skeptical.

"More the whatever really."

Jennifer returned with the drink.

"Cheers." Sol took a hearty sip and sighed. "I needed that."

"So I've told everyone about the séance tomorrow, Dr....Sol, and we're all up for it except Beth. Angus is coming though. You'll meet him later. He had to work today. His dad's a bit under the weather, and the garage has a few cars coming in. Anyway, as I've said, I've told Sol all about the Big Hoose, and she's intrigued, aren't you, Sol?" She spoke breathlessly as if she felt the need to fill any possible gaps in the conversation and looked expectantly at Sol.

"Have you told your friends about the history of the place?"

"She's told us a bit and, of course, the superstitions about it and about the crossroads." Letty barely suppressed a shudder.

"You know you shouldn't believe everything you hear or read."

"But, Sol—"

The woman placed her hand on Jennifer's and said, "I know how interested you are in all this, Jennifer, but we should proceed carefully and with a large dose of healthy skepticism."

A flush spread across Jen's face. Beth thought it was caused partly by embarrassment at being thought of as naive and partly by the touch of Sol's hand. She couldn't remember seeing the normally regal Jennifer looking so skittish before.

"I'll tell you why I'm here. I am fascinated by a great deal of what Jennifer tells me about the house's history. Among my other interests, I like to dabble in genealogy. I know that I'm descended from slaves, so the tale of the mute housekeeper from the past moves me. However, my prime purpose here is not to contact her spirit. Or anyone else's for that matter."

Despite Jen's obvious disappointment, Beth looked relieved.

"And superstitions often have a variety of interpretations. Take those surrounding places like crossroads, for example. You've probably heard about their associations with evil spirits or meeting a dark man or the devil himself if you visit them regularly. But a tradition relating to crossroads among African Americans that undoubtedly came across with the slave trade was that of the Kongo Cosmogram. That is associated with the rising and setting of the sun or the human cycle of death and rebirth. It has links with voodoo, but there was a belief that you could visit a crossroads and ask for desired skills— without selling your soul."

They laughed uneasily.

"As for Jennifer's planned séance, well, I don't want to preempt anything, but I doubt very much whether we'll be in contact with the house's ghosts."

Jennifer interrupted, "But what about the story of the séance that Gaylord Latimer conducted? Two people died, and one was driven insane."

Sol was not to be drawn but continued, "A lot of very smart people have debunked séances and mediums and the like in the past, people like Harry Houdini, for example. One of the mediums he proved was fraudulent was one Mina Crandon who used to hold séances in the nude and apparently produced ectoplasm from various bodily orifices, including her vagina."

The girls looked embarrassed at Sol's bluntness. Darren, in a weak attempt at levity, said, "Sounds as if she exposed herself before Houdini exposed her."

Sol smiled indulgently. "In more recent times, illusionists like Derren Brown and his collaborator Andy Nyman have demonstrated the trickery involved in these so-called communications with the other side. What interests me is the psychology involved and a lot of interesting research has been done on the subject. They reveal the role of such things as the ideomotor effect in table turning and Ouija board sessions *involuntary* and subconscious muscle reactions that inform the participants' responses and lead to them unconsciously spelling out messages.

"You'll all have heard of the power of verbal suggestion and the ability of self-styled spiritualists to use cold reading. That is, they make probable guesses and pick up on clues from their subjects' responses. Then there's the Barnum effect where the spiritualist makes statements that are general and universal such as 'You have a great need for other people to like and admire you,' which the gullible listener imagines is an intuitive insight into their own individual mind."

Sol paused to take a drink, and the others realized that they had been listening in rapt silence to her, partly fascinated by her knowledge but equally lulled by the timbre of her voice. Darren, of course, had been unable to take his eyes off her since she had joined them.

As if to break the spell, Jennifer said, "Can I get you another, Sol?"

"Let me get these." After taking their drinks order, Sol moved to the bar. Several pairs of eyes watched her progress, and Colin Sark almost sprang to attention to serve her. The friends sat in silence until she returned.

"I don't get it," said Letty at last. "If you're so skeptical about séances and the like, why did you agree to come here?"

"Because Jennifer seemed so wired by the whole situation, and the least I could do for one of my former star students was to help set her mind at rest. I'm only sorry she decided to switch to history in her second year." She looked warmly at Jen, whose face reddened once more. "Besides, who says we won't find out something of interest? There have been some dark goings-on in this place, both now and in the past, that have made an imprint on the fabric of the town. We might even get a clue about some of the awful recent events here. Anyway, it can't do any harm."

"Well, I'm up for it," said Darren, almost puffing out his chest.

"If you're sure it won't be harmful, I suppose I could come along for a bit," said Beth hesitantly.

Darren gave her a light punch on the shoulder. "That's the spirit, Beth, if you'll pardon the pun."

"To tomorrow then. Cheers." Sol raised her glass, and the others followed suit though both Letty's and Beth's responses to the toast were half-hearted, and they continued to look uncomfortable as Sol gave them an enigmatic smile.

CHAPTER 9

Newcomers

Nan was dispatched with one of the DSs they had brought in from Edinburgh to interview Hugh Syme, Arthur Bauld, and Len Sark. She was relieved to leave the station. There was an uncomfortable atmosphere created by the local coppers' obvious resentment at the interlopers from the city. It wasn't helped by the attitude and approach of DCI Carpenter.

She was almost out of central casting for the role of the feminine but tough, attractive but no-nonsense senior policewoman. She oozed confidence and was immaculately turned out in a pin-striped jacket and skirt and pristine white blouse. Her highlighted hair was styled in a pixie cut, and she wore heels, probably to make her look taller, Nan thought.

When she addressed the assembled officers, her subtext was clear. She patronized DI Bruce and his team by unenthusiastically praising them for their hard work to date, but the underlying message was that they had been getting nowhere and that now the big guns had arrived, progress would be made at last. She felt sorry for Bruce who stood beside her and gazed at the floor. Next to the DCI, crumpled and unshaven, he looked more like a guilty suspect they had dragged from the street for questioning rather than a police officer.

Sergeant Gerard—"Call me Gerry"—Eastman was a loquacious Glaswegian with ginger hair and a neat beard who kept up a constant stream of patter as they made their way in Nan's car to Hugh Syme's house. Annoyingly, he kept addressing her as "hen" and was less than complimentary about the Law and its citizens as they drove toward the run-down housing estate where Syme lived.

"I mean don't get me wrang, hen. I've been in some shitholes in my time. Run-doon schemes wi' run-doon folk. I mean there are hooses in Govan where ye wipe yer feet on the way oot, y'know? But these wee rural places are the pits. I mean you've got the sea and a' that and some braw views, but look at some of the locals and their hooses."

He pointed out a downtrodden-looking young mother wheeling a pushchair that appeared to have one wonky wheel along the pavement. "I mean look at the state o' that lassie, she looks like a character fae Wallace and Gromit efter they ran oot o' Plasticine. Probably inbreedin'. Ye never have tae leave the hoose when ye want a lumber if ye've got sisters, eh?"

He accompanied his offensive remarks with a cheeky grin. Nan was quiet, hoping he would shut up. They reached Hugh Syme's address. To her surprise, it looked better maintained than its neighbors. The front gardens of the houses next door consisted of patchy grass and overgrown weeds with an old bicycle and pram in one propped against an overflowing wheelie bin and a car engine in the other, leaking oil onto the path. By contrast, Syme's lawn looked recently cut and was surrounded by a neatly planted border.

Eastman was on his way up the path before Nan had finished locking the car. She caught up with him as he banged unnecessarily loudly on the front door. A startled-looking Syme opened it. His rake-like frame was accentuated by an Armani T-shirt and a pair of skinny jeans. Eastman held up his warrant card.

"Sergeants Eastman and…" He hesitated and looked at Nan.

"Wilson," Nan responded, giving him an exasperated look. She smoldered with resentment at the manner in which he had assumed the lead, and him forgetting her name only served to exacerbate her annoyance.

"Just a wee visit fae the polis, pal. Nothin' to worry aboot. Can we come in and ask ye a few routine questions?"

Grudgingly, Syme admitted them. His entrance hall looked recently decorated. Nan had expected the house to smell of unwashed laundry, booze, and recent takeaways, but there was a dish of potpourri on the hall table, emitting a pleasant odor. When he lead them into a small living room, it continued the impression of someone determined to keep his private space in order almost as a revolt against his chaotic neighbors.

Nan knew his wife had left some time ago, but the three-piece suite with its floral pattern and embroidered cushions looked as if they had been chosen by a woman. The units housed a collection of books—mostly on military history as far as Nan could observe—and there was an old-fashioned turntable on one unit flanked by neatly arranged vinyl records.

There was a modest TV set in the corner, showing horse racing, and Syme immediately went to switch it off and sat on the edge of the settee, looking small and nervous. He didn't ask them to sit.

"Noo, Mr. Syme—"

"If you'll allow me, Sergeant Eastman?" Nan was damned if she was going to let him put her in the corner. She knew her deliberate hesitation and question mark before saying his name were childish, but she wanted to signal her irritation.

"We're investigating the murder of Janine Gunning and questioning anyone who knew her."

"I already spoke to that inspector in the pub."

"I appreciate that, Mr. Syme, but we have to follow everything up. How well would you say you knew Ms. Gunning?"

"Hardly at all. Just from chattin' in the pub like. I was that sorry about what happened. Naebody deserves that. The funeral was quite upsettin'."

"What sort of things did you talk about?"

"Just the usual shit everybody talks about in the pub. Bit of banter and that, you know."

Eastman, who had been surveying the room as if he might find some incriminating evidence, suddenly chipped in, "I've heard she was a bonny lassie. Did you have a wee fancy for her mebbe?"

Syme became flustered. "No, that is, she was nice lookin' and that, but I never thought of her in *that* way."

"What *way* is that, Hugh?" Eastman eyed him with faux innocence.

"I mean, she was young so—"

"Nice tits though, eh?"

"Sergeant!" Nan looked at him angrily. "Where were you last Tuesday night?"

"Last Tuesday? At the pub as usual and then back here wi' a fish supper. Watched some shite on the telly and went to bed."

"Anyone with you?"

"I live on my own."

"And why is that again?" Eastman had dropped his naive expression and moved over to Syme, looming over him in a manner that Nan presumed was designed to intimidate him.

"Oh, I get it. Go after the sad, lonely guy. He must be desperate since his wife left him."

"Was that no' because ye were a bit too ready to lift your hands tae her?"

Syme rose and moved away from Eastman. He stood with his back to them as if he was examining his books. He said quietly, "I see how this is goin'. Track record of violence to women. Must be a likely suspect. Let me tell you, there isnae a day goes by I don't regret my behavior toward my wife. I used to lose my temper, especially after I'd been drinkin'. I miss her. And I could never do the things that were done to that young lassie."

"What things?" Eastman wasn't prepared to let him off the hook.

"This is a small place, Sergeant. Word gets about."

"Thanks for your time, Mr. Syme. We may need to talk to you again at some point." Nan moved toward the door, but Eastman held back. He moved to Syme and stared at him pointedly for a moment before following her.

As they drove off, Nan struggled to contain her anger. "What was that all about? In which book of police procedure does it say we should antagonize a possible witness from the start and then try to browbeat them?"

"That was mild, hen. Men like that get my goat. Weedy wee bastards that try tae prove their masculinity by hittin' women. Saw it a' the time in the west. The aftermath o' an Old Firm game was carnage for the poor wives and girlfriends o' the supporters whose side had lost."

Though he infuriated her, Nan could not think of a fitting response. She abhorred domestic violence. At last, she said, "Don't call me hen. It's Sergeant Wilson to you." As soon as the words left her lips, she realized how petty she must sound, but Eastman seemed unperturbed, merely gazing serenely out of the window.

When they reached the High Street, he said, "So where's Mr. Bones the butcher's shop?"

Nan knew he had been briefed on Bauld's record of harassment and suddenly wished he hadn't been. His balls-out approach to Syme didn't bode well for their next interview. It was Saturday, so the street was busy, but fortuitously, a car pulled out ahead as she negotiated the traffic slowly. "There, three doors down."

The butcher shop was doing a roaring trade. She and Eastman were met by glowers from the customers who were queuing as they went straight to the front. They were unlikely to be placated by Eastman's shrug of the shoulders and apologetic smile.

Nan asked one of the middle-aged women serving if Mr. Bauld was available. She eyed them suspiciously till Nan produced her warrant card and then exited to the back of the shop. After a moment, she returned and ushered them through.

Arthur Bauld was busy chopping up a side of pork, surrounded by animal carcasses hanging from hooks. He wore a traditional striped apron over a white coat, and both looked to be straining to contain his considerable gut. His disposable gloves were flecked with blood as was the hair on his arms that was spilling from the sleeve of his coat. He paused in mid cut when he saw them, the wicked-looking cleaver he was wielding raised. Nan thought he looked menacing.

"Whit's this aboot?"

"Mr. Bauld, we're in the process of interviewing everyone who knew Janine Gunning."

"I already spoke tae the inspector in the pub."

"We're following up on that. How would you describe your relationship with Ms. Gunning?"

"I wouldnae describe it as a relationship. Look, could this no' wait? I've a busy shop to run, and it doesnae look good to have the police in here questioning me."

"This won't take long. So Ms. Gunning?"

"I already telt your colleague. I only knew her tae speak tae in the pub."

Eastman had been standing quietly, staring at the butcher, but now said, "Did you like her?"

"She was all right. Cheery. Up for a laugh."

"Fancy her?" said Eastman casually.

Nan gave him a warning look.

Bauld put down the cleaver and pushed back the white hat he was wearing with the back of his hand. "Aye, I suppose. I mean she was a good-lookin' lass, and she always wore clothes that got your attention like. Why are you askin' me that? A lot of the regulars probably fancied her."

"One of them obviously fancied her a wee bit too much, eh?" Nan thought the sergeant couldn't seem to stop himself from being provocative.

"What are you gettin' at? If you think—"

"It's just that you've a wee bit of a history of likin' girls too much."

Bauld looked thunderous and grasped the handle of the cleaver once more. "Now you look here—"

Nan held up her hand. Eastman's bullish, adversarial approach was less than helpful in eliciting information. She took out her notebook and consulted it. "You'll be aware that what the sergeant is referring to in his usual subtle manner is your previous *difficulties* with a Ms. Amanda Leadbetter."

The man visibly sagged. He had a haunted look in his eyes, and as he raised his blood-spattered hands as if to ward off the past, Nan thought he resembled a bad actor in a production of *Macbeth*.

"Listen, just because…listen, Mandy and me…that was a terrible misunderstandin'. I explained to the police at the time. I thought I was in love wi' her, and she might feel the same."

Eastman favored him with a cruel sneer. "Really?"

"Mr. Bauld, we understand it went a wee bit further than crossed wires about feelings. You harassed Ms. Leadbetter to such an extent that she left her job and the town."

Bauld looked anxiously toward the door to the front of the shop. Nan couldn't decide if he was worried about eavesdropping customers or staff or whether he was looking for an escape route.

"Okay, I admit things went too far."

"Send her pictures of your meat, did ye?"

Nan glared once more at Eastman.

"I never did anything like that. I did send her some messages and tried to see her a couple of times."

"A bit more than some messages and trying to see her a couple of times. Effectively, you were stalking her and you ignored an official restraining order." Nan bit back her aversion. She was only too aware of how stalking could evolve into more violent, sometimes lethal, action. Bauld hung his head.

"I knew even while I was doin' it that it was wrang, but I couldnae seem to help it. I had a' these thoughts in my heid about maybe her and me havin' somethin' together. Deep down, I knew I was kiddin' masel', but I thought that if she saw how much I cared aboot her, she might see me differently." He looked close to tears, but Eastman was relentless.

"Have you taken a good look at yoursel' in the mirror, pal?" he said, his words dripping with contempt.

"I knew she was too good for me, but when you're on your own like me, you get desperate."

"Let me ask you again, Mr. Bauld, did you have any of these feelings toward Janine Gunning?"

He had been avoiding eye contact but now looked at them fearfully. "No, no. She was a nice lass, but no' really for me. She was a bit too interested in the men, if you ken what I mean."

"So you like a girl wi' high moral standards, Mr. Bauld," Eastman said sarcastically.

"It's no' that. I just meant she was popular wi' a lot o' men. She could more or less have had her pick, so I knew I had no chance."

"Pity you hadnae thought of that wi' that poor lassie that was so scared of you she took to her heels. Maybe if you had—"

Nan cut Eastman off. She decided that they weren't getting anywhere and brought the interview to a close by handing the butcher her card and telling him to contact her if he should think of anything else that might help with their inquiries.

She looked back at the great bulk of him against a backdrop of pig corpses as she exited. He stared after them with wet eyes that reflected regret and shame and perhaps grief for a life he could never have. She noticed that he had bitten his bottom lip so hard he had drawn blood.

Despite herself, she felt sorry for Bauld. She knew lonely, frustrated men like him were capable of desperate acts, and his grisly trade was perhaps at odds with his romantic ambitions. Yet her instincts warned her against jumping to conclusions. He might wield sharp knives and meat cleavers for a living, but Janine had not been killed by one of them though her assailant had certainly been carrying a knife.

Back in the car, Eastman seemed to read her thoughts. "Do you like our overfriendly neighborhood butcher for the killing then?"

"He has to be a suspect, but somehow I don't see it."

"What a fucking place this is. Do they no' have access to internet porn here? You could practically smell the sexual frustration off those two, and I expect the local boozers are chockablock wi' others like them."

She turned the car to return to the station.

"Speakin' of lonely men lookin' for company, I havenae had a chance to get to know anyone here, so if you fancied a wee drink later?"

Nan couldn't believe her ears. Was he actually asking her out? Not only that, but doing it in such an asinine way. She wondered just how good a detective he was when evidently he had failed to perceive her constant irritation with and growing antipathy toward him in their time together.

"Sorry, I make it a rule never to socialize with fellow officers, especially when we're in the throes of a major investigation."

He looked straight ahead and muttered, "It was just a drink. I'm no askin' to sleep wi' you, hen. I even thought this inn we're goin' to next might fit the bill."

Great, Nan thought. Now she was going to have to deal with his hurt male ego as well as his jaundiced attitude to suspects. Their last port of call for the morning was the Cross Inn to speak to Len Sark, and Nan wasn't relishing the prospect of an even more disgruntled DS Eastman delving into the sordid details of Sark's past.

The landlord was bustling around behind the bar when they entered. Though it was early, there were a few customers. Nan thought they were either there for a palliative hair of the dog after a heavy Friday night or they were topping up their alcohol levels for whatever afternoon activities they were planning.

Sark seemed unsurprised to see them. He called for his son to take over at the bar and led them back to the room where Nan and Bruce had conducted their initial interview.

Without preamble, Sark exclaimed, "Look, I know you've been looking into everyone's previous records, and I admit I havenae always done things I'm proud of but a' that was years ago."

Eastman opened his mouth to speak, but before he could come up with one of his scathing belittlements, she said, "We're not interested in your soliciting charges, but a sex worker went missing around the same time as your offences."

"I knew aboot that, of course, but that had nothin' to dae wi' me. I mean the lives these lassies lead, they've practically got victim tattooed on their forehead. Anythin' could have happened to her."

Nan could feel herself getting angry. "You've got that correct, Mr. Sark. These *lassies* are victims all right, victims of their backgrounds, their pimps, and of men like you who go to them seeking sex."

He hung his head just as Margaret Sark entered. She didn't acknowledge them but gave her husband a withering look as she went through to the front of the bar.

Sark lowered his voice as he said, "I telt ye I'm no' proud o' what I did then. My heid was a' ower the place at the time, and I've never done anything like it again. And there's no way I'd ever harm a woman. As for Janine, I really liked her, and I think whoever did what they did to her should be strung up."

"Were you ever questioned about the disappearance of Carol Chalmers?"

He looked flustered, and Nan glimpsed a fleeting moment of panic crossing his face before he found his voice. "I think everyone was questioned at the time. That poor girl. Your man DI Bruce was like a dog wi' a bone."

Eastman leaned in. "Are you trying to tell us you have respect and sympathy for women when you're prepared to pay some of them to suck your prick? You no' think that's a tad degrading?"

Sark almost visibly shrank and shut himself off. *Another triumph for the diplomatic approach*, Nan thought bitterly. She realized they were going to make no further progress and signaled to Eastman that they should leave.

"That man reeks of guilt. He's fucking hiding something. I feel it in my water. But then all of these C U Next Tuesdays are suspicious."

Nan was barely listening to him and realized she was subconsciously scanning the bar to see if Dr. Chapelle might be there. There was no sign of her, and Nan inwardly chastised herself when she realized she was disappointed by her absence.

She was relieved as she and Eastman split up on entering the station, but her respite was short-lived as she went to the incident room and was met by a flurry of activity. Everyone was either animatedly speaking into phones, urgently consulting computer screens or pulling on coats to go out.

Only DCI Carpenter was looking collected and still as she stood at Malcolm Bruce's desk, addressing him quietly. Bruce was slumped in his chair. Nan thought it was like one of those tricks of filming where two figures were frozen in frame while all the activity around them was in accelerated motion. As she approached, she heard the DI saying, "In the grounds of the Big Hoose? But where?"

"Ma'am, sir, may I ask what's going on?"

There was a pause while Bruce looked at her with dead eyes. Carpenter said finally, "Human remains have been discovered near the Big Hoose. The owners had commissioned a Dundee firm to build an orangery in the grounds north of the house. When work-men were digging the foundations, they came across human bones. Forensics are on the scene, and I've been trying to persuade DI Bruce to wait for their report. There's nothing to be gained by racing off to the scene."

"Another murder?" Nan couldn't hide her dismay.

"Initial findings indicate that the remains are *not recent*."

Nan felt the world going off kilter. For a moment, she was back in a stairwell in Edinburgh, her thoughts scattered by the sudden hammer blow that blinded her. So that was why Bruce was looking as though he had just witnessed an atrocity that had sucked out his life force. He suspected that they had found Carol Chalmers at last.

CHAPTER 10

Nosy Bastard

Colin followed his father when he left the inn, trying to keep some distance between them so he wouldn't be spotted. He had felt alarmed when the female police sergeant from before had turned up with a stranger. The latter reminded Colin of someone out of a Western who enters a saloon in an untamed town, eyeing up the customers with distaste and as if expecting trouble to erupt at any instant. He could only be another cop.

After they had questioned him through the back, his father had appeared in an agitated state and, after an obviously fractious exchange with his mother, had gone out. Colin didn't know what made him want to find out where his father was going, but the bar was quiet, and they had a couple of the temporary Saturday staff in, so he was able to slip out without telling his mother. He thought he could be back before he was missed.

He welcomed the brisk breeze that blew into his face as he walked. It was a relief to get outside. There had been a febrile atmosphere in the bar after one customer had entered with the news that there was more police activity up at the Big Hoose.

What the fuck had happened now? The Law was becoming like one of those quiet villages in the television crime dramas his mother watched so frequently where an unlikely proportion of the inhabitants of an apparently rural idyll harbored murderous intentions. At least St. Mary Mead had Miss Marple to restore order, thought Colin, before wondering to himself if he was actually fucking losing the plot.

His father had not taken the car, which was curious in itself, though Colin reflected he had been drinking so much into the small hours lately that he might still be over the limit. There was an urgency in his father's step as if he had to be somewhere quickly.

Colin nodded and smiled at familiar faces as they moved through the village. He and his father were well known in the community, and some of them must have wondered why they weren't walking together. He hung back as his father turned into McKissock's garage. Its owner appeared from the workshop. They didn't speak but merely raised their chins in mutual acknowledgment. Then they stood together as if they were waiting for someone to join them. Even from a distance, Colin thought, they both looked edgy and uncomfortable.

He glanced anxiously at his watch as minutes ticked by. The last thing he wanted was a confrontation with his mother when he returned to the inn. He was beginning to think this was a waste of time and that he ought to be heading back when a Volvo S90 drew up in the garage forecourt.

To his surprise, Campbell Lake and the man who had been with Janine's mum at the funeral tea got out. After shaking hands with his dad and McKissock, Lake looked up and down the street as if he was fearful of being observed. Colin ducked down behind the corner of the wall where he was standing. After a moment, he raised his head tentatively and peered out. The men were disappearing into the garage workshop.

Colin was perplexed. What business did his father have with the MSP that involved meeting in McKissock's dingy workshop? Unbidden, the thought entered his head that Lake would have been too worried about getting oil on his expensive suit to venture anywhere near it. It was not for the first time he wished he was a fly on the wall.

In the inn, he often caught tantalizing snippets of the customers' conversations that piqued his curiosity and led to him finding some task near them to eavesdrop more efficiently. When he regarded his behavior in a beneficent light, he thought it was evidence of an inquiring mind that would serve him in good stead in the police.

When he was less sparing of himself, he simply thought he was a nosy bastard.

As he dithered there distractedly, Angus McKissock came out of the house adjoining the garage, and after a curious and admiring look at the Volvo, he began to walk toward him at a rapid pace. There was no time to evade him, so Colin merely stood and waved. Angus regarded him with a mixture of uncertainty and hostility. "What the fuck are you doin' here, Sarky?"

"Headin' for the pub, Angus? I'll walk along with you." Colin realized how lame he must sound as he began to retrace his steps. After a pause, Angus walked alongside him.

"Flattered as I am that you should come here to escort me to the pub personally, I ask again what are you playin' at? Surely you and your old man are no' so desperate for customers that you have to resort to persuadin' them in aff the streets."

Colin realized there was no point in dissembling. "It's my old man I was followin'. He's been in a funny mood lately, and I was worried when he left the inn. He came here and met up wi' your dad, Jennifer's dad, and a guy who was at Janine's funeral wi' her mum."

Angus stopped suddenly, causing a couple who were walking behind them to swerve around them, muttering curses. "Lake is wi' my dad? Maybe I should go back and find out what's goin' on."

"Best to leave it till after they're gone. You can speir him later."

Angus stood hesitantly, looking back toward the garage with narrowed eyes and a furrowed brow. Then as if he had resolved his internal debate, he set off toward the inn at a redoubled pace. Colin struggled in his wake, attempting to keep up with him.

"This other guy, was he tall, well dressed, kind of stooped, big beaky nose?"

"Sounds about right."

"That's Dixon. He's been to the garage a couple of times to meet with my dad. He's some big-shot accountant. It's been an uphill struggle at the garage this last wee while. But then recently business has really picked up. I thought maybe he was givin' financial advice though why he'd concern himself wi' a small business like ours, I don't know. He usually swims in a pool wi' bigger fish. I think he does stuff for Lake."

"Maybe your dad's doin' some deal to service the MSP's official cars." Even as he spoke, Colin knew how improbable this sounded.

Angus scoffed openly, "Aye right."

"I'll be honest, Angus. It's the same story wi' the inn. Could our dads be involved in some scheme to restructure their businesses or whatever it's called?"

"That would explain their meetin' wi' an accountant, but where does Lake fit in?"

By the time they arrived back at the inn, they were both quiet, realizing they were no nearer to solving the puzzle.

"I'll ask my dad later what's goin' on and you do the same." With this tacit agreement, Colin went back behind the bar and Angus moved over to join his friends who had already assembled.

His mother came from the kitchen to berate him. "It's gettin' busy in here, and you and your father disappear to leave me to hold the fort. What's goin' on?"

Colin was relieved when Angus interrupted to buy a round. With a baleful look at him, his mother returned to the kitchen. The group around their habitual table looked more subdued than usual. "What's up wi' your mates, Angus? They a' look like they lost a tenner and found a pound. Apart from Darren, of course, who's his usual carefree self."

"He's perpetually stoned, that's why. Na', they're miffed because we cannae meet at Jennifer's the night as planned wi' the police bein' there diggin' up the grounds and that."

Colin had heard enough from their conversation in the bar a few days before to know that the meeting to which he was referring was supposed to be a séance and had already surmised that the exotic Dr. Chapelle was involved. Again, he wished he was part of the clique. It all sounded like a bit of excitement.

"I heard somethin' about the police bein' up there. Jennifer say what it's about?"

"She's as much in the dark as everyone else. But don't worry, you'll hear soon enough. You know this place, news travels faster than shit through a goat wi' salmonella."

As he ferried the drinks back, Dr. Chapelle entered and came up to the bar. She was wearing a dark formal-looking jacket over a dress that was a vivid shade of yellow. She looked stunning, and Colin thought she couldn't have attracted more attention if she had come in naked. She ordered a whiskey and ice, but before she could pay, Angus returned to collect the remaining drinks and insisted on including it in his round.

Colin observed the friends' reactions to her. As she addressed them, her words immediately lifted Jennifer's mood though he thought the other girls looked as ill at ease as they had the other night when they were discussing the séance. It made him think that their earlier gloom might have been a sympathetic response to Jennifer, that perhaps they had been secretly relieved at the cancellation. And now evidently an alternative was on the table.

He saw that they had only begun their drinks, so he couldn't go over under the pretext of collecting glasses to better hear their conversation. His attention was so focused on them that he almost missed his father's quietly furtive return. *So many mysteries here in the Law*, he thought.

Under other circumstances, he might have been brightened by the departure from the mundane routine of his life, but Janine's death and his father's clandestine meeting cast a cloud of doom and dread over everything. He was quickly becoming aware that being a nosy bastard could bring you pain.

CHAPTER 11

Remains

Nan stood with Bruce outside the station as he fumbled a pack of cigarettes from his coat pocket and lit one with a match. He must have noticed her raised eyebrows because after taking a deep drag on it, he said apologetically, "I know. These will kill me. I gave up eight years ago, but here we are. My excuse is that the stress might finish me off just as quick. What is it they call that? Cognitive dissonance?"

DCI Carpenter had just given them the news about the recent findings at the Big Hoose. She began with a long preamble in which she outlined the work of forensic anthropologists in determining the age of remains by examining pubic bones and the surface of the cranium. They could work out if the person had been young, under twenty, say by the extent of the fusion of the epiphysis.

At this point, Eastman had intervened to say that his old science teacher, Chalky White, always maintained he was an imbecile at the subject so could the DCI speak in English. The look she gave him suggested she wished she could reduce him to a skeleton, but Nan suppressed a smile, grateful for the first time that day for the sergeant's bluntness.

"If you'd give me the chance, Sergeant, I was about to explain that the caps on the ends of long bones fuse completely with the bones after the age of twenty. They can also work out the height of the person using a formula based on the length of the femur and tibia."

Nan sensed the anguish of the DI at her side. His clenched body language spoke of his dread that the senior officer was about to reveal that the skeleton was of a female of around five feet six who had been under twenty when she died.

"To cut a long story short—"

Eastman muttered, "Thank fuck," under his breath.

Carpenter pretended she hadn't heard him and continued, "Preliminary findings indicate that the bones were of a male of average height, and they looked as if they had been there for many years."

Bruce cleared his throat as if to disguise a sudden exhalation that revealed he had been holding his breath. Someone in the station had told Nan that the DCI had been a fast-track graduate recruit whose degree was in forensic science. Despite herself, Nan was impressed with her erudition, but she wished she had been more sensitive to the agony of her fellow officer before choosing to show it off.

She and Bruce had been dispatched to the Big Hoose. Nan was relieved to be working with him again rather than the overbearingly assertive Eastman, but she was pessimistic about their chances of discovering anything that would bring them closer to Janine Gunning's murderer.

In the grounds of the Big Hoose, they stood outside the police tape that surrounded a recently excavated crater. A mechanical digger stood off to the side, its bucket and tipping lid hanging down as if it was in mourning for having been abandoned. One of the forensic crew came over. She introduced herself as Dr. Sheila Grant after they showed her their ID.

"Any guesses about how long the remains have been there, Dr. Grant?"

She removed her face mask. Nan thought she would have been pretty if she didn't look so severe, but then, she reasoned, opportunities for smiling in her line of work must be few and far between.

"I don't guess, Inspector." She paused as her rebuke hung in the air. "But based on the preliminary evidence, I'd say he had been there for some time. Perhaps over a hundred years."

"Thank you, Doctor. We'll look forward to your report."

As they headed up to the house, Bruce said, "Well, at least Carpenter won't be bellyaching about having to bring in extra resources to solve another recent crime. I heard her complaining about the budget being stretched even further by having to employ the services of forensic anthropologists." He spoke lightly, but the worry lines etched on his brow told the story of how much the wait to find out if the body was that of the disappeared girl had cost him.

A cheery round-faced woman showed them into the impressive entrance hall, all carved wood and oak floors, though Nan found the stained-glass window at the top of the stairs rather incongruous. However, from what she'd heard about the house's history, the nudity and violence depicted there were not so surprising. The woman showed them into a downstairs room she described as the drawing room and said she would fetch Mrs. Lake.

The room looked as if it was rarely occupied. The oak floors had been polished so much that Nan was afraid if she looked down, she might see a reflection up her skirt. They were covered here and there with oriental-style rugs.

The antique furniture included an elaborately carved cabinet on a stand: a Victorian-looking mahogany bookcase, two leather Gillows armchairs, and a scroll end chaise longue that clearly had not been sullied by many bottoms sitting on it. Though she would never have admitted it, Nan was a fan of television antique shows, and she reckoned some of the pieces must have been worth thousands of pounds.

The room contained none of the comforts of diversion. There was no TV or music player of any kind, and the gilt and bronze mounted mahogany bureau looked too delicate to be practical, and certainly there was no sign of a computer or even pen and paper on it. While Bruce stared out of the large bay window at the expanse of lawn, Nan examined the cabinet more closely.

She was running a hand over its elaborate design when she became aware suddenly of the tall elegant woman who had entered the room so silently that she might have been on castors. "That is seventeenth century, you know." Nan started as if she had been caught rummaging through it. "And the bureau there is in the style of Louis XVI."

Nan stammered, "They're very impressive."

The woman held out a perfectly manicured hand and said in a cut-glass accent, "Eloise Lake. I'm afraid if you're after my husband, he's out presently."

Nan shook her hand, getting a subtle floral scent of the woman's perfume, and introduced herself and DI Bruce. She watched as Eloise Lake drifted over to perch on the chaise. "This piece is Regency. I think antique dealers must see me coming." She smiled faintly.

She was what Nan would have called a handsome woman rather than a pretty one; though in a blue ruffle-pleated cotton midi dress complemented by a single string of pearls, she certainly had an arresting presence. Nan became aware that she was staring. The dress looked expensive, but the unusual style and cut didn't really suit the woman. "The dress is Alexander McQueen, if you were wondering."

Both she and Bruce hovered awkwardly as if discomfited by the woman's patrician air. "Of course, my stepdaughter has told me about that poor girl. One doesn't like to think too much about the awful people that must be out there." She waved a hand vaguely toward the window as if some of the criminal inhabitants of the Law were skulking outside on the lawn. "And now this recent development. Honestly, what's next? Bodies in the attic?"

"Have you discussed any of this with your husband, Mrs. Lake?" asked Bruce.

"My husband doesn't really discuss things—he pontificates on them, Constable."

"Inspector. And what has he pontificated about these cases, the dead girl and the remains found on your property?"

"I'm afraid I'm rather squeamish, so I tend not to listen too closely when he's talking about such things. It all seems terribly sordid." She looked at them as if one of them had just broken wind in her fragrant presence.

"I think Campbell believes the remains might be those of a previous owner of the house who went missing in the nineteenth century. A dreadful man, by all accounts, who got up to all sorts of nefarious activities if you believe the stories. My stepdaughter seems unhealthily fond of telling them to everyone. The original house dates back to the eighteenth century, so I expect there are all sorts of bodies buried out there."

Again, she gave an airy wave toward the outside. "A distasteful thought." She sat up even straighter on the chaise as if to reinforce her stoicism in the face of the unpleasantness that had intruded with her visitors.

Bruce seemed at a loss as to how to make headway against this woman who sat there among her expensive antiques in her designer dress, protected against the unsavory or abhorrent activities of others that might take place beyond the walls of her carefully constructed room. For some absurd reason, Eloise Lake made Nan think of Dickens's Miss Havisham. Though this woman was certainly better dressed and less desiccated and scarred by the male sex than the fictional character, and her surroundings were certainly not decayed; she clearly had the same impulses to live with the past and keep the outside world at bay.

While Bruce hesitated, Nan interjected, "In relation to the death of Janine Gunning, did you know she had been in your house on the night she was murdered?"

"When?"

"Last Tuesday."

"My bridge night, so no doubt I wasn't here. Anyway, all sorts of people traipse through here on a daily basis, Constable, including Jennifer's rather loud friends and the people my husband works with. I try to avoid contact with them as much as possible. Particularly my husband's political colleagues. Even the women among them give off the anxious aroma of ambition. If the girl was here, I certainly did not encounter her."

"When we find out more about the remains in your grounds we will, of course, inform you, Mrs. Lake, and if you should recall anything that might be relevant, please contact me or Sergeant Wilson." They handed over their cards as if to conclude the interview.

Eloise Lake rose and took the cards gingerly as if they might be infected with a virus. Nan had no doubt that she would wash her hands as soon as they had gone. "I'm sure I know nothing else that might be useful, Officers. And I am less than curious about the remains, so just let my husband know of your findings." The plump smiling woman from before materialized, as if she had been summoned — though Nan had detected no bell or buzzer that Mrs. Lake could have pressed—and showed them out.

As they walked toward their car, Bruce said, "Well, there's a woman who thinks her shit smells like Chanel."

"I can't believe she's so uninterested in things that are happening on her own doorstep, especially when her husband is in the public eye so much. And she and Campbell Lake are an unlikely match surely."

"She was married to his brother before he killed himself, threw himself in the Forth. Lake was sniffing around her before his corpse was cold."

Nan reflected again how a small place like the Law had seen more than its fair share of tragedies over the years. She spent the rest of her shift filing reports of her recent interviews, which only made her more acutely aware of how little progress they were making.

She felt that the remains up at the Big Hoose were an unnecessary distraction from their main purpose, which was to find the killer of Janine Gunning. She pored over her interviews searching for anything they might have missed. All they had so far was a series of tenuous suspects. While she knew from hard experience not to judge people by appearances, was it really possible that men like Syme and Bauld were capable of a frenzied sex attack and brutal murder? They seemed more to be pitied than feared. And the link between Len Sark's ten-year-old conviction and the disappearance of a prostitute around the same time seemed equally insubstantial.

She believed that Campbell Lake was a slippery operator who would be ruthless in his pursuit of his ends both political and otherwise, and he had some links to both the murdered girl and Carol Chalmers, but that seemed nebulous too. Was it likely that underneath the suave surface, the bespoke suits, and custom-made shirts, there was a beast who couldn't control his craving for young flesh?

Other questions and speculations chased one another through her mind, tormenting and frustrating her. They reminded her of a recurrent dream she had in which she was pursuing an elusive figure sometimes through a forest but more often in an urban setting of poorly lit streets and shadowy closes and stairwells. She knew it was vital that she should catch up with him or her before they did something awful.

She could never get close enough to see them, but she knew they were only a few steps ahead of her because of tantalizing glimpses of a heel or the hem of a coat. She even imagined she could smell her quarry, but they were forever just ahead of her, taunting her; and when she woke with her bed sheets and her insides in a knot, she had an overwhelming sense of disappointment and failure.

Finally, she couldn't sit at her desk in the station any longer. It was late anyway. She had a vague intention of revisiting the Cross Inn. Perhaps there was more to be gleaned from the younger inhabitants of the Law—Jennifer Lake and her friends or Colin Sark. When the DI was not at his desk, she crept out of the office. She just managed to avoid Eastman as he stood with his back to her, talking on the phone. The last thing she needed was having to field any barbed questions from him.

She took out her car keys but then hesitated. It wasn't that far to walk to the inn from here. Her elbow ached from her repetitive pounding on a keyboard, and her knee was stiff from sitting too long. It would do her good to walk some of the discomfort off.

She could leave her car at the station and perhaps have a drink. The anesthetic properties of a couple of stiff vodkas would be just what she needed. And it was Saturday night after all. Part of her was hoping that she might bump into Dr. Chapelle, and even as she acknowledged that, she realized she ought to quell her dangerous and foolish anticipation.

CHAPTER 12

Faith Healing

The bar was busy when she eventually reached it. Her leg hurt, and she reflected that she might have been somewhat overambitious in undertaking the walk. The group of friends was at their favorite table, but they seemed more animated and louder than usual. Their voices were raised, and they burst into frequent bursts of raucous laughter.

Her initial disappointment of not seeing Solange Chapelle with them changed to a quickening of her pulse when the latter emerged from the toilets and glided over to the noisy coterie. She was breathtaking in a vivid yellow dress. Nan was debating whether or not she had the temerity to join them under the pretext of asking them if they had remembered anything relevant to the case when Darren waved and beckoned her over.

"Hey, Sarge, caught any interesting criminals the day? Sol, you'll no' have met the long arm and legs of the law, the legal law, I mean, no' the toon of Law. This is DS Wilson." He obviously had too much to drink, and Dr. Chapelle gave Nan a wry smile of greeting.

Jennifer said, "For God's sake, shut up, Darren, you're embarrassing her."

Nan noticed that she, too, was slurring her words. She looked flushed and kept casting hero-worshipping glances at Chapelle, who simply looked amused. "Great news though. Dr. Chapelle couldn't do the séance tonight because of the police activity chez moi, but she's agreed to come back next week when the fuss has died down and try again."

"Séance?" Nan looked questioningly at the group.

Dr. Chapelle merely smiled as if she was enjoying a private joke. Letty cast her eyes down while Jennifer glared at Darren. Nobody offered an explanation.

"You joinin' us for a drink, or are you still on duty?" asked Darren with an impish grin. "Another round everyone."

"You've had enough, Darren," said Letty, who seemed more sober than the others. Even the normally phlegmatic Beth was smiling inanely, and Angus gazed unfocusedly into the remains of his pint. "In fact, we've all had enough. I've called my dad to pick me up, so he'll be here any minute. Better give me your car keys, Darren. I'll get Dad to bring me to the van tomorrow and drop them off."

"Come on, Let, do you honestly think I'd try to drive?" Darren looked like a petulant schoolboy who had been summoned unjustly to the headmaster's office. Letty merely continued to hold out her hand till Darren slammed his keys sulkily into it.

"Think we should all be calling it a day," Jennifer agreed.

"Talk later," said Nan and went to get herself a drink. Colin Sark and his father were serving. The former eyed her warily as she ordered a large vodka and tonic and hoisted herself with some difficulty onto a barstool.

She nodded over to the group of friends who had begun to disperse. "Having a wee party over there."

"They've been in for most of the afternoon. Think they're drinking to drown their sorrows after their weekend plans were cancelled."

Nan took a large sip of her drink and sighed as she savored the burn of the alcohol. "Know anything about that?"

"Something about a séance up at the Big Hoose. No' that I was listenin' in or anything." He suddenly found an urgent need to empty the glass washer. Nan looked into the mirror behind the bar. Though her view was disrupted by optics, she saw a large ruddy-faced man appear at the door of the bar, and Letty Vance was hurrying over to him.

As they left, Jennifer leaned over to kiss Sol Chapelle on the cheek, and she hoisted a protesting Darren Boyd from his seat and linked arms with him as they exited too. Beth March and Angus McKissock appeared to exchange angry words before the latter weaved erratically between the tables toward the toilets. Beth looked after him for a moment before grabbing her bag and exiting hurriedly as if she wanted to catch up with her friends.

Nan downed her drink and smiled at Colin Sark and indicated she was ready for another. He served her with alacrity but dropped the coins of her change on his return and fumbled for them behind the bar. Nan sipped her second drink more slowly, trying and probably failing to look casual as she stole furtive looks in the mirror at Dr. Chapelle, who sat quietly finishing her whiskey.

Nan had stopped feeling uncomfortable about being a woman drinking alone in a bar many years ago, her feminist instincts putting it down to outmoded concepts of pubs being exclusively male territory. But she knew she had never possessed the poise of the academic, who seemed oblivious to everyone around her as she inhabited her own space.

She looked down at her drink, conscious that she was beginning to stare. She felt her spirits sinking once more and recognized the warning signs of the relentless introspection and questioning of her life choices and abilities that frequently led her to depression and kept her from sleep.

A voice at her side startled her from her reverie. "Mind if I join you, DS Wilson?" Chapelle slid gracefully into the barstool next to her without waiting for an invitation. "I know in these days of gender equality, I shouldn't admire women who have the courage to come into bars on their own, but generally, drinking holes are still bastions of the male species. And you're always liable to get hit on by some guy who looks into a mirror after a few drinks, and instead of seeing a guy who isn't going to win any beauty contests, he sees someone who's catnip to the chicks."

Nan thought, *For fuck's sake, say something instead of sitting like a tongue-tied teenager*, but she found the proximity of the woman overpowering. Apparently, undaunted by her silence, Chapelle went on, "I always find the hundred-yard stare pretty effective in dampening down their romantic notions. Is it this place or the things that have been happening here that are getting you down?"

Nan found her voice at last. "Dr. Chapelle—"

"Please call me Sol, and forgive me for prying."

"And I'm Nan. There's no need to apologize. Must be kind of obvious I'm not in my happy place since I'm sitting here with a face like a wet weekend."

"I think if I did your job, I'd be permanently gloomy. You've obviously seen a lot of stuff that doesn't exactly square with a rosy view of humanity."

"You might say that." She found herself smiling and overcame her reserve sufficiently to look at her companion directly for the first time.

Chapelle regarded her with wide wise brown eyes that seemed to look inside her. "At least you can still smile sometimes." In a surprisingly intimate gesture, Sol reached up and moved a lock of hair that had escaped her chignon away from Nan's eye.

Nan tried to conceal her discomposure by asking, "So séances, do you often conduct them?"

"No, not at all. But I do find them fascinating on a psychological level. And I'm fond of Jennifer Lake. Underneath that rich woman confidence, there's something of the lost little girl about her. Even at uni, she was going through a lot of stuff: her parents' marital discord and the whiff of scandal surrounding her dad. She's scrabbling around like the rest of us to find some meaning and purpose. So when she asked me to come here, I said yes.

"I thought it might allay some of her fears about malign influences at work at her house. But from my point of view, it would also provide some insights into her and her friends. Séances are more about reading the psychology of the individuals that participate than an opportunity to contact the dead."

"I'd be grateful if you'd share any of your insights with me. We're stumbling about in the dark at the moment."

"Don't sell yourself short." She caught Colin Sark's eye and nodded at both their glasses.

He looked at the two women obliquely as he fetched their drinks as if he was disturbed by their joint presence at the bar. It occurred to Nan that if Sol had been matching drink for drink with Jennifer and her friends, she was showing none of the signs of inebriation they had evinced.

Sol continued, "What I mean is you strike me as someone who has already worked out certain things about the case. You have some suspects, but up till now, none of them does it for you. And you take what you see as lack of progress personally. You lose sleep over it."

Nan was slightly perturbed by the woman's accurate analysis but said lightly, "I suppose the bags under my eyes are a dead giveaway."

"You have rather beautiful eyes in fact." Nan couldn't prevent the warm glow that suffused her cheeks. "And of course, you hide your feelings beneath a veneer of tough humor. Sorry, I'm being presumptuous. I promise, I'm not trying to psychoanalyze you."

"No, go on. We could use your powers of detection in the police."

"See, *humor*, I would say you feel a constant need to prove yourself. Maybe in the background, there's a pushy parent who doesn't approve of your choices?"

Nan was startled but replied, "Try two pushy parents."

"Besides, you've confirmed their worst fears by putting yourself in harm's way. You probably have a bit of posttraumatic stuff going on, too, that you've had to seek professional help for. You constantly question whether you've made the right decisions, and because you're a woman in a tough job, you feel the need to suppress your softer feelings in case they're mistaken for weakness."

Nan attempted to cover up her surprise at the accuracy of Sol's dissection of her character by taking a sip of her drink. "And you've worked out all this about me even though we've only just met?"

"The jury's still out for me on whether there's really such a thing as psychic ability. I was trying to explain to our young friends earlier how there are a lot of charlatans out there who use cold reading, guesses, and the use of statements that are general and universal to convince people they can read their minds."

"And that's what you've just been doing with me?"

"Yeah, sorry but kinda. You were looking sad when I came over so it's not rocket science to guess some of the reasons. Any woman in what is still a predominantly male profession probably feels the need to bury her femininity, and parents always worry about their children, especially those children who have chosen to work at the front line or in stressful occupations. My folks were mightily relieved when I stopped being a firefighter and became an academic."

Nan stared at her in surprise.

"Joke."

Nan laughed in spite of herself. She had been hovering between disquiet at Sol's revelations and vexation at her simple explanations. The woman had the unerring ability to wrong-foot her.

"And the physical clues are kinda obvious too. Looks like you've suffered a couple of serious injuries, and it isn't a quantum leap to guess they could have been sustained in the line of duty. Were they?"

Nan simply nodded.

"Look, I'm not just trying to show off here or be a smart-ass. I suspect I'm really trying to impress you and maybe to persuade you that this séance might throw up some things that could help to find out what's going on here."

Again, Nan was torn. She was both flattered and flustered that Sol should be making the effort to impress her, but her professional instincts told her she should be telling her to desist and that in her experience, any kind of amateur sleuthing would only serve to muddy the waters in what was already a murky and stagnant pond.

Before she could voice her concerns and objections, Sol reached out and touched her damaged elbow. "Still hurts a lot."

The bold statement and the woman's compassionate look made tears well up in Nan's eyes. Sol seemed to sense her emotional reaction, and as if to ward off embarrassment, she said brightly, "What say we put another couple of drinks on my bill and take them up to my room? There's something I'd like to show you."

The conflicting thoughts and emotions that rushed through Nan made her feel dizzy. Her sensible head told her she should decline the invitation, perhaps pleading tiredness after a long hard day, but part of her wanted to prolong her encounter with this fascinating woman. And she couldn't deny the excitement that coursed through her. She could still feel the warmth of Sol's touch through the jacket of her suit.

Sol took her silent vacillation as agreement and called to Colin, "Could you arrange to have these drinks brought to my room?" She continued to hold Nan's arm as she helped her from her barstool.

The young barman gawped at the two women open-mouthed. Nan couldn't decide whether it was because of Sol's audacity in assuming room service was available in a place like the inn or because of his astonishment that a police officer should go so blatantly to the room of a stunning-looking guest. She shuddered to think where his imagination was leading him.

They made their way out of the bar and up the narrow staircase. Sol had to duck frequently to avoid low beams. "I swear if I stay here too long, I'll have a permanent mark on my forehead." She giggled. At the door of her room, she said, "Do you think it's the done thing here to invite visitors to your room? That young barman looked shocked."

"It was probably because you asked him to bring the drinks up."

Again, there was that girlish laughter. It made Nan wonder if perhaps Sol was a little bit drunk after all. The room was intimate with a low ceiling and a Georgian-looking window with small panes of glass that reflected the glow from an old-fashioned standard lamp that stood in one corner.

A queen-size bed with an elaborately embroidered bedspread took up most of the space so that the narrow armchair and wardrobe and tiny bedside table that were the room's only other furniture looked like cramped afterthoughts.

With her apparently uncanny ability to read her thoughts, Sol said, "Yeah, bet you're glad you didn't bring your cat 'cause there's no room to swing it here. You kinda have to sidle around the bed."

Nan stood uncertainly, wondering if she should take the armchair when Sol took her bag and placed it with her own on the chair before sitting down on the bed and inviting Nan to join her by patting the cover beside her. Nan perched awkwardly. She was conscious that the other woman was so close that their thighs were touching.

Sol placed a hand lightly on her damaged knee. Nan could only shake her head. "Hurts here too, huh?"

"My knee and elbow were injured in the *accident*." She had always been self-conscious about her leg but found herself being surprisingly unfazed when Sol pushed her skirt a little higher and examined her knee more closely. She quickly pushed it back down when there was a light tap at the door.

Sol crossed to open it. Colin Sark stood there looking gauche and ill at ease with two drinks on a tray. She took the drinks, put them on the bedside table, and said to Colin, "Here, let me give you something."

She was reaching for her bag when he stammered, "No, no. You're a'right, honest," and closed the door hurriedly.

"God, did you see his face? Wonder what he expected to see." She gave a ribald laugh, handed Nan her drink, and rejoined her on the bed. "Cheers again."

"I shouldn't really. These are going to my head. Feeling a bit squiffy already." *For fuck's sake*, she thought. *Squiffy?* She sounded like a character in a P. G. Wodehouse novel. "You said you wanted to show me something?"

Sol took her drink and said, "Lie back on the bed. Here, let me take your shoes and jacket." She smoothly removed Nan's suit jacket before leaning down to take off her shoes and gently swinging her legs up onto the bed. Nan thought she did all this with a natural ease as if it was simply etiquette to do this for a stranger you'd invited to your bedroom.

"I'm going to just hold my hand over your elbow without touching it but close enough that you should sense it there." Nan watched her elegant fingers hovering over her elbow. "Close your eyes. Feel anything?"

"I don't think so." Nan felt her loosening her cuff and trying to roll up her sleeve, but her blouse was close fitting, so it could go no farther than her lower arm.

"Let's just slip this off a little. Do you mind?"

Nan's eyes sprang open as she felt the other woman's fingers beginning to undo the buttons of her blouse. "I really don't think—"

Sol smiled at her reassuringly and said in a breathy voice, "Relax." In a smooth movement, she slid the blouse from her shoulders. Nan looked down bashfully at her pale skin and her purple bra that had once been expensive and had lived up to its lingerie tag, but now the color looked faded after too many washes. "Just close your eyes and please relax."

Reluctantly, Nan obeyed.

"I'm holding my hand just above your elbow again. As I move it around, you should feel your elbow getting warmer and warmer." As she listened to the smooth milk chocolate tones of the woman's voice, Nan was astonished to find that she was indeed beginning to feel a warmth radiating from her arm. "And that warmth is soothing, soothing, taking away any pain."

And it was true; the nagging discomfort that was always with her was gradually easing away. She didn't know how long they sat there like that. At one point, she felt she was drifting till Sol said gently, "Let's do the same for your poor leg."

As she moved her hand away, Nan felt an almost physical longing to have it back there. She didn't know if it was the woman's soporific voice or the effects of the alcohol she had consumed, but she wasn't perturbed when she felt Sol undoing the button and sliding down the zip at the side of her skirt. Nan even raised her bottom so it could be slid off more easily.

"Pantyhose just get in the way." Nan didn't open her eyes as her black tights were removed. Partly, it was because she was aware that the navy knickers she was wearing were wildly unsexy and didn't match her bra but also she was in an almost dreamlike state where these things hardly seemed to matter.

"Once again, I'm just going to hold my hand over your knee. Feel it getting warm?"

Nan felt the same heat suffusing her leg that she had on her arm. "Yes, I do feel something."

"And you only feel the warmth. The ache is receding, floating away."

Once more, Nan had no sense of time passing. She felt only gratitude for these moments of respite from the pain that usually was her constant companion. When she opened her eyes at last, Sol was studying her as if she were a fascinating creature she had just discovered.

Suddenly, Nan became uncomfortably aware that she was lying half naked in a strange hotel room and crossed her hands over her breasts self-consciously. Sol said softly. "Unfortunately, I can't cure you, but I can make you feel better for a while." She traced her fingers in a line from below Nan's breasts to her stomach. The woman's actual touch was a shock at first, but Nan felt a more intense kind of heat. "You have beautiful skin."

Nan tried to lighten the atmosphere by saying, "My body never sees the sun. I'm as pale as a ghost."

"Would you just lie there for a few more minutes? I have to pee."

The moment Sol disappeared into the en suite bathroom, Nan felt nonplussed. What did she think she was doing? The woman was involved with a number of suspects in a case she was supposed to be investigating. This could compromise her. And yet she felt unable to move as if her body had floated free from her mind, which was urging her even more vehemently, as she heard the toilet flush and the sound of running water, that she had to leave before it was too late.

And then it was too late. When Sol reappeared, she was naked. Nan's breath caught in her chest as she took in her large high breasts and muscular legs. Between them was an unapologetic shock of dark pubic hair. Nan knew she was lost even before Sol moved to her, and the soft pillows of her lips were on hers and then on her neck and moving onto her nipples.

She was scarcely aware of her underwear being removed, and the ridiculous thought occurred to her that perhaps this woman did possess mysterious powers after all. In spite of her heightening arousal, her mind refused to let go of the sense that this was unreal. She even reflected that if anyone could look down on the scene, they would be struck by the contrast between them—Sol's body dark as night against the milk of her skin. And then there were no more thoughts as Sol's tongue and soothing fingers moved onto her vagina, and she gave herself up to the primal urgency of desire.

After, as her own tongue explored the secret hollows between Sol's legs and that majestic arse, she reflected that there was something elemental about the encounter. She tasted of the earth and the sea. When they lay together, limbs entwined, hair wild, and skin damp, Nan couldn't stop herself from asking, "All of the healing thing, was that just a device to seduce me?"

Sol regarded her with amusement in her eyes. "I told you, I could make you feel better for a while."

Nan had no inclination to pursue it. "You certainly did that. I'll be back." She rose reluctantly, retrieved her phone which she had left switched off in her bag, and went into the bathroom. As she sat on the toilet, she turned the phone back on. As it started up, she noticed Sol's bright-yellow dress hanging at the back of the door, but she could see no sign of discarded underwear.

Before she could reflect on the kind of woman who walked around naked under her dress, she discovered she had three missed calls from DI Bruce. He answered on the first ring. "Where the hell are you? I've been trying to reach you. Beth March and Angus McKissock were attacked on their way home from the pub."

Nan was stunned by this development. "I'm at the Cross Inn. Could you send a car round? I've had a couple of drinks."

In the bedroom, she scrambled around for her bra and pants, which had been discarded carelessly on the floor. "I'm sorry, Sol. I have to go. Something's come up at work."

"That's okay. I realize you couldn't stay the night anyway. Probably wouldn't do anything for either of our reputations."

She leaned on her elbow, her heavy breasts above the crumpled sheet, candidly watching Nan dressing with no attempt to pretend casual disinterest. Nan felt herself lapsing back into awkward coyness under her frank gaze. Almost simultaneously, it seemed that her knee and elbow began to ache once more. As she struggled to think of something suitable to say before she left—"Thanks for the amazing sex. We must get together and do this again some time?"—Sol rose and embraced her silently. It seemed enough.

CHAPTER 13

Hospital Visits

Nan was dismayed to find Sergeant Eastman at the wheel of the car that was waiting outside the inn. The last thing she needed was his impertinent questions about her night. Sure enough, as soon as she slid into the passenger seat, he regarded her inquisitively. Her hair was still down, and she'd barely had time to draw a brush through it.

"Good night?"

"Yes, thanks."

"You're lookin' a bit flushed. Bit of a heavy session was it? Drinkin' to forget your troubles and that?"

"Something like that."

"Kinda late. Hope you havenae been participatin' in any illegal lock-ins wi' the locals." When Nan didn't respond, he conjectured, "Unless you met a handsome stranger, eh? They have plenty of rooms upstairs in that place?"

Nan ignored the salacious grin on his face. "Just drive. What's the story on these attacks?"

He smirked knowingly and said, "That's what we're goin' to find out. They've been taken to the community hospital."

"So their injuries aren't too bad then?" Nan knew the small hospital only had a minor injuries unit and no A&E (accident and emergency).

"No' life-threatening apparently."

"This has to be connected to the Janine Gunning case."

"That's why Carpenter and Bruce are at the hospital while we speak."

When they arrived, they were directed to a small waiting area. Nan texted Bruce to tell him they had arrived, and a few moments later, the DI appeared and took them up to a corridor that was painted in a garish shade of yellow. There were a few doors leading off to individual wards.

Lowering his voice, the DI said, "McKissock's in the one at the end, and Beth March is just here. DCI Carpenter is in with him. Eastman, you're with her. Sergeant Wilson and I will speak to Beth."

When Eastman had made his way along the corridor, Bruce said, "She's badly shaken, but apart from that, there are no serious injuries, and there's no indication of sexual assault."

"What the hell happened?"

"The bare bones of it are that they both left the pub rather the worse for wear."

"I can vouch for that. I saw them. Beth March went after Jennifer Lake and Darren Boyd."

"Jennifer wanted to pay for a taxi, but the others decided to walk to clear their heads, so they split up outside the inn. McKissock was on his own. He admits he had had one too many, and when he was heading home, someone struck him from behind on the side of the head, and he went down dazed. By the time he'd recovered enough to be able to stand up, his attacker had disappeared. Whoever it was, it made no attempt to grab his wallet or phone. He hadn't paid any attention to them at the time, too busy trying to put one foot in front of the other without staggering."

"What the hell is going on, Malcolm? Are all of these incidents connected?"

"Fuck if I know."

When they entered the ward, Beth March was perched fully dressed on the side of the only bed in the room. Her sweat-dampened dark hair contrasted the pallor of her skin. She looked up at them sheepishly. "They say they want to keep me here in case I have concussion or something, but I need to go home. Mum will be worried sick."

Nan said, "Can't you call her?"

"She never answers the phone when I'm out, and even though I'm always on at her to get a mobile phone, she insists she wouldn't be able to work one."

"Ms. March, I know you've had a frightening experience, but do you feel up to answering a couple of questions about the attack? Afterward, we'll clear it with the doctor and arrange for a car to take you back."

Beth looked at Bruce gratefully for a moment and then glanced down at her lap and nodded.

Nan stepped in, "First of all, did you get a look at your assailant?" She knew she was sounding like a formal cliché, so she tried to soften her approach by sitting next to the girl on the bed.

"No, I left Darren and Jennifer at the pub. They offered to walk me to my door, but to be honest, Darren was at that silly drunk stage, and I just wanted to get rid of him." She stopped and stared out of the window. Her expression suggested she was unwilling to revisit a painful memory.

"And then what happened?" Bruce prompted.

"I had almost reached my gate when something struck me from behind, and I went down on my knees." Nan stole a glance at her legs; her knees were grazed. "With the drink—I don't usually drink so much, so I was already a bit unsteady—and the shock of it, I suppose, I was really disorientated, and then what felt like a foot pushed me down onto the pavement. I must have hit my head because I don't remember much of what happened next. I know when I came round, I was sprawled face down on the pavement."

"Have you got any idea—any idea at all—why someone might have attacked you?" Bruce asked.

"None. My handbag was lying next to me. It was open, and some of my stuff was scattered next to it, but my purse and my phone were still there. Later when I checked, there didn't seem to be any money missing, and my credit card was in my bag."

"What did you do next?" Nan asked.

"I got up as quickly as I could and looked all around in case whoever it was might still be nearby. The street was deserted, so I dashed into my house and dialed 999. Thank God Mum was in bed and didn't see the state I was in. I waited by till the police and ambulance arrived. I mean, I was shaking like a leaf. I kept thinking of Janine and that other girl that disappeared."

A shadow crossed the DI's face as he murmured, "Carol Chalmers."

"Yes, I couldn't help thinking I might have been next. That maybe somebody had been watching me in the pub, waiting for the chance to abduct me o-or worse."

Nan said softly, "Sorry, we have to ask you this, Beth, but when you were dazed and didn't really know what was happening, do you think this person might have *touched* you inappropriately?"

The girl looked toward the window again as if to avoid their scrutiny. "They…they've examined me, and I wasn't *you know*. And I think I'd know if someone had, well, touched me up, you know. Only…"

There was a long pause during which Beth's discomposure was evident.

"Only what, Beth?" Nan asked gently.

"M-my underwear was gone."

Nan exchanged a worried look with Bruce.

Beth went on, "I know I was *fully dressed* before…before I was hit. I mean, I'm not the sort to go out without pants on." Her face flamed. "I was so confused after I was attacked, I didn't even notice till I was home and waiting for the police and ambulance to arrive and I had to use the loo."

"Okay, we'll go and have a word with the doctor, and if he gives you permission, we'll organize for you to get home." Bruce seemed keen to leave.

Nan patted the girl's hand. "But have a good think, Beth. If there's anything else you remember—anything at all, however small—let us know right away."

Nan followed Bruce out. They had barely closed the door to the ward when he hissed, "What the fuck?"

"Quite. This case just keeps getting more and more bizarre. Does the missing underwear mean there's a link to Janine Gunning?"

"You think there's some nutcase out there who wants to steal girls' knickers? Wouldn't it be a hell of a lot easier to just steal them off clotheslines? And then what? Sometimes they resist too much, so he ends up killing them?" Bruce ran his hand exasperatedly through his hair, making it stand on end even more.

"And where does the attack on Angus McKissock fit in, or was it just a random coincidence?"

"Better check with Carpenter and Eastman that he's still got his underpants on."

The ridiculousness of the remark coupled with Bruce's perplexed appearance gave Nan the sudden urge to giggle. As she tried to suppress the mirth bubbling up inside her, she caught Bruce's eyes, and then both of them were snorting with suppressed laughter and moved away from the door in case Beth might hear. It took at least a minute to get themselves under control.

Nan wondered if she was looking as shamefaced as Bruce at their entirely inappropriate behavior. There seemed to her to be an edge of hysteria to it though she reflected it was no doubt similar to the impulse that made people want to laugh at funerals.

Fortunately, they had assumed more grave expressions before Carpenter and Eastman appeared. Bruce brought the DCI quickly up to speed on the Beth March attack. Of course, Eastman couldn't resist saying, "Better put the word out to look out for any more panties thefts, especially the ones where the owner's still wearing them."

Carpenter said haughtily, "May I remind you this was a serious assault, Sergeant, and there's nothing remotely humorous about it." Eastman seemed unrepentant after the reprimand.

Nan intervened, "What about McKissock? Has he got any idea who might have attacked him?"

"None. He speculated it might have been a spontaneous attack by a disgruntled customer from the garage. Maybe someone who had bought a dodgy secondhand motor from his dad. Apparently, there were a few of them. But apart from that or a random attacker, he doesn't have a clue."

It was up to Nan to put into words what the others undoubtedly were thinking. "Surely this can't be coincidence. Two of a group of friends who met regularly at a pub where a young barmaid was murdered recently get attacked on the same day? What are we missing here?"

With a shake of his head, Bruce went off to find a doctor.

"There must be CCTV along the main streets. Let's see how much of it is deployed around the shopping area and get onto traffic to see if their cameras have spotted anyone showing an unusual interest in the group that left the pub together. Then we knock more doors around McKissock's garage and Beth March's street. See if anyone saw anything. Sergeant Eastman and I will head back to the station to get the ball rolling. If the March girl is allowed to go home, you and DI Bruce take her and then meet us there."

She set off down the corridor briskly. Before Eastman followed her, he looked glumly at Nan and murmured, "Shit," under his breath. They both knew the hours of tedium ahead: the routine door-to-door inquiries and poring over CCTV footage. Shoe leather and red eyes—the monotonous grind of police procedure. But, Nan reflected, they had to hope it would uncover something useful.

They took Beth March to Bruce's car. As if to underline Nan's pessimism, a dense haar had drifted off the Forth. It seemed to her that they were stumbling around in a dense fog that only deepened and darkened as they peered into it, trying to find their way.

CHAPTER 14

Hair of the Dog

Colin watched Dr. Chapelle moving across the inn's car park to a Ford Focus. He thought that such an unusual woman might have something a bit more exotic, like an Aston Martin perhaps or a Dodge Viper. When she checked out, she gave him her mobile number with instructions to make sure Sergeant Wilson received it. She accompanied this with a twenty-pound tip and ignored his protestations with an airy wave.

He rubbed at his eyes. Even though he had finished his Saturday shift late and was worn out, sleep had eluded him. His overactive imagination conjured up lurid scenes of the two women he had seen in the bedroom when he took up their drinks. The policewoman had been sitting on Dr. Chapelle's bed, and to Colin, she looked brittle and on edge, as if she had been interrupted in a guilty act. He wondered what had happened after he had closed the bedroom door.

But it wasn't just salacious speculation that kept him from sleep. His mind raced from one troubling image to the next—Janine Gunning, alive and laughing; Carol Chalmers running through the school grounds in her school uniform; and Jennifer Lake flicking her long hair and laughing up at him as she called him Clipper. And why was he thinking of Jennifer in the same context as the other two girls, one dead and one lost? Was it some kind of premonition that she might suffer the same fate?

More dark thoughts made him toss and turn. Why was his father behaving so suspiciously, and what was the guilty secret from his past that his mother had referred to? Though he had told Angus he would ask his father why he had been meeting with Campbell Lake and Angus's dad, he had no intention of doing so. He had no desire to provoke him, and besides, part of him was afraid of what he might find. Everyone in this town seemed to have something to hide.

And now one of the morning cleaners had told him about the attacks on Beth March and Angus McKissock. It made him feel he was living through a nightmare in which everyone was wearing a mask that could slip at any moment and reveal something monstrous and foul underneath.

He tackled his usual bar chores in a desultory and frequently clumsy fashion. In his distracted state, he managed to smash two glasses and a large empty vodka bottle when he was changing the optic. He was in the process of sweeping up broken glass when he was surprised to see Angus McKissock entering the bar. He had a spectacularly colored bruise above his right temple, and his eye was beginning to blacken.

"Surprised to see you in here so early on a Sunday especially after… No' working on Darren's car the day?"

"Pint please, Sarky. Waiting for parts for it. It's a piece of shit. I keep tellin' him I won't be able to keep it on the road much longer." He sank half of his beer in one swallow. "Christ, I needed that."

"Heard about what happened to you and Beth. What the fuck is happenin' in this place?"

"Beats me."

"You have any idea who did it?"

"If I had, I'd be round there with a tire iron. I told the filth I never saw what hit me far less who. Told them I thought it might have been a dissatisfied customer from the garage. Christ knows my old man's sold on some right cut and shuts in the past."

"Have you heard how Beth is?"

"Gave her a bell this mornin'. She said she was fine, but she sounded really spooked. Mebbe delayed shock or that. She didnae give me many details but seems somebody came up to her from behind as well. When I plucked up the courage to ask if she'd been robbed o-or molested, she just said no in this dead quiet voice. Fuck knows what really happened."

"Do you think this is connected with Janine somehow?"

"Put another one in there will you, Sarky? Cannae work out how. If it had just been Beth, I could have seen it, but if it's the same psycho out there that did what they did to Janine, what the fuck would he want to attack me for?"

Colin left him staring into his pint while he went to serve Bauld and Syme, who had come in together. When he returned, Angus said, "Found out anythin' fae your dad about yesterday?"

"Havenae had a chance to ask." He hoped that Angus couldn't tell that he was lying. "You?"

"I asked him, and he looked a bit furtive like and told me to mind my own fucking business. No, but here's the thing, the garage has been on its knees for months. I mean, our reputation's shit wi' everyone round here. But just lately, Dad's been dealin' wi' a lot more upmarket motors than the crap he usually sells, and the repair side's picked up as well. We even took on another mechanic. His English isnae great, but he's a good worker and kens his way around cars, like."

Colin lowered his voice. "That's funny. A couple of months ago, my dad's credit card was refused at the cash and carry. He tried another one, and it was declined as well. I was wi' him. I was fucking mortified. We havenae been gettin' as many passin' tourists as we used to. If it wasnae for the regulars, fuck knows how we'd stay open. And my mum and dad seemed to be arguin' all the time about money. Heads up."

He turned away to put Angus's money in the till as his mother appeared and came over. "Angus, look at the state of you. Betty Lennox told me what happened to you and Beth March, as if she didn't have enough on her plate wi' her mother. How are you both?"

Angus looked uncomfortable. "Nothin' serious, Mrs. Sark. Thanks for askin'."

"I don't know what this place is coming to. It's like the wild West. Folks are going to be scared to walk the streets at night." She paused a moment as if to see if Angus was going to be more forthcoming and, disappointed, went out to the kitchen.

"I swear that Betty Lennox knows what's happenin' in the Law before it even happens," Angus said irritably.

"Aye, it was her that told me an' all. Anyway, as I was sayin', we seemed to be havin' money worries, then we get the catering gig for Janine's funeral, and we have another two lined up for next week. The Rotary Club have asked if they can have their weekly meetings here instead of the Royal Hotel, and that arsehole Paul Rand is havin' a leaving do for his PA here. The old man was even talkin' about how the place needs a face-lift, and I seen him lookin' through a catalogue for pub furniture and fittings."

"You think it's connected wi' them meeting up wi' Campbell Lake?"

Colin leaned closer. "Bit of a fucking coincidence, that accountant bein' there as well. And do you no' think there's somethin' funny about both your dad and mine being on their uppers one minute then suddenly business is boomin'?"

Angus's shoulders slumped, and he cast his eyes around as if he was looking for an escape route. "You think they might be involved in somethin' illegal?"

"Fuck if I know, but you must admit there's somethin' fishy goin' on."

"So what do you suggest we do?"

"There's nothing we can do except keep our ears to the ground. The good thing is if they are involved in some shady business arrangement, the police have too many other priorities to be payin' attention to that at the moment."

The worry in his eyes and the set of his mouth showed Colin that Angus was unconvinced. "I'd better shoot the craw."

"You find out anythin', let me know, and I'll do the same."

Angus merely nodded. He left most of his second pint and went out as if he was walking to the gallows.

CHAPTER 15

Shoe Leather and Red Eyes

The following week seemed to pass for Nan in a blur. Angus McKissock came into the station on Monday, the side of his face sporting a colorful bruise, and she had taken his statement that added nothing that might be helpful in finding his attacker. The team had examined the available CCTV footage taken around the time of the assaults.

A number of people had been out and about in groups or in couples, and the ones who were alone were mainly dog walkers or joggers. They had traced one man who looked as if he had been acting suspiciously when one of the PCs identified him as a well-known homeless figure who often slept rough. He turned out to have been raking through bins in the area, and far from seeing him as a suspect, Nan felt a stab of pity at his squalid predicament.

No one on Beth's street had seen or heard anything. Traffic cameras had identified a number of cars in the area, but none of them triggered any alarm bells.

On Tuesday, she and Bruce went round to Beth's house to take her statement. The DI thought it would save her having to come into the station, and once again, Nan felt a mixture of warmth and pain at his sensitivity. The house smelled of bleach and a cloying floral air freshener, both failing to cover the underlying whiff of sickness that pervaded everything.

They were surprised to find Darren Boyd in the living room. He sat next to Beth's mother's wheelchair, clutching a plastic beaker with a straw. Clearly, he had been helping her with a drink, but his reaction to their appearance suggested he had been caught trying to burgle the place. The room seemed cramped. Nan thought some of the furniture had been pushed together to accommodate the wheelchair.

The air crackled with tension as Beth fussed around them offering tea and then hovering uncertainly as if she was in an unfamiliar space rather than in her own surroundings. Her mother sat small and fragile, her eyes darting between them like a nervous animal as she gamely tried to make small talk. There was a haunted look in her eyes, and Nan could only imagine her distress at the news of her daughter's attack. Perhaps it had emphasized the precariousness and vulnerability of the two women's situation.

Getting down to business, Bruce said, "Actually, Darren, it's fortuitous to find you here. You were on the list of people we were getting round to seeing."

"Not sure how much help I can be. I was pretty out of it. Too much drink, you know?" He added this hurriedly as if they might jump to the wrong conclusions and make the connection to his drug habit.

"You didn't see anyone hanging around that night?" Nan asked.

"To be honest, I dinnae really mind much about it. I cannae even remember how I got back to the van. Woke up in the early hours of the next mornin' lying on my bunk. Still had my jacket and boots on. There were a bunch of wee devils inside my skull tryin' to tunnel their way out wi' pneumatic drills." He tried to smile apologetically at Beth's mum, but it emerged as more of a grimace.

"Obviously, if I had seen the cu—the person that was attackin' Beth, I'd have jumped in, like."

Beth appeared preoccupied with trying to arrange a large vase of flowers that was on the sideboard till her mother said, "Beth, will you sit down. You're making me nervous fidgeting about there." She said it lightly in a thin reedy voice, clearly at pain not to antagonize her daughter. Beth sat suddenly on a dining chair as if an invisible hand had pushed her into it.

"Beth, if you're feeling up to it, we'd like to go over what you said earlier just after your ordeal and check that there's nothing else that you might have remembered since then. Obviously, if you'd like to go into another room…" Bruce looked pointedly at her mother and Darren.

"I've told Mum and Darren all about it, even th-the embarrassing stuff."

Darren rose stiffly, looking around as if he was uncertain what to do with the beaker till Mrs. March indicated the tray that was attached to her chair.

"I was just going anyway. Beth, you want me to pick you up later for the pub?"

Beth glanced at her mother before answering, "That's probably not a brilliant idea at the moment, Darren."

Darren's face reddened further. "No. Right. Sorry."

"We'll have to pay you a visit at some point, Mr. Boyd," said Bruce.

"Sure. Nae blue lights and sirens though, eh? My neighbors in the other caravans might get the wrong idea." Realizing his weak joke was doing nothing to lighten the atmosphere in the room, he said, "I'll come in again, Beth. Look after yourself, Mrs. M." He patted Beth's shoulder as he shuffled out.

When he had gone, Beth said, "I'm sorry, but I can't really think of anything else that might help. Seeing Darren again just reminded me of what happened before the attack. The rest is just as confused as I said before."

Nan took her through the statement she had made after the assault, conscious all the time of the presence of the diminished woman in the wheelchair who seemed to hold her breath at the violent details and fluttered a hand in the air helplessly as if trying to ward them off.

There was an uncomfortable silence after she had finished broken by Beth, saying, "How's Angus?"

"He came into the station yesterday. He' s a bit bruised, but he's recovering."

"And he was attacked around the same time as me?"

Nan looked to Bruce, who said, "Similar time line. We think perhaps a short while before your assault."

"Don't you think that's weird? Was there some random nutter roaming the Law that night lookin' for folk to harm?"

Bruce squirmed in his seat. "We haven't found any evidence of—"

"I mean, why me and Angus? Maybe Darren was lucky, whoever it was didn't go after him, and do you think Jen and Letty might be in danger as well?"

"We have no reason to believe that there's someone targeting your friends." Even as she said it, Nan realized how feeble and inadequate she sounded.

"But what if they are?"

"Can you think of someone you and your friends might have had a run-in with recently or someone who might have a grievance against you all?"

Beth shook her head.

"Then it's hard to go down that avenue." The girl looked so hopeless that Nan had to resist an impulse to go over to her and put her arm around her.

As she showed them out, Nan said quietly, "How are you coping really, Beth? Believe me, I know how hard it can be in the aftermath of something like this." She was aware of Bruce loitering awkwardly in the doorway as she went on, "And what with your worries about your mum and everything."

"Thanks, but I suppose we're all right considering. Mum has carers coming in four times a day, and the routine of it helps, I think."

As they drove off, Nan could see in her rearview mirror the girl standing at the garden gate watching them till they were out of sight. Her forlorn figure seemed like an accusation. Waves of inadequacy crashed around Nan, threatening to drown her spirits.

The DI said, "What do you say we pay our friend Darren Boyd a wee visit now, when he isn't expecting us?" Without waiting for a reply, he turned the car toward the coast road that would take them to Nirvana Caravan site.

It was situated on the cliff tops with good views over the Forth. To Nan's eyes, some of the static caravans there looked old and neglected though a few owners had made more of an effort than others by fencing them off and planting flower beds. She seemed to recall that when vans reached a certain age, they had to be removed or replaced by newer models, but that didn't appear to be a rule that was being enforced rigidly here.

Darren's van was much smaller than the ones that surrounded it, and it had seen better days, but its situation on the outskirts of the site afforded a better view than those caravans that were in the centre. His car was there, but when they knocked, there was no answer, and there was no sign of him when they looked into the large front window. Nan was surprised that the interior of the van appeared to be tidy and well kept. She had expected it to be as disheveled as its owner.

Bruce waved her over and pointed toward the cliff top where she could discern a figure crouched over a small bonfire. Dark smoke was being blown inland toward them. Darren rose so hastily when he saw them approaching; it looked like something had stung him. Nan couldn't decide if it was their presence that alarmed him or if he had been caught doing something suspicious.

He held out his wrists as if he was about to be handcuffed. "A'right. It's a fair cop. Guilty." When they both looked puzzled, he went on, "We're no' supposed to burn stuff on the site." When he noticed them eyeing the fire, he said, "I had so much junk in the van to get shot of I couldnae be arsed takin' it to the dump. Better stand upwind, Officers, or your clothes will stink of smoke."

Nan tried to make out the contents of the bonfire. It blazed with a mixture of what might have been old clothes and paper. She could just see what looked like the smoldering cover of a lad's mag, an impossibly solid pair of breasts blackening in the flames.

"We could go back to the van. Wasnae expectin' you quite so soon, but as you can see, I've been tryin' to tidy." As they walked back, he added, "Dinnae get many visitors. Let's face it, when the gang get together, if it's a choice of goin' up to Jen's place or squeezin' into mine..." He unlocked the door to the caravan, and they went in after him. "See what I mean? Couldnae get a decent-sized telly in here, far less a pool table."

The three of them seemed to take up all the available room, so she and Bruce sat on the bench seat that ran beneath the window. Its upholstery was rather worn and threadbare, but, as Nan had observed from outside, the space was clean and uncluttered. In fact, there was very little that indicated the van was occupied apart from a couple of paperback books and a tablet that was charging on a pullout table.

Bruce nodded toward it. "You get a decent signal up here?"

"Reasonable. There are some long-term residents here, and the owners have to keep them happy. I'm pretty dependent on my tablet and my phone for entertainment."

Once again, Nan's nose was assaulted by the artificial scent of air freshener though she thought in this case, it wasn't to disguise the smell of a sick room so much as to conceal the smell of weed, a function it was failing conspicuously to fulfill.

"I'd offer tea or coffee, but I havenae had the chance to get to the shops yet."

As the three of them sat uncomfortably close together, Nan took him again through the day of the attack, but he stuck to his earlier insistence that his memory was hopelessly clouded by drink.

"What I don't get is why Beth and Angus? I mean none of us are involved in anythin' shady." He must have noticed Nan and Bruce's skeptical looks, and he at least had the good grace to look chastened. "All right, I get it. You ken about my *past misdemeanors*, but you cannae think the likes of Beth March would take anythin' stronger than a paracetamol."

Bruce turned up the heat. "And you're behaving now, Darren? If we were to get a warrant to search your caravan, we wouldn't find anything incriminating?"

Darren licked his lips nervously. "You wouldnae have any grounds. Look at my record. There's nae violence in it, and I'd never do anythin' to hurt my mates."

"We'll be in touch." Darren looked relieved as they left. Nan had no doubt he had been sweating at having two police officers in close proximity to wherever he had hidden his stash. Bruce seemed to read her mind. "You think he was burning some fragrant herbs on that fire?"

"I'd be surprised if he was. Let's face it, he's no big time dealer, and he couldn't afford to lose a valuable source of income."

"But he must have a supplier, and there's always someone up the line who's pulling these guys' strings, usually someone with very dirty hands and no conscience."

"But what's the connection? Besides, he had a point. He has no history of violence and no motive that I can see for the attacks on his friends." Nan was troubled, too, that in the case of Janine Gunning, by his own admission, he had enjoyed one or two sexual encounters with her, so what reason would he have had to subject her to a barbaric assault?

She couldn't rule him out as a suspect, of course. He had close connections to all of the victims. But she was nagged once more by the feeling that this case was uncovering more questions than answers.

The DI interrupted her jumbled thoughts. "He did seem to be burning clothes though. I haven't seen much evidence of him having an extensive wardrobe that he renews regularly, so maybe he was burning them to get rid of evidence."

Despite her doubts about Darren's involvement, she said, "Worth getting forensics to check."

After the tedious task of writing up reports, she found herself almost on automatic pilot as she drove to the Cross Inn. She had no clear idea why she had gone back there. She knew Sol had returned to the world of academia.

The bar was dead. There was no sign of Darren and his friends, and Nan suspected they were lying low after the attacks on two of their group. She was debating whether to have just one drink when Colin Sark sidled up to her with a piece of paper. "Dr. Chapelle asked me to give you this."

Nan felt her cheeks burning and a fluttering in her groin as she realized it was Sol's mobile number. Outside the bar, she took out her phone and added the number to her contacts and then spent the next few minutes in an agony of indecision about whether she should call her.

*****

She spent a restless night, waking at one point from her recurrent nightmare. This time, she was pursuing her shadowy prey along precipitous cliff paths and only surfaced from the dream when she found herself standing at the end of one of the paths looking down at a turbulent sea, watching waves crashing on rocks that looked like jagged blackened teeth. Even when she was awake, she thought she could still hear the boom of the sea and smell the rotten tang of seaweed.

The next morning, she phoned Sol's number before cold feet could stop her. There was no reply, but she left a halting message on her voice mail, thanking her for leaving her number and asking her to let her know when she was next in the area.

There were some sorry-looking faces at the station when she got there, a couple of them sporting bruises and black eyes. DI Bruce called her over and told her that there was, what he described as, an altercation the previous night at the Queen of the Forth pub. Apparently, some of the local ne'er do wells had taken umbrage at Sergeant Eastman and his colleagues' aggressive style of questioning, and one of the drunker customers had thrown a punch. What followed sounded to Nan more like a Western-style barroom brawl than an altercation, and uniform had been called in to break it up.

Nan was unsurprised and secretly wished that she had been there to see Eastman's heavy-handed methods coming unstuck. The DI said that three men were currently in the cells charged with assaulting police officers. DCI Carpenter had called a case review meeting at ten. Nan thought that under the circumstances, it would be a short meeting.

As they gathered in the incident room, Nan noticed that Eastman, rather than engaging her with his usual flippant cheek, avoided contact with her and seemed much more subdued. Her granny had had an apt expression for it: "His gas was at a peep." No doubt he had felt the sharp edge of Carpenter's tongue.

Sure enough, she immediately pinned him and some of the officers whom she had brought in with her with a steely glare and launched into a diatribe about how damaging and self-defeating it was to antagonize the people of the town when some of them might be harboring evidence, however unaware they might be of its significance, that would help them to find the perpetrator not just of Janine Gunning's murder but also of the recent assaults. She talked in complex sentences without pausing for breath.

Though her demeanor was calm, she appeared to Nan to be struggling to bottle up her fury and frustration. She had a twitch in her left eye, which she hadn't noticed before. She stopped and turned to the pinboard, visibly composing herself before addressing them again.

"I am aware of everyone's exasperation and disappointment at the lack of significant breakthroughs in the case, but we must proceed with patience and professionalism. Now we have some findings through on the human remains found in the grounds of the Lakes' house. They indicate they are those of a man, and he appears to have been there for around a 150 years or so."

There was an audible groan from some of her audience. Nan knew they were thinking it was another dead end, but her thoughts went to the colorful stories Jennifer had told about the house's history. Could these be the remains of the notorious Confederate major who had owned the place in the mid-nineteenth century? She forced herself to concentrate on the DCI's address.

"I have, therefore, authorized a search of the areas around the recent assaults, the street where Beth March was attacked and the vicinity of the McKissock garage."

Nan was surprised to hear PC Elsie Telfer asking what they were looking for or hoping to find. Normally, Elsie worked away in the background largely unnoticed and self-effacing.

"Perhaps whatever was used as a weapon to attack Angus McKissock. And as you know, an article of clothing was taken from Ms. March. Meanwhile, we'll continue to monitor the activities of their friends. In the light of DI Bruce and DS Wilson's discovery that Darren Boyd was burning materials at the Nirvana Caravan site, forensics are up there gathering evidence. Also I'd like to bring into the station some of those who have been interviewed already in connection with Janine Gunning's murder and a team of officers is revisiting the files on Carol Chalmers."

She noticed DI Bruce looking vexed and rigid. She could guess what he was thinking. Did the DCI not recognize that he had already been through this material many times with a fine-tooth comb? She could feel herself bristling with indignation as well at the suggestion that they had to recheck her own previous interviewees so soon.

Still she tried to rationalize that perhaps it would put more pressure on the likes of Syme, Bauld, and Sark if they were taken out of their comfort zone. Sometimes the formality of an interview down at the station concentrated a suspect's mind. Nevertheless, it felt like a slight and part of her thought they were wasting time going over old ground.

When the meeting broke up, a young DC that Nan didn't recognize approached Bruce and said, "There's a Mr. and Mrs. Chalmers at the front desk asking to see you."

Bruce's shoulders sagged, and he blanched visibly. Under his breath, he said, "What the fuck do they want?"

Nan suggested that she sit in on the meeting, and he seized her offer gratefully. When they were seated across from Liam Chalmers and his wife in an interview room, there was a silence after the introductions and exchanged pleasantries in which Nan could sense the tension in the room. It was like the prelude to a storm where you can smell rain and the air itself seems charged. Nan thought that they must have been a handsome couple once, but the dark rings beneath his eyes spoke of many sleepless nights, and grief had etched small but aging lines around her mouth.

To Nan, it seemed the wife still made the effort to keep up appearances with her smartly tailored trench coat and a designer handbag whose straps she continuously twisted as it sat in her lap. Liam Chalmers, on the other hand, looked somehow uncared for. He wore a shabby anorak over his crumpled suit, and she could see what looked like an ink stain on his striped tie. There were patches of stubble on his cheeks and chin that his razor had missed.

Bruce eventually prompted them. "What can we do for you, Liam? Mrs. Chalmers?"

"Diane, please. I didn't want to come but—"

Her husband interrupted brusquely, "We heard that you had found *remains* up at Lake's house."

"They had been there since the last century apparently, so—"

They both seemed to unclench at once. "What about this latest murder? Have you found anything?"

"Our inquiries are ongoing, but I'm afraid we can't discuss the case." She could tell he was ashamed to hide behind a wall of formal clichés.

"Do you think it might be linked to—"

His wife put a hand on his arm as if she couldn't bear to hear him speak their lost daughter's name.

"As I said, Mr. Chalmers, Liam, we can't talk about the case, but rest assured we are pursuing several lines of inquiry." The more he rolled out the tired phrases, the more his knuckles whitened as he clutched his chair. Nan thought he looked as if he wished to be anywhere but here.

Chalmers went on, "My wife's heard some gossip in the town. Apparently, Brenda, Lake's PA, has been shooting off her mouth. She's told people that the girl who was murdered was up at the Big Hoose on the night she was killed."

Nan and Bruce exchanged a worried look.

"Bit of a coincidence, don't you think? What with Carol spending time up there before she—"

At the mention of her daughter's name, Diane Chalmers put a hand up to her mouth. Nan noted that though she had tried to disguise the damage with varnish, her fingernails looked bitten and ragged.

"I told you before, I had my suspicions about Campbell Lake. It took me a while to see what a sleaze he was. He even came on to my wife a few times."

"Now, Liam, he was just flirting a bit."

He ignored her and went on, "And my daughter was naive and easily impressed. Even though he was old enough to be her father, he might have used his position to take advantage of her. It wouldn't have been the first time."

"Liam, you're a lawyer. You of all people should know there's nothing to substantiate a claim that Campbell Lake's behavior toward your daughter was inappropriate. I interviewed him several times and could find no evidence to link him to Carol's disappearance."

"He puts on this front. Look at me, I'm a man of the people, a respected member of the Scottish government. No matter how much shit gets thrown at him, he comes up smelling like freshly mown grass. You seem to forget I helped with his political campaign. I know all the things people accused him of."

"And did that include an unhealthy interest in young girls?" Nan interjected.

"Well, no, but he's a past master at burying stuff that might hurt him if it came out."

"This is all pretty vague, Liam, if you don't mind me saying so. Unless you have concrete allegations to make against Campbell Lake, I don't see what you expect us to do."

"I expect you to find out what happened to our girl." And then he was broken. He bowed his head but not before they saw the silent tears running down his face. His wife clutched his hand helplessly. She looked distressed but remained dry-eyed. Perhaps, Nan thought, the river of her own grief had run dry over the years.

After a few minutes, he appeared to collect himself and blew his nose.

Nan said, "Would you like me to fetch you a cup of tea or coffee?"

Diane Chalmers spoke up, "No, thank you. We'd better go." She rose firmly, still clutching her husband's hand, and with head down, he rose to follow her out. At the door, she turned and said, "Thank you at least for not saying you know how we feel."

This last seemed to stab Bruce more deeply than if she had accused him of abject failure. His hand shook as he took out his cigarettes and headed outside for a smoke. Nan checked her phone and, to her delight, found a message from Sol Chapelle:

Got your message. Back at the Cross Inn
on Saturday. Know you disapprove but going to

do the postponed séance. Will let you know if
I find out anything. Maybe we could hook up
afterward.

X

Nan's excitement at the prospect of seeing Sol again was tem-
pered distinctly by a feeling of foreboding. She feared nothing good
could come of Saturday's meeting. While she no more believed in
ghosts and spirits than she did in fairies and unicorns, she was afraid
that something might be stirred that was more dangerous than any
fictitious demon.

CHAPTER 16

Developments

Angus McKissock had spent Thursday evening drinking alone. There was no sign of his usual companions, and he had asked Colin to have a quiet word when he wasn't busy. The worried expression on his face made the young barman edgy. For the third night in a row, the bar was quiet. When his father appeared to take over serving, Colin nodded toward the exit to the car park, and Angus followed him out there.

"Any further forward on who attacked you?"

"No, but get this, last night, I was working late in the workshop, and my dad came in. He was on his mobile. He never knew I was there 'cause I was under a car at the time, so I kept quiet and listened. He was havin' this really urgent conversation wi' whoever was on the other end of the line, sayin' he wasnae doin' it anymore, and he wanted out. Then this mornin', a Jag XJ rolls up wi' two heavy-lookin' dudes in it, askin' to see him. Fuck knows what they said to him, but after they'd left, I found him in the kitchen knockin' back whiskey. I tell you he was physically shakin'."

"These men, was one of them short and squat, ex-boxer maybe who'd been in the ring a few times, and he was wi' a big blond guy who looked as if he mainlined steroids?"

Angus seemed taken aback. "Aye, that's them."

"I saw them comin' out of the bar when I got back from the cash and carry. And they got into a Jag. When I asked my dad who they were, he said they were from the brewery, but I could tell he

136

was lyin', and he went rushin' out somewhere just after. You think it might have been these guys that attacked you?"

"Might have been. But why? And I would think by the look of them that these two would have inflicted more damage. What the fuck have the two stupid cunts got themselves into?"

They stood in silence, looking into the mostly empty car park as if they might find an answer there. Whatever their fathers were involved in, it was clear that it was corroding their spirits and making them very afraid. Colin wondered if Angus was feeling the same chill premonition clutching at his bowels that a reckoning was coming soon.

*****

That same night, a search team found a pair of women's knickers that had been discarded in a bin normally used for storing grit in the winter at the end of Beth March's street. For Nan, it was too much of a stretch to think that they were simply lost in the heat of a possible tryst between a courting couple or as the result of some poor woman being caught short on the way home.

Reluctantly, she asked Beth March if she could come in to identify them. They were barely giving the poor girl time to recover from her attack by continually reminding her of it. Besides, it was a bit of a long shot. The panties were generic-looking plain white cotton. DNA testing would confirm if they were hers, but Nan wanted some indication of possibility before proceeding down that route.

When Beth arrived at the station on Friday morning, Nan took her to look at the evidence. The knickers were in a clear evidence bag, and the girl examined them closely before saying, "I think they might be mine. I can't be sure, I expect lots of women wear similar ones, and I have loads of pairs of plain white pants in my drawer at home, but they do look like the ones I was wearing that night."

Beth's embarrassment was tangible, but Nan had no choice but to explain to her that they would be tested for DNA—both hers and her possible assailant's—and then she asked permission to conduct a DNA swab. She was relieved when she at last showed the flustered girl out.

Later, she recognized the figure of Dr. Grant from the dig up at the Big Hoose leaving DCI Carpenter's office, so, curious, she contrived to meet her on the stairs and asked her if she had time for a coffee. There was a moment before a flash of recognition crossed the forensic scientist's face. After all, their encounter in the grounds of the Lakes' house had been brief. She was hesitant but accompanied Nan to the staff canteen.

"Dr. Grant, or may I call you Sheila?"

"I think we should keep this on a formal footing, don't you?" She grimaced as she sipped the brew that was loosely described as coffee in the canteen, but Nan had at least bought her a KitKat.

"Sorry, I should have warned you about the quality of the refreshments here. Have you discovered anything interesting that might help with our murder inquiries?"

"I've already told your superior officer of my findings. Perhaps you should ask her."

Nan thought, *God, this woman is hard work*, but as Grant bit into the biscuit, she seemed to lighten up. "I suppose you'll know eventually. The team did some more digging around the site to see if there were other remains nearby. That seemed to antagonize the lady of the manor somewhat."

From her tone, Nan could easily imagine just how a meeting between the frosty doctor and aristocratic Eloise Lake would have gone.

"While we didn't discover any more remains, we did dig up some artifacts."

"What kind of artifacts?"

"Specifically a metal box. It contained a leather-bound journal of some sort that seemed to be in reasonable condition. The box it was buried in must have given it some protection from the soil and the elements though the last few pages were loose and had sustained some water damage. We've sent it for more analysis."

While Nan was curious about this discovery, she failed to see how it might progress their current case. Dr. Grant thanked her for the coffee even though she left most of it.

"Perhaps I can return the favor some time." Nan was surprised that the woman would make any kind of gesture of goodwill. Perhaps her coolness was part of her professional demeanor.

That night, after a frustrating day of tracking back over aspects of the investigation—she hesitated to call them leads—she found herself back at the Cross Inn. She was surprised to find the five friends there. When Beth saw her, she came over. "Would you like to join us, Sergeant?"

"If you're sure I'd be welcome."

Darren had already fetched an extra chair for her when she went to the table and said, "We have to stop meeting like this." Though the remark was light, there appeared to Nan to be little of his usual humor in its tone.

"This isn't your usual night, is it?"

Jennifer replied, "We thought we'd have our normal pub night tonight because we're all getting together at my house tomorrow night."

"Ah yes, the postponed séance." She tried to keep her voice neutral. Not only was she being careful not to offend Jennifer with her skepticism, but also she didn't want the group to detect the frisson that ran through her at the thought of Sol Chapelle's return.

Darren said bitterly, "Your lot seem mad keen to examine our clothes. I noticed folk going over the stuff I'd burned on the bonfire. You'll no' find bloodstained shirts or whatever and what with Beth's knickers getting checked out."

"Darren!" Beth looked around uncomfortably.

"You know as well as I do that we have to explore every possibility even if it's just to eliminate certain things from our inquiry." This failed to placate Darren, who stared at the others moodily as if he expected them to back him up.

Finally, he said impotently, "You're barking up the wrong tree if you think any of us had somethin' to do wi' Janine's death."

"I'd better leave you to it. I'm obviously killing the mood here." Before she could move away, Letty said, "Tell her, Beth."

"It might be nothing."

Nan had half risen but sat back down. "Tell me what?"

"It's just I told Letty that I remembered that I was aware of a bit of a smell just before I went down on the pavement."

"What sort of a smell?"

"Like a really musky cologne or aftershave. It was like somebody had sprayed it all over themselves, as if they were trying to hide another odor."

"Like what?"

"I don't know, maybe just body odor or, you know, something to do with their job. You know how chefs always tend to smell of cooked food or people working in the fish factory have trouble getting the smell of fish off them. And what about the smokery? The folk who work there must always smell of smoke and smoked haddock or salmon."

Nan knew there was a well-known smokehouse down the coast that cured fish and sold them all over the country, but for some reason, her first thoughts were of Arthur Bauld. The butcher seemed to carry the scent of blood around with him no matter how much he washed.

"Do you think you'd recognize it if you smelled it again?"

"That's just it. I'm sure I've smelled the same thing before somewhere, but I can't think where."

"Beth, do me a favor and have a wander round the room and see if you can pick up any familiar scent."

"I'll feel like a prize idiot."

Nan opened her purse and gave her a ten-pound note. "Go to the ladies, and then get yourself another drink at the bar."

Beth looked doubtful but walked stiltedly to the toilets and returned a few moments later, still looking gauche, and went to the bar. Nan paid particular attention when she moved into the proximity of Bauld and Syme, who were occupying their usual barstools.

When she returned with her drink, Nan said, "Anything?"

"No. It might not have been in here that I smelled it before. Sorry." She handed Nan her change.

"No worries. But keep your senses sharp in case you come across it again." She was just about to go out when Colin Sark stopped her. He looked decidedly jumpy and couldn't have looked more suspicious if he'd been found removing large quantities of cash from the till.

Without looking her in the eye, he murmured, "Can I have a word? Outside?"

Nan went out to wait. Just when she thought he had changed his mind, he appeared and ushered her away from the front of the inn. He looked around as if he was afraid he was being watched before saying in a low voice, "This might be nothing, and I dinnae want to get anyone in bother but—"

"Spit it out, Colin."

"It's just that my dad had two visitors this mornin' that looked a bit suspicious."

"Suspicious in what way?"

"Dad said they were from the brewery, but I'd never seen them around here before, and they looked, well, they looked like a couple of heavies."

"Can you describe them?"

"One was a tall blond guy, looked like he spent a lot of time liftin' weights in the gym, and his mate was short and broad and looked as if he'd done a bit of boxing. His nose looked as if it had been broken a few times, and he had that look around his eyes like he'd had a few cuts repaired. They were well dressed, and they got into a fancy wine-colored Jag. Angus reckons it was an XJ."

"Angus McKissock?"

Colin looked furtive suddenly as if he'd given too much away before blurting out, "They'd been round to see Angus's dad as well. Look, it might be nothin', but there's a lot of shit going on round here, and these two looked kind of sinister. They looked like trouble."

"Could you come down to the station tomorrow and look through some pictures? The two men could be on police files somewhere, and you might be able to identify them."

Colin hesitated. "I'm working tomorrow."

"If your father and Mr. McKissock have got themselves into some kind of a scary situation, you may be doing them a favor."

Colin looked fearful. Nan didn't know if it was because he was concerned for his father's safety or because he was worried he'd betrayed him by bringing this to the attention of the police.

At last, he said, "I'll try to get away for a while in the morning."

"Thanks, Colin, you're doing the right thing."

"Am I?" With a tormented look, he left.

Nan stood for a moment in the street. It wasn't just the chill wind blowing off the river that made her shiver.

CHAPTER 17

Rogues' Gallery

Colin entered the police station on Saturday morning full of trepidation. If his and Angus's dad were involved in something illegal, he could be instrumental in getting them caught. On the other hand, the kind of men they appeared to be mixed up with might do them some serious harm.

He asked for DS Wilson at the reception desk, and he had only just seated himself in the waiting area when she appeared. It seemed to him that she looked paler than ever, like a porcelain doll and just as fragile though he knew that in her job, she must be tougher than she looked.

"Colin, I'm glad you came. Any problems getting away?"

"I told my mum I had a dentist's appointment, so I can't be too long."

"This won't take long. Come this way."

She took him up to a room that buzzed with activity and introduce him to a uniformed PC who sat at a computer screen. "This is PC Telfer. She's going to show you a range of photographs that you've probably heard described as mug shots. Please alert her if you can identify either of the two men you saw at the inn yesterday."

The officer was tall and, in Colin's view, rather masculine looking though her features softened when she smiled at him, and he caught the scent of her perfume when he sat beside her. She offered him a coffee, which he declined, and then told him to take his time scrolling through the photographs on the screen and let her know if he recognized any of the people in them.

Colin had heard this called a rogues' gallery, and it certainly lived up to the description. The series of photographs revealed one sullen-looking individual after another, usually staring blankly at the camera. The majority looked like the kind of people you would cross the street to avoid.

After only around fifteen minutes, one face was blurring into another, and Colin had to force himself to concentrate. After all, he wanted to join a group like the one in this room, where both uniformed and plain clothes officers exuded a kind of desperate energy as they went about their various tasks. Surely, as well as his innate curiosity, his powers of recall and observation would be assets if he were to succeed in his ambition.

After a futile trawl through what seemed to him to be hundreds of head and shoulder shots, he was about to pass over one of a scowling blond man when his attention was arrested by something. Perhaps it was the hair, but when he looked more closely, he thought it could be one of the men he had seen coming out of the inn.

In the photograph, he looked younger certainly, and the face was less full, but Colin alerted PC Telfer, and she called Sergeant Wilson over. "You think this was one of the men?"

"I cannae be sure, like, but it could be."

"Carry on looking to see if you can see the man he was with." She reached across him to put a print command into the computer, and the two women went over to a nearby printer to consult the photograph and, Colin presumed, the information about the subject. They both looked serious.

He tried to concentrate on the sorry parade of glum-looking men, but after another fifteen minutes, he had found no one that resembled the ex-pug. He was stretching back in his chair to ease his stiffening neck muscles when the sergeant returned. "No more luck?"

"Sorry. Don't see the other guy."

"Never mind. Thanks, Colin, you've been really helpful."

"The one I recognized, has he got a record?"

"Oh yes. I can't go into too much detail, but I will say this, if your father's involved with men like the one in the photograph, he's playing with fire."

*****

After the perplexed-looking young man left, Nan and Elsie Telfer sought out DI Bruce. He examined the photograph and the record that accompanied it, the worry lines etched more deeply in his brow.

"And this is the man that Colin Sark thinks was with his father and Angus McKissock's dad? Shit."

PC Telfer looked in turn at the expressions on their faces as if she had come late to a conversation and missed the key points.

"Okay, he's done time for a couple of grievous bodily harms, but that was a few years ago, and his record's been clean since."

"Tip of the iceberg, Elsie. We're pretty sure he's not clean. He just hasn't been caught."

Nan elaborated, "Graham Neeson is a well-known face across the river. He's been working as an enforcer for Tom and Barbara Tweedie for the last few years."

When the PC still looked blank, Nan explained, "They're a brother-and-sister team that we know is behind a good deal of the major criminal activity in the capital, like drugs, prostitution, people trafficking, fraud, extortion. You name it, and the Tweedie family have their blood-soaked prints all over it.

"They took over when their old man went in to Saughton for a fourteen-year stretch. For years, he was the most vicious thug in the east of Scotland, and his kids are real chips off the old block. They've been pulled in countless times, but from a combination of the best advocates money can buy, witnesses that mysteriously disappear or change their minds about giving evidence, some less than watertight investigating, and the rumors suggest bribery at the highest levels, nothing has ever been pinned on them."

The DI added, "That, and some of their employees being paid to hold their hands up and take the fall for a generous pension when they've done their time. And of course, brutality inspires loyalty among the members of the organization, particularly when it's being dished out by men like Neeson."

Nan said, "I've come across some of his victims when I was with the force in Edinburgh, and none of it was pretty. One of them had all the fingers on his left hand broken. Another was beaten so badly he'll never walk again. Neeson's a coldhearted sadist."

PC Telfer's eyes had been growing wider as she listened to their accounts. "And this man was in the Law? Why?"

Bruce stood. "That's what we need to find out and quickly. It's bad enough that we've got an unsolved murder, a disappearance, and two assaults to contend with. The last thing we need is notorious underworld characters roaming the streets."

Nan looked bemused. "I'm still not seeing the connections here."

"Maybe there aren't any, but if there are, we're not going to find them sitting round on our arses here. Take Neeson's mug shot and show it to our local publican and mechanic. Let's see if they can explain why he might want to visit them. Take Eastman with you."

"What are you going to do?" Nan didn't want to sound as accusatory as she did, but she was peeved by the thought of doing more legwork in the company of the nut-cracking sledgehammer that was Eastman.

"I'll have to fill in the DCI and then get in touch with CID in Edinburgh to see if they know anything about some of the shit flowing down the river from their patch and ending up here."

She went reluctantly to inform Eastman of their mission. As they drove away from the station, the sergeant was less than his ebullient self. To break the awkward atmosphere, Nan asked him what had happened at the Queen of the Forth, but the look he gave her suggested he thought it was an attempt to gloat. She persevered, "I've never been in it, but it's a rough joint frequented by local ne'er-do-wells."

"Fuck, you sound like you stepped out of a Sherlock Holmes story, 'ne'er-do-wells.' Fuck." When he saw her color rising, Eastman went on, "It's fu' of mouthy scum that cannae hold their drink, that's what it is."

"How did it kick off?"

Putting on a dreadful RP accent, Eastman said, "One of the scoundrels present insulted a lady, so I was forced to challenge him to a duel." Then in his normal voice, he said, "This loud cunt said Janine Gunning was askin' for it. She was well known as the town bike. I gave him a bit of a slap, and some of his mates started to pile in, and me and the two plain clothes PCs with me were gettin' the worst of it till uniform arrived."

Despite herself, Nan was impressed that he would leap in to defend the dead girl. "I think I'd have done the same thing if I'd been there."

He looked surprised at her conciliatory tone for a moment but then said, "And DCI Carpenter would have had you in her office takin' your pants down and skelpin' your bare arse just like she did mine."

They went to McKissock's garage first. He greeted them at the entrance to the workshop, looking decidedly unhappy at their presence. When Nan showed him Graham Neeson's photograph, he wiped off his hands with a filthy-looking rag before making a show of squinting at it. "Couldnae say. We're gettin' a lot of folk in and out. Business has picked up a lot in the last wee while."

Nan thought it couldn't have been more obvious that he was lying than if his nose had suddenly grown a few inches. "He was probably with another man, shorter, uglier."

"Cannae remember anybody like that."

Eastman was looking round the garage's forecourt. "Business must be good. You've got a few fancy motors for sale here."

Nan didn't pay much attention to car makes and models generally but even she recognized that there was a Lexus, a Mercedes Coupe, and even a Porsche Boxster among the vehicles for sale, all for prices north of £25,000. The cars seemed out of place sitting on the crumbling tarmac outside the dilapidated-looking garage.

As if sensing their suspicions, McKissock said, "I just got a new partner recently who put a bit o' money into the business, a long-term investment and that."

Eastman held the photograph up once more. "Take another look at this guy. You sure you havenae seen him?"

McKissock barely glanced at it before pursing his lips and shaking his head. Nan said, "I hope you haven't seen him, Mr. McKissock. I really do. The last man we suspect he visited is still in hospital. Been there for six weeks."

"Well, he hasnae visited me."

Nan noticed the tremor in his voice and a fleeting look of fear in his eyes.

"Aye. Some nice cars here. If this man does happen to drop by…" Eastman raised his eyebrows and cast a last meaningful look at the vehicles. As they walked away, McKissock scurried back into the workshop. Eastman muttered, "If he was tellin' the truth, I'm the archbishop of Glasgow's secret love child."

*****

When they entered the Cross Inn, Colin was behind the bar. In a cod cowboy voice, Eastman said to him, "We've come for your pa, son."

Colin nodded nervously to the back of the pub. "Just go through." As Eastman left, the young man stuttered, "Please don't…" He broke off, but Nan saw the look of entreaty in his eyes. She saw that he was afraid they would divulge to his dad that he was the source of their information.

*****

Len Sark paled visibly when they showed them Neeson's photograph. There was a pause as he stared at it, and Nan could sense him furiously searching for a plausible reaction. "Mr. Sark?"

"No, I don't think they've been in the pub."

Eastman's exasperation boiled over. "Listen, could we just stop fannyin' around. We know this guy was here wi' an equally charming sidekick. Your son—"

Nan interrupted hurriedly, "What Sergeant Eastman was about to say was that your son and you could be in danger from this man and his associates." She hoped that Eastman caught her expression, warning him to keep quiet. Meanwhile, Sark's eyes resembled those of a cornered rat desperately searching for a way out.

"All right. This guy and another man were here. They were quite threatening. I think they were part of some kind of protection racket."

Eastman looked skeptical. "Why didn't you report them to the police?"

"There was no need. I sent them away wi' a flea in their ear."

Eastman laughed openly. "Look, pal, you don't send guys like these away wi' fleas in their ears. That is unless you want them to come back and nail *your* lugs to the wall wi' a couple of nine-inch nails."

Sark's fear was evident now. Nan wondered whether it was caused by Eastman's grim projection or by whatever it was he was hiding from them.

"You're right, of course. I should have ta'en their threats more seriously. If they come back, I'll be straight on the phone to you people."

Eastman addressed him as if he were a particularly recalcitrant child. "Look, sunshine, if you think those two were bad, the people they work for are ten times worse. If you've got yourself mixed up in somethin' that involves them, your best bet is to come clean now and spare yourself a lot of grief. They might not stop at hammerin' nails into your ears."

"I don't know what you're insinuatin'. I don't know people like that."

Eastman huffed in frustration, shook his head, and headed for the door.

Nan held back for a moment and said, "Sergeant Eastman's manner may be a bit too blunt at times, but he's right. If you're not concerned for your own safety, think about your family."

"You dinnae think this hasnae something to do wi' what happened to Janine?"

"I can't say for sure. Perhaps if you told us everything you know, it might help us to lay her ghost to rest too."

She left him staring into space as if he expected some creature from his nightmares to appear before him and he was helpless to prevent it from devouring him. In the bar, as she passed Colin, she shook her head subtly at the unspoken inquiry in his eyes.

Outside, Eastman was pacing and sucking on a cigarette as if he was gulping in life-saving oxygen rather than toxic chemicals.

"What the fuck is goin' on in this town? Everybody we speak to is as straight as a fuckin' corkscrew. Both those two are hidin' somethin', and whatever it is, they'll have nae use for laxatives any time soon."

CHAPTER 18

Séance

The friends met up at the Big Hoose at eight o'clock on Saturday night as arranged. Jennifer had wanted them to meet at midnight, but Beth refused point-blank, and the others were also fearful that she was making the occasion too corny. When she protested that she wasn't trying to be all Grand Guignol, they just looked at her blankly. Letty and Darren arrived first together, followed shortly afterward by Angus.

Unfortunately for Jennifer, her father and stepmother were staying in that night. Campbell Lake meandered out apparently casually into the hall when he heard the door full of his usual fake bonhomie. Jennifer couldn't have been more embarrassed if he had greeted them in a silk dressing gown, holding a cigarette holder. Worst of all, she noticed the way his eyes swept over Letty appraisingly and nearly popped out of his head when Sol appeared.

He insisted on being introduced to "this beautiful young woman" and was oversolicitous in his attentions to her. Letty surreptitiously put her fingers in her mouth and gagged theatrically behind his back, which did nothing to alleviate Jen's embarrassment. They hung around in the hall waiting for Beth to appear.

Darren voiced Jen's anxious misgivings. "Mebbe she'll no' show. She's had enough excitement this week."

Sol fended off her father's offer to give her a tour of the house while they were waiting by saying, "That would be interesting but perhaps later."

Jen wished he would just leave them alone and go back to doing whatever he did on the rare occasions he was home on a Saturday night, watching TV or porn or his old speeches in the parliament.

Just when she was about to give up and take the others up to the turret room, Beth arrived, looking frayed and sounding breathless.

Letty said, "For God's sake, you didn't walk here on your own, did you?"

Darren chipped in, "I did offer to pick her up."

Campbell Lake put an arm around Beth's shoulder and, with his well-practiced concerned voice, said, "Dreadful shock for you, love. I honestly don't know what my constituency's coming to, and the police seem to be worse than useless."

Jennifer winced inwardly both at her father's fake sincerity and the fact that he left his arm draped around Beth.

The latter moved pointedly away from him and said defiantly, "I live here, and I'm not going to spend my time looking over my shoulder at every fox shrieking or car backfiring just because I was the victim of some random pervert. I'm not wrapping myself up in cotton wool."

"That's the spirit, Beth," said Jen. For a moment, she was about to punch her on the shoulder, but she noticed the frowns on the faces of her friends, and her hand hovered impotently in the air. "Well, if you're ready, Sol, let's get to it."

To her further discomfiture, her father continued to tag along, trying to engage Sol in conversation as she led the way up the staircase. "So you contact the dead, Dr. Chapelle?"

"No."

He was undeterred by Sol's monosyllabic response but noticed her interest in the stained-glass window. "You like it?"

"Very much. Diana and Actaeon, I always like it when representations in art depict men as the victims for a change."

Lake didn't rise to the bait. "Of course, I don't entirely approve of Jennifer's plans, but if there are any ghostly presences in the house, the turret room is the best place to start. You'll no doubt have heard the stories about the Hoose's history."

"Yes. Is there a safe place where we could leave bags and mobile phones?"

Lake indicated his study. "You can leave them here and pick them up on the way out."

Jennifer gathered the others' phones and put them in her own bag, then took the two girls' handbags.

Sol shook her head when she went to take the large bag she was carrying and said, "I need this, honey."

"If your guests want anything, Jennifer, just give me a shout." Jennifer thought he wasn't usually so interested in them when they visited, apart from his scarcely disguised lascivious looks at the girls, not that the reason for his new attentiveness wasn't obvious. "Perhaps you'd like to join me for a nightcap, Sol—may I call you Sol?—before you leave."

"Maybe some other time. I find it takes me a while to settle myself down after these things."

"Well, if you change your mind…" His disappointment was plain as he entered the study.

"Sorry about my father, Sol."

Sol merely smiled knowingly in reply.

Jennifer led them deeper into the house. To her knowledge, none of them had been up here before, and they seemed rather intimidated by the dark-paneled wood of the corridor and the portraits on the walls of some of the previous owners of the Big Hoose and their ladies, all of them grimly unsmiling and looking uncomfortable in their stiff formal dress.

Sol stopped at one that stood out in marked contrast to the others. Jennifer was secretly pleased that she had singled this one out because it was easily her favorite painting in the house. "I take it this is the infamous Major Latimer," Sol said.

The portrait depicted a man in the full dress uniform of the Confederacy. Unlike the historic photographs Jen had seen of slovenly and dirty-looking Confederate soldiers who often wore mismatched and improvised uniforms, the gray of Latimer's double-breasted coat and matching trousers seemed to shine out from the painting, as did his riding boots, sword, and the single star he wore in the middle of his collar.

Long fair hair flowed from his slouch hat, and his blond beard looked neatly barbered. He was holding aloft a tattered flag—the Southern Cross of the Confederacy—as if he had just won a heroically fought battle.

"I love me. Who do you love?" said Darren disparagingly.

"Does look rather dashing though," said Letty.

"Obviously, he wanted to keep up the good ol' boy image even when he moved to this place," added Sol.

Angus had given the portrait only a cursory glance and was now looking around the dimly lit passage as if he thought he might be being watched. "Don't forget this guy vanished just after a séance here," he said.

"Thanks for reminding us, Angus," said Beth with a shiver.

Sol chuckled reassuringly. "Let's not get each other spooked before we've even started. Lead on, Jennifer."

At the end of the corridor that Jen took them along, they came to a steep set of metal stairs that wound their way in a spiral up to the next level. Jennifer warned, "Take care on these stairs. They're a bit tricky."

"Aye, we don't want any more bodies to be discovered at the foot of them, eh?" Darren's tongue-in-cheek comment was rewarded with a slap in the chest from Letty. He began to protest but was quickly distracted by the movement of Sol's backside as she negotiated the stairs in front of him.

At the top of the stairs, they queued while Jennifer took a large metal key and inserted it into the lock of a door that was paneled in green oak. Darren piped up again, "Behind the green door, wasn't that the title of an old porn movie?"

Letty said, "Shut up, Darren," but her admonition seemed half-hearted as her voice was tight with nerves. Jennifer reached for a light switch at the entrance, but it cast only a subdued light on the room they now entered in single file. They were quiet as they took in its unusual shape. It was paneled in wood all around, and the combination of this and the presence of all their bodies in the small space made the atmosphere oppressive and claustrophobic.

It was sparsely furnished with a round table in the centre made of a lighter wood than the wall paneling and six plain upright chairs arranged in a semicircle at one side of the table. The only other furniture was a small curved dresser that appeared to be designed to fit against the wall. Several candles in holders were placed on it.

"We don't use this room much. Dad holds the occasional small scale meeting in here, but I often come up to look out over the grounds." Angus edged round to the two small rectangular windows. "Too dark to see anything tonight," Jen said. "Why don't we sit down?"

Sol sat on the farthest away chair from the door. She already seemed to dominate the space. After steeling herself, Beth moved firmly to the chair farthest from Sol. Jen thought she gave Angus a peculiar look as he sat beside her. The others shuffled into the other chairs. Before she sat down in the chair next to Sol, Jennifer took an electronic lighter from the dresser, lit the candles, and switched off the room's light.

"Is that really necessary?" Beth asked shakily, and indeed, the flickering shadows cast by the candlelight had added another layer of foreboding to the surroundings.

"I thought it would be a bit more atmospheric," said Jennifer, clearly trying to sound cheerful for Beth's benefit.

"Wooooo!" went Darren, but he soon appeared to realize no one was in the mood for laughing and held up his hands apologetically.

Sol placed the voluminous bag she had been carrying on the floor by her chair and took out from it what looked like a large chess board. It was folded into four, and when she opened it out, it revealed the letters of the alphabet done in a heavy dark print arrayed in semicircles above the numbers 0 to 10 and the words *Yes* and *No* in the uppermost corners.

"What's this, a homemade Ouija board?" said Darren. "I thought we were just going to hold hands and ask if there was anyone there, 'knock once for yes and two for no' sort of thing. Why aren't we in a circle?"

"You've watched too many movies," said Angus. Again, Jen thought that Beth seemed to start at the sound of his voice.

"I guess it kind of is, Darren," said Sol. "In earlier séances, a technique called table turning or table tipping was used. The participants would speak the alphabet aloud and the table tipped at the appropriate letters. But it was too easy to fake. This is sort of modeled on the original Ouija board, but it's much bigger and so is this."

She took out an object that was made of light-colored wood rounded at one end and pointed at the other. There appeared to be some kind of felt material at its base. "It's based on the planchette, but it's not heart shaped like the traditional ones. It means more people can place a finger on it to spell out messages."

Jennifer said excitedly, "Sol had it specially made by a shop in St Andrews that sells mystical stuff—crystals, dowsing rods, pendulums, dream catchers—that kind of thing."

Jen noticed Letty and Darren exchanging a skeptical look.

Sol explained, "I wanted it bigger and clearer. The letters and numbers are done in a font called Matchbook JNL so more people can participate, and there's less room for ambiguity. Just relax and keep your minds clear. Everyone place a finger lightly on the round part of the device."

As they moved to comply, it became clear why the chairs had been arranged the way they were. It facilitated everyone managing to reach the makeshift planchette without anyone having to reach across the table awkwardly and obscure some of the board.

Sol said, "Is there anyone present who wants to pass on a message?" Her voice was flatly conversational, without drama or increased projection. There was silence. Sol asked the same question three times though Jen noted she stressed different words each time: *is*, *anyone*, and *message*.

The silence seemed to stretch out more tensely each time till Darren said, "Must all be out at the pub, which is where I suggest we go to commune with some other spirits."

Letty began to upbraid him but broke off as the wooden object under their fingers shifted almost imperceptibly, and she said instead, "Did anyone else feel that?"

Sol repeated her question, and after a moment, the pointer moved to the word *Yes* on the board. With a startled cry, Letty withdrew her hand as if she had been scalded. "Everyone please keep a finger on the planchette," instructed Sol quietly, and with some reluctance, Letty complied.

"For whom is the message?" Sol continued as if she was asking for the weather forecast. The silence in the room thickened so that everyone was conscious of one another's quickened breaths as the pointer moved to the *A* and twice to the *L*.

"All," said Jen and then whispered, "Ask it if it's Latimer."

"Or maybe Janine," Letty murmured fearfully.

Sol hushed them gently before asking, "Who are you?"

Jennifer spoke the letters aloud as the pointer moved though some of the others were moving their lips as they followed it. When it stopped, Jennifer said, "It's spelled out 'A Keeper of Secrets.'"

"What does that even mean?" Darren scoffed.

"Please, I must ask you to stay quiet," Sol said firmly. There was a lengthy pause. Just when it appeared that nothing else was going to happen, the pointer moved again. It spelled out "All here have secrets."

Sol asked, "What secrets?"

Sotto voce, Jen said, "I'm not sure we should ask it that."

The pointer spelled out, "Father is to blame."

They exchanged looks that were half puzzled and half alarmed.

"Who's it talking to? Whose father?" murmured Angus.

The movement of the pointer became quicker and more purposeful as it spelled out in succession, "You are alone with your guilt," "Some secrets are worse than others," then "There is death in this place."

"Sol, I think we should stop now," said Letty.

But Sol continued, "Whose death?"

There was no movement. It seemed that all of them were holding their breath, fingers frozen on the planchette.

Darren eventually broke the spell. "This is a waste of time. These riddles don't mean anything." His voice lacked conviction.

Before he could continue, the pointer moved again, spelling out "Carol and Jan—"

With a cry, Beth sprang up, knocking over her chair. She ran to the door and wrenched it open, the sudden draught from the hall extinguishing one of the candles nearest to it.

Angus was the first to react, calling out, "Beth, wait," and chasing after her. The others heard a high-pitched scream and moved to go after them, but they got in each other's way in the restricted space.

When they eventually crowded together on the landing, they looked down to see Beth lying in a twisted heap at the foot of the spiral staircase with Angus kneeling awkwardly on the step above her, pushing her hair from her face.

He looked up and called, "Darren, help me wi' her."

Jennifer's face was ashen as she said, "Wait, we shouldn't move her."

Sol stood at the back, looking as distressed as the others at the turn of events. Campbell Lake came hurrying along the passage. "What's going on? I thought I heard a scream."

Jennifer said, "Call an ambulance, Dad. Beth's fallen."

He dithered uncertainly before moving back along the corridor. A low moan came from Beth. Jennifer held up a hand to stop the others from rushing to her on the narrow stairs. "Let's not crowd her. Give her space to breathe." She joined Angus at the foot of the stairs, carefully stepping over and around Beth, who looked up at them groggily. Jennifer pulled down Beth's dress, which had ridden up in the fall.

"What happened?"

Jennifer said, "Try not to move. You've had a fall. An ambulance is on its way."

Despite Jen's warning, Beth began to push herself up on one elbow.

"Keep your head still. You might have damaged your neck or your spine."

Again ignoring her, Beth raised herself up farther and moved her head around tentatively. "Feels okay, and my back seems fine. Help me up."

"I really don't think you should..." but Angus was helping her to her feet. Again, Jennifer thought she gave him an odd look as he held her arm. Darren brushed past her and supported Beth at her other side as they began to make their way back along the corridor with Letty and a worried Jen bringing up the rear.

When she saw that Beth appeared to have no serious injuries, Sol disappeared back into the room to retrieve her equipment and bag, Jennifer supposed.

When they got back to the hall, Campbell Lake made Beth sit in one of the occasional seats placed there and tried to press a brandy on her, saying, "For the shock," which she declined. Shortly afterward, Sol rejoined them, and he tried to persuade her "to have that nightcap after all," but she, too, refused his offer.

They all stood around in the hall, waiting for the arrival of the ambulance. Everyone seemed lost in their own thoughts, and no one spoke. If anyone accidentally caught someone's eye, they looked away sheepishly.

It seemed to take an age before Lake admitted the paramedics though it couldn't have been more than twenty minutes. They asked Beth for details of the fall and gave her a brief examination. When they established she could walk under her own volition, they ushered her out into the waiting ambulance.

Jennifer called out, "Do you want one of us to come with you, Beth?"

Beth shook her head and said, "I'll be all right," as she was issued into the back of the ambulance.

They watched its departure from the front of the house.

Campbell Lake said, "Anyone want to tell me what went on in the turret room?"

As they all hesitated, Jennifer said, "We're not really in the mood to talk about it tonight, Dad, but I'll tell you all about it tomorrow."

He looked around the chastened group, his gaze lingering on Sol as if he wanted to say something more to her. But clearly gauging a diplomatic retreat was his best option, he went back inside unhappily.

After an uncomfortable pause, Darren said, "Pub?"

Letty said, "I'm not particularly in the mood after that, but I could certainly do with a drink."

There was muttered agreement from the others.

Darren said, "Think I should swing by Beth's and let her ma know what's happened?"

Sol offered to give a lift back to anyone who needed it. Jennifer said firmly, "I really think we should leave it till we've managed to contact the hospital to find out how Beth is first. You know how she hates to worry her mum."

As they made their way to the cars, Darren intoned theatrically, "In Hill House, whatever walked there, walked alone." Nobody laughed.

CHAPTER 19

Psychoanalysis

Colin Sark thought the group of friends that gathered in the bar later were more subdued than usual. He knew they had come from the Big Hoose after a séance, and his curiosity was piqued. He contrived to move nearer to them at every opportunity to try to eavesdrop on their conversation, but their exchanges were muted and halting.

One thing was clear—something had happened earlier that had distressed and dismayed them. Colin caught himself wondering if perhaps they had encountered a supernatural entity that had drained their spirit before giving himself a mental shake.

He approached their table though their glasses were still half full. "Hey, guys, needing any refills?" He knew how lame he must sound.

"Table service now, is it, Clipper?" Jennifer asked, then added, "We're fine for the moment, thanks."

"Beth not with you tonight?"

No one answered. Angus took a large swig of his beer, Letty seemed to find something fascinating at the far end of the bar, and Dr. Chapelle sat impassively. Darren and Jennifer glanced at one another uneasily before the latter said, "She had a bit of a fall, but she's going to be okay."

"A fall?"

No one met his eye. It became obvious that they weren't going to elaborate, so itching with frustration, he was forced to retreat to the bar. As he moved away, he heard Darren saying more loudly, "Come on. If one of you was messing with our heads back there, own the fuck up."

Sol waited till the young barman was out of earshot before replying calmly, "Darren, what happened in that room might have been alarming in many respects and certainly scared poor Beth into panicking, but in my experience, that was typical of these *occasions*."

"Typical in what way? Beth ran because she thought we were receiving messages from or about Carol and Janine." Jennifer's face was animated with eagerness and misgiving.

"Her mind simply jumped to that conclusion. Remember, I told you all about the ideomotor phenomenon that scientists think inform these sessions. We make motions unconsciously or reflexively in response to certain stimuli."

"You mean someone in that room was subconsciously moving the pointer to those answers?" Letty seemed unconvinced.

"Yes. Perhaps more than one person."

"So rather than being prompted by spiritual activity, the answers are generated by what's going on in someone's head," said Angus.

"Exactly."

"I'm no' sure I'm relieved by that. I think I'd rather it was ghosts."

"Think about it. Did we receive a single clear message? There was the stuff about secrets. Well, we all keep secrets. The father is to blame? You don't have to delve too deeply into Freudian theory to realize most of us have daddy issues. It told us we're alone with our guilt—guilt is a very lonely emotion. And how old is that house, Jen? Of course there's death in that place—it's obvious it has seen its fair share of deaths over the years."

Darren said, "But it was about to message us about Carol Chalmers and Janine Gunning."

"It mentioned death. Whose deaths are at the forefront of everyone's thoughts right now?"

As Sol paused to sip her whiskey, Letty admitted grudgingly, "I suppose when you explain it like that, it does make a kind of sense."

"But if what you say is the case, it means that someone there tonight has some pretty deep shit going on in their heads," said Darren.

Sol smiled. "Everyone has shit going on in their heads, Darren." At that moment, she was distracted by the entrance of Nan Wilson, who looked over at the group and raised a tentative hand in greeting. Her limp seemed more pronounced as she made her way to the bar, but even Darren and Angus seemed to sense the energy that passed between her and Sol. The latter said, "Excuse me for a moment, would you?" and went to join Nan.

Jennifer looked flushed as she followed her with her eyes.

"Since when did Sol get pally with our pretty Ms. Plod?" said Darren.

Angus added worriedly, "You think she'll tell her about what happened tonight? I mean, it might be interestin' to the police, especially the Carol and Janine stuff."

They all sat in perplexed silence till Letty grabbed her bag and said, "I'm going to go outside and phone the hospital to see how Beth is."

"Good idea, Let. I'll come with you." Jennifer appeared grateful for an excuse to leave the bar.

*****

Nan could scarcely disguise her pleasure as Sol joined her. Once Colin Sark had poured her drink, he hovered near the two women till Nan gave him a pointed look, and he skulked off to the other end of the bar.

"Well, how did the séance go?" she asked with a pretense of making casual conversation though she was burning with curiosity. She became increasingly agitated as Sol told her of the evening's events in her rich composed voice only interrupting her when she got to Beth's accident.

"Is she all right?"

"She was taken to hospital, but she didn't appear to have any serious injuries."

"I ought to go over there, but first, I'd like to hear the details of these messages."

"Let's go somewhere more private. I have the same room as last time." She raised her eyebrows and nodded subtly in Colin Sark's direction. The young barman was attempting to feign nonchalance, but his frequent glances toward them gave away his fascination with them.

"I'll get my drink."

Nan was conflicted. On the one hand, she wanted to get as many details of the evening's events as she could glean from Sol. On the other, she felt that it would be better to conduct their conversation openly, where there was no question of her professionalism being compromised. Besides, hadn't she crossed a line last time? And was there any guarantee she wouldn't again? There was no denying the frisson of excitement she experienced when she was around this woman.

Meanwhile, Sol was taking her leave of the others. "Off to help the police with their inquiries then?" Despite the lightness of Darren's tone there was an edge to his question.

Sol's self-possession remained intact. "I think they should know all about tonight, don't you?"

Angus was more explicit. "You think this could get us into trouble wi' them?"

"Why would it? No one's done anything wrong tonight, have they?"

Sol's sangfroid clearly failed to placate them as Angus's frown deepened. "They might blame us for causin' Beth's fall."

At that point, Letty and Jennifer returned. Letty said, "We phoned the hospital, and there's nothing wrong with Beth but a few bruises. She hasn't broken anything."

Jennifer added, "They're going to discharge her. I think we should go up there. How much have you had to drink, Darren?"

"Just the one pint."

"If you think you're still under the limit, maybe we could offer her a lift home. Or perhaps Sol you might—"

"I'd be happy to, but I promised Sergeant Wilson I'd fill her in on what happened. Maybe after that I could—"

"No, don't worry. No sense in us all traipsing up there anyway. I could go with Darren." She gave Sol an unreadable look and bit her lip before adding, "Do you think it's wise to tell the police all about tonight?"

Sol put a reassuring hand on her arm. "We have no choice. However tenuous the link is to their inquiry, they'll get round to asking us all about it sooner or later."

There was an uncertain hiatus before Jennifer said, "We'll probably have time to come back if you guys are staying." Her question appeared to be directed more toward Sol than to the others.

Angus replied, "I wouldn't mind another pint. Let?"

"I might have one more and then phone my dad."

"And obviously, I'm staying the night, so I'll be here." Sol smiled but touched her hair in a self-conscious gesture. "I'll let the sergeant know about Beth. She was talking about going up to the hospital so…"

They shuffled off, leaving Letty and Angus seated at the table. "What a horrible night," said Letty. Angus was staring so intently at Sol and Sergeant Wilson as they exited toward the inn's bedrooms that she thought they must feel the heat of his gaze on their backs.

At last, he turned his attention back to her. "Aye, too right. I'll get them in."

As he rose, she asked, "Angus, what actually happened outside that room tonight?"

He hesitated and sat back down. "What d'you mean?"

"You were the first to go after Beth when she bolted."

"What are you gettin' at?"

Letty seemed startled by the hostility in his voice. "Nothing. I just meant what did you actually see when you went out on the landing?"

Making an evident effort to conceal his annoyance, Angus replied, "It all happened that fast. I mean, she'd already fell by the time I got out there. I just rushed down the stairs to her. You saw the state she was in. She must have tried to take the steps too fast and missed her footing or something."

Letty nodded, and he went to the bar. She closed her eyes as if she might erase the unpleasant images of that night that played on a continuous loop inside her head.

*****

Nan felt self-conscious as she followed Sol into the familiar bedroom. She was both relieved and disappointed when Sol sat in the room's only chair and indicated that Nan should take the bed. It seemed that Sol sensed the policewoman's discomfort and was making a deliberate effort to remain businesslike and not to compromise her role as a potentially useful witness. Nevertheless, the memory of their last encounter here hung in the atmosphere like a lingering scent.

She retrieved her notebook from her bag and asked Sol to relate again the events of the evening up to Beth's fall and departure by ambulance. Nan could scarcely restrain herself from interrupting her account but waited till Sol finished and sat quietly, awaiting her reaction. So many questions crowded her mind that she found it difficult to know where to begin. At last, she said, "So do you think someone in that room was moving the pointer?"

"Almost certainly."

"But that means…what about what was spelled out? What does that tell us about them?" Nan recognized that her fumbling attempts to find explanations were making her less coherent.

"Good question. The first thing that emerged was that the messages were for all of those present. That could indicate someone in the group had an issue with the others, but equally, it could be an attempt at obfuscation, and let's face it, there was plenty of vagueness in the answers."

"That bit about being alone with *your* guilt. Was that directed at an individual, or did it refer to collective guilt. And guilt about what?" Sol gave her a sympathetic smile and gentle shrug.

"Then there was the stuff about the father being to blame. Knowing what we do about the backgrounds of the participants, we can surmise a few of them had issues with their fathers."

"It might not refer to their own fathers."

Nan considered this for a moment, but going down that path could only lead to a dead end, so she continued doggedly, "Jennifer Lake is pretty down on her father, alienating her mother with his less-than-moral behavior, trying to keep his daughter on a tight leash. I got the impression there's a distinct lack of respect there. And there was the message about there being death in that place. Okay, it could refer to history but might it also point to recent history."

"You mean it's possible Campbell Lake killed Janine and was involved in the Chalmers girl's disappearance."

"He knew both girls. But really I'm just trying to join up the dots, and frankly, I'm still not seeing the complete picture. Moving on with the father theme, I don't know much about Letty's father, but she seems a bright girl. Maybe there's some resentment simmering for being stuck working on the family farm."

"Do you think this kind of speculation is helpful?" Sol softened the question by reaching across and touching Nan's hand.

Nan held it for a moment but continued, "Isn't this the process how we unlock the psyche?"

"Okay. How about Beth March?"

"She's been left to nurse an ailing mother on her own. Her father buggered off with someone else in the early stages of his wife's illness by all accounts. And isn't it interesting that she seemed most affected by the messages? Terrified, in fact."

"How about the boys?"

"Darren's father spent most of his son's childhood in prison. And then his mother died when he was young. You don't have to be a psychologist to work out how he might feel about effectively being abandoned. And without telling you tales out of school, Angus is worried his father is involved in something dodgy. And there's his old man's drinking."

"You make a persuasive case for any of them to be unwittingly unburdening themselves through the machinery of the séance. But how does this help with your investigation?"

"What was one of the last messages, some secrets are worse than others? Who among those present there is carrying a particularly terrible secret. And that was followed by the apparent reference to Janine Gunning and Carol Chalmers."

"You think one of them was responsible?"

"I don't know. But one or more of them is involved in some way if your theories about séances and Ouija boards are correct."

Sol removed her hand and rose. "Oh, they are. But I can't imagine your superior officers would use these things as the basis for developing their investigation."

Nan rose too. In the small space, she found herself so close to Sol that she could smell her musky perfume and the sweetness of whiskey on her breath. She said, "One thing's for sure, I need to speak to them again, starting with Beth."

Nan stood for a moment, realizing she was rigid with sexual tension. Then Sol leaned into her and kissed her gently on the lips. "I have no wish to make things any more difficult for you than they are already, but any time you need a gentle touch again, I'm here."

"Thanks, Sol. I'd like that very much. Only tonight—"

"I get it, and there are too many hungry eyes and ears around anyway."

Their lips touched briefly once more, and Nan moved to leave the room, feeling the other woman's eyes on her and feeling more self-conscious than ever about her limp.

CHAPTER 20

Suspicious Scent

Nan sat at her desk the next day with an aching head and eyes that felt full of grit. She had gone to the hospital after leaving the pub only to find that Beth March had been discharged. She decided not to attempt to interview her that night when the poor girl was still in shock probably, and she didn't want to add to her distress. Besides, she thought she ought to run Sol's account of the evening's events past DI Bruce.

So she had gone home but had only found sleep briefly in the early hours of the morning as her mind poured relentlessly over what had happened. After a fitful few hours, she gave up, rose and showered, and came in early to the station. She only realized she had been sitting there immobile and staring when Eastman passed her desk and said, "Too much bed, no' enough sleep, Sergeant." He accompanied this with a lewd wink.

She sprang up when DI Bruce finally came in. "Have you got a moment, sir?"

He nodded toward his desk, but before she could embark on her narrative, he said, "The reason I'm a bit late is that Carpenter asked me to liaise with a team of forensic accountants. We're going to get a warrant to look into the financial dealings of the Cross Inn and McKissock's garage."

"You think there's something shady there?"

"A couple of enforcers for a criminal gang don't show up to make social calls. What can I do for you?"

Nan filled him in with the details Sol had given her. He listened with a mixture of fascination and disbelief. When she got to Beth's fall, he interrupted, "You think she was pushed?"

"On the face of it, it seems to have been an accident caused by her panicked reaction to the séance, but who knows? There's something suspicious about that bunch."

"I don't know, Nan. I'm not sure where this gets us. All seems rather airy fairy to me. Séances and messages and what have you. This academic, Dr.?"

"Chapelle. Sol Chapelle."

"What are your impressions of her? She a bit flaky?"

Nan hoped Bruce didn't notice the blush that suffused her cheeks. "She's obviously very clever, and I'm pretty sure she doesn't buy into the whole table tapping, communing with the dead stuff. Seemed to me her psychological insights might prove valuable."

She hoped her tone was objective and that she wasn't appearing too partisan in her defense of a woman who had been her lover after all. Bruce regarded her doubtfully for a moment before saying, "All right. How do you want to proceed?"

"Speak to Beth March in the first place. Get her take on last night."

"Fair enough. Give her a bell and tell her we'll call in."

"We?"

"One of a group of people who legitimately might be called suspects in a murder inquiry takes a header down a flight of stairs. I trust your instincts, Nan, and I'd like to pursue this."

*****

Beth March answered the door almost as soon as they knocked and said in a hushed voice, "I saw you coming from the window. Mum's still in bed. She's not too bright this morning, so I'm trying to let her sleep."

"We'll try not to disturb her," Bruce said as she led them into the living room.

After they had refused Beth's offer of tea or coffee, Nan said, "How are you?"

"Okay, just a bit sore. I take it you're here to ask me about last night. The truth is I'm not sure what happened really. I guess I got really spooked by the messages about…about Janine and Carol. I know I just had to get out of that room. I must have tripped, I suppose." She had been speaking with her eyes cast down as if trying to recall the incident but now looked at them. "You must think I'm really daft."

"Not at all," said Nan. "But this is the second time in a week you've been hurt."

"I know. Mum's worried sick. But surely the two things aren't related. I've just been unlucky, I suppose."

Bruce said, "What do you think is going on?"

"What do you mean?"

Nan prompted, "Was there anything suspicious about anyone's behavior last night?"

Nan thought that for a moment, the girl looked like a startled deer which had just picked up the scent of a possible predator. "I'm not sure. I mean, someone in that room must have been pushing the pointer around and spelling out messages, mustn't they? I think that's what frightened me really. I don't believe they came from the other side or whatever."

The DI leaned forward in his chair. "Any idea who?"

"No, but…" They waited tensely as Beth's eyes darted around the room. Again, Nan was reminded of a wary animal that might bolt back into the woods at the slightest provocation.

At last, Beth said, "It might be nothing, but you remember I told you about a smell I'd noticed the night somebody pushed me down?"

Bruce gave Nan a puzzled glance, and she realized she hadn't yet filled him in on what Beth had told her in the pub.

"Beth told me about a smell she thought she recalled on the night of the attack, sir. A heavy kind of cologne or aftershave, wasn't it?"

"Yes, to cover up another odor, I thought."

"And?" Bruce said abruptly.

"I thought I smelled it again last night in that room." She hesitated once more, and Nan willed the DI to curb his impatience. "I smelled it on Angus."

"Angus McKissock?" Bruce was leaning so far forward he was practically on the edge of his chair.

"I know he does a lot of welding in his job, and you know how that kind of burnt metal smell almost seems to get into their skin. I mean it occurred to me that might be the odor he was trying to cover up."

Beth obviously noticed the charged look that Nan and Bruce exchanged because she exclaimed hurriedly, "But I could be wrong. I expect lots of people must use that kind of aftershave. And I just can't believe that Angus would do anything to harm me. And don't forget he was attacked that night too. It couldn't have been him. Oh, God, have I got him into trouble?"

She looked so distraught that Nan said reassuringly, "I'm sure you're right, but we just need to have a word with him to straighten this out. How well did he know Janine?"

"Oh, God, you can't think he'd..." Beth rose as if the chair in which she was sitting had administered an electric shock. She moved to the window. "I suppose he knew her as well as the rest of us. She was often serving in the bar. I don't think they had any kind of relationship outside that. Not that I know of anyway—"

Bruce interjected, "And Carol Chalmers?"

"I think he had a crush on her at school. But then most of the boys did. Some of the girls too." Her attempt to smile died on her lips, and she rubbed her hands on the sides of her jeans as if they were damp.

Nan crossed to her. "Angus was the first person to come after you when you dashed out of the room last night. I hate to ask you this, Beth, but is it possible he might have pushed you?"

"I-I wasn't conscious of anyone's hands on my back, if that's what you mean, but then it all happened in a flash. One moment, I was in the room. The next, I was lying at the foot of the stairs."

They left Beth at her door looking anxiously after them.

Nan said, "What are you thinking, sir?"

"Without jumping the gun, I'm thinking this might be the first decent breakthrough we've had. We've always thought that lot were involved somehow, and here we have suspicions cast on McKissock by one of his close friends. He was a regular at the bar where Janine Gunning worked, and I'm not getting my hopes up here, but how far did this crush on Carol Chalmers at school go?"

Nan thought that getting his hopes up was exactly what DI Bruce was doing.

Confessions 2

You can't help feeling the police are closing in, breathing down your neck, in fact. Their presence seems to be everywhere. Maybe that's just paranoia talking. Things aren't going exactly to plan, it's true, but surely they can't suspect you. They've been questioning loads of possible suspects, and as far as you know, they haven't eliminated anyone definitely from their inquiries.

And now they have a lot more to think about. If you can just keep sowing the seeds of confusion, all those suspicious incidents and weird happenings. They're occupying them, pushing them further and further from the truth.

That pretty police sergeant is nobody's fool, it's true, but there's no sign she's getting any closer or even that her professional instincts are twitching, alerting her senses that the one she's after is right there under her nose.

Besides, she's distracted by the impressive academic. You don't need to be Sherlock Holmes to detect what's going on there. She's got a nerve, getting involved like that with someone who's so close to the investigation. Maybe somebody ought to report her for professional misconduct or whatever it's called.

You have to calm down, a bit of the green-eyed monster going on there.

Focus. You just have to make sure there's no evidence that might lead them back to you. It was stupid compulsive behavior that got you into this mess, and you're still capable of it obviously. Look at what happened tonight. You can't help feeling you slipped up there.

But you just have to stick to the plan. Lead them further and further into the swamp till they've lost their bearings. There'll be more casualties along the way certainly, but that's too bad. All those hypocritical arses deserve everything they get. They hold their noses at what they see as everyone else's sordid and unsavory behavior, but they're oblivious to the stink of their own dirty laundry.

You might have been stupid, but now you're playing the game much more cleverly. You just have to keep the authorities constantly on the back foot, keep them off balance. And you have plenty of other tricks up your sleeve.

CHAPTER 21

On the Scent

Nan and Bruce found Angus McKissock in the garage work-shop, leaning into the bonnet of a new-looking top-of-the-range Mercedes. Across from him, another young man in overalls was working on what looked to Nan like an upmarket Porsche.

"Working on a Sunday, Angus?"

The young mechanic rose and spun round so abruptly at the sound of Bruce's voice that he struck the bonnet prop. For a moment, Nan had a ridiculous vision of him being snapped inside, with only the lower half of his body visible like Robert Shaw disappearing into the shark's mouth in *Jaws*.

When he had recovered his composure, Angus said, "Aye. We've got a bit o' a backlog. These last few weeks, it's been nuts."

The DI walked around the vehicle, examining it. "Bit more fancy than the bangers you usually get in here, isn't it?"

Angus shifted from foot to foot uneasily. "Well, we've been gettin' a few cars like this in recently for sale or repair."

"Outside investors?"

Angus ignored Bruce's barbed question, and nodding at the car, he said, "I have to get on, so what can I do for you?"

Nan tried to sound casual as she asked, "We see you're busy, Angus, but we're talking to everyone who was at the Big Hoose last night. We've just come from Beth's, so we'd be grateful if you could come down the station to answer a few questions."

"Is that really necessary? I mean, I could answer them here just as easy."

"We'd prefer it down the station," said Bruce in a tone that brooked no argument. "We'll wait if you want to tell your dad."

"Nae need. He's already had a few cans, and he'll be sleeping in front of the TV. Just give me a minute to get oot o' these overalls and get the oil aff my hands." He called across to the other mechanic, emphasizing each word, "Havel, I am going out for a short time. I will be back soon." His companion nodded and raised a hand in acknowledgment.

*****

When she was sitting across from Angus in the interview room at the station, Nan found herself sniffing the air in an effort to detect any obviously strong cologne he might be wearing. There was none though she did notice a faint odor of engine oil and welding fumes, so it was possible he might try to cover these up when he was socializing.

"This seems really formal. Am I in some kind o' trouble?" Angus asked though he seemed unperturbed.

Bruce looked at Nan to indicate she should take the lead, so she said, "Not at all. In fact, would you like a cup of tea or coffee?"

"Tea. Milk and two sugars." Nan nodded at the young PC standing by the door, and he went out.

"As I said, we just wanted to get everyone's take on the events of last night."

"I don't get it. Why are the police interested in that? Do yous no' have a special unit for huntin' doon ghosts?"

"A young woman was injured," the DI said brusquely.

"Aye, but that was an accident."

"Just tell us in your own words what happened," Nan said more delicately.

"We met up at the Big Hoose around 8:00 p.m. as arranged. That arsehole—I mean Jen's dad—was there sniffin' roond the lassies as per usual, especially Dr. Hottie."

"You mean Dr. Chapelle," Nan interjected before she could stop herself.

"Aye. There was nae other doctors there."

The PC returned with a plastic cup of tea and resumed his stance by the door, preventing Nan from overreacting to Angus's sarcasm.

"She was cool as a cucumber, mind. Everyone else was actin' as if they had an army o' soldier ants marchin' through their underwear. When we got into that turret room, I must admit, the atmosphere was beginnin' to get to me tae. Candles and Ouija boards and that. And then a' that weird shit started happenin'."

"Weird shit?"

"The messages aboot secrets and death and guilt and that. At first, I thought it was probably just Darren arsein' aboot as he usually does, but then I began to get a bit freaked oot. When Janine and the other lassie's name came up, that's when Beth bolted as if somebody had set her on fire."

"You went after her," Nan prompted.

"One minute she was sittin' next to me, the next she was oot the door. I was just tryin' to get to her to calm her doon. Just as I got to the door, I heard her scream, and when I got out on the landin', she was lyin' on the stairs, so I went doon to her. Me and Darren got her up even though Jen was gettin' her knickers in a right twist aboot spine or neck injuries. Then we waited for the ambulance."

He paused and took a sip of the tea.

"Are you sure that's the way it happened, Angus?" The DI failed to conceal his impatience.

"Well, no' really."

Nan wondered if she looked as confused as Bruce did.

"What do you mean?"

"The hale thing was so surreal like. When I woke up this mornin', I thought I might hae dreamed it a'."

"What brand of aftershave or cologne do you wear?"

Angus looked surprised by the DI's question as if the police interview had morphed into a consumer survey. "I think it's called Joop or somethin'. I probably shouldn't be tellin' you guys this, but it was one o' Darren's wee sidelines. He had acquired a couple o' cases of it and was floggin' it around the pub at knockdown prices. Back of a lorry job nae doubt."

Nan was quick to realize the implications of this. If half the customers of the pub were wearing the same fragrance, it hardly could constitute evidence against Angus. Evidently, Bruce had the same thought because he suddenly asked, "Didn't you have a romantic relationship with Beth March at one time?"

"We went oot a couple of times ages ago."

"What happened?"

"Think we baith realized it wasnae gaun anywhere."

"Why not?"

"No' that it's ony o' your business, but there was nae spark there, especially in the physical sense. I got the impression she wasnae that into me, and when I got *a bit amorous*, she always stopped things."

Bluntly, the DI asked, "Did you push Beth March down the stairs last night?"

Angus was slack-jawed with astonishment. "What?"

"Did you push her down the stairs?"

"What kind o' question's that? Of course, I fucking didn't."

"Did you attack her in the street the other night and remove an article of clothing from her while she was lying on the pavement?"

"This is fucking ridiculous. Are you forgettin' that somebody attacked me the same night?" Angus's incredulity was quickly turning into anger. "If you're serious, I'm answerin' nae mair questions till I have a lawyer here." There was a lull in the interview during which something seemed to dawn on the young man. "What did Beth tell you?"

Nan thought that it was time to cool the rising temperature in the interview room. She was annoyed that her boss had been so direct. She would have preferred to come at the apparently suspicious evidence by a more subtle and circuitous route.

"There's no need for that, Angus. We have to ask these questions if only to eliminate you from our inquiries."

Angus slumped back in his chair and eyed them sullenly. "Can I go?"

Nan detected an almost inaudible sigh from Bruce as he said, "Yes, you're free to go, but we may need to speak to you again."

"Aye well. Next time, I'll hae a lawyer present." He rose, pushing his chair back so forcefully that the PC by the door was suddenly on alert, but Bruce indicated with a gesture he should show the interviewee out. As he was going, Angus turned and said, "Your tea's shite by the way."

When they had both left, Bruce shouted, "Fuck!" and slammed both hands down on the table. Nan waited till he looked at her at last and said, "I know what you're thinking, Nan, and you're right. I blew it by going in so hard. Sorry."

"I'm not sure I bought his righteous indignation, but we could hardly hold him on the evidence, sir. Beth March's impression of a suspicious smell?"

"And now we know half the fucking town probably smells like that."

"She did say she noticed it on Angus at the séance."

"Did she though? I mean she could be mistaken. It might have been Darren. He probably wears it to cover up the smell of weed. And she doesn't strike me as the most reliable witness." He picked at the skin around the nail on his index finger, which already looked ragged and sore. His frustration was palpable.

"How do we proceed from here, sir?"

Bruce rose slowly, his joints cracking. He stood there in thought for a moment before saying, "Okay, we haven't got much, but we have to go with the little we have got. I'll run this by DCI Carpenter. Try to persuade her to sanction surveillance on McKissock. We keep an eye on our young friend for a day or two. See where that leads us."

As they left the interview room, Nan thought they were as far away from solving this case as ever and was troubled by a niggling feeling they were missing something. But the straws were waving in the wind again, and there was nothing else to do but grasp them.

CHAPTER 22

Journal

A few days later, Nan was due to do a night shift on the limited surveillance operation that DCI Carpenter had agreed to reluctantly, given the paucity of evidence. She was trying to grab a few hours' sleep when she was surprised to receive a text message from Sol:

> Any chance you could swing by the university? We've got something interesting you might like to see.

> X

Nan swallowed back her absurd excitement on seeing the closing kiss in the message. She gave herself a mental slap at reacting like a lovesick teenager. She had been failing miserably to sleep anyway with daylight streaming into her room and the noises of the day outside, so she texted back to see if Sol was available later that afternoon.

The drive up to St Andrews was around twenty-five minutes. The venerable university town was looking cheerful under a watery sun. Its narrow streets were busy with what looked like a mixture of tourists and students. Nan was early for her appointment with Sol, so she stopped for a moment beside the expanse of the Old Course and its familiar hotel that looked down onto the course.

She gazed down toward the shore. The beach had a scattering of dog walkers and some hardy families braving a stiff breeze from the sea. She could hear the excited voices of their children as they dug in the sand and the shrieks of those who ventured to the edge of the chill white waves.

At the university, a receptionist directed her to Dr. Chapelle's office. It was large and impressive. Nan took in the wooden bookshelves groaning with books and the large bay window that looked out toward the university's sports fields. Sol sprang up from her chair behind a deep mahogany desk to greet her with a kiss on both cheeks and a squeeze on her shoulder.

"Can I fix you a drink?" She pointed to a side table with a coffee machine that might have dropped there from space, so alien did it look in its gleaming modernity in the old-fashioned surroundings of the office.

After Sol had made her a coffee that appeared to Nan to demand a great deal of palaver that included frothing the milk, she pulled a chair round to her side of the desk so that they might sit together. The coffee was strong, and Nan could feel the caffeine hit instantly, making her feel more awake.

A battered old journal lay on the desk.

"Is that what I think it is?" said Nan.

"It's the book Dr. Grant found in the grounds of the Big Hoose, yes. She actually does the odd guest lecture here and thought that we would find it of academic and cultural interest though she did say the police might be interested in our findings also. She mentioned you by name in fact. You must have made an impression."

Nan ignored the mischievous glint in her eye and, indicating the book, said, "May I?" Sol produced a pair of paper gloves, and Nan pulled them on.

"I have a friend in the history department who lent me it on the condition I took good care of it. I mentioned you might come up to see it."

"Have you read it?"

"Yes. And it riled me and heartened me and saddened me by turns."

Nan opened the journal. On the inside page, there was a title written in a neat hand.

> If anyone whomever find this, know it be
> the record of Harriet Jackson. May God forgive
> me and all them who done wrong by me.

Sol said, "You'll probably want to skip the early parts, but to summarize, it's what you might expect. Her early life as a slave was grim enough, but her owners seemed enlightened for those dark times, and she appears to have formed a close friendship with one of the white daughters of the house and her brother. Importantly for her story, the daughter taught her to read and write even though it was against the Slave Laws, the son taught her how to handle a gun. Then they must have fallen on hard times because her family was sold on to the Latimers, and that's when her troubles really began."

Nan turned the pages carefully. Each one was written in the same tight script. She stopped at one that was headed "I go into hell and meet the devil." It detailed the backbreaking work that was the lot of slaves on the cotton plantation.

> That summer, my mammy and daddy and
> my little brother and sister were all took by the
> fever one by one. There was days I wanted to die
> and join them in heaven, so I kept on pickin' the
> cotton under that big orange sun, sure that one
> day I'd just fall down in the dirt and pass away.
> Then one day, the young masta came to call. He
> said I stunk and ordered me to strip off my filthy
> close and wash myself at the pump. He stood and
> watched me standin' there neked. Then he took
> me inside to the shack and forced hisself on me.
> He left me bleedin' and cryin'. This happened
> a lot. He came to me most days. If it hadn't of
> been for the old wise woman Betty and Clay, her
> man, I woulda threw myself in the creek, but she

kept tellin' me there was better days to come. She teached me some of the old ways and about herbs and plants and such. How they had the power to heal but if need be the power to kill too. Her eyes was gleamin' when she said that, so I planned. Before I could do nothin', the war came. That was a hard time. We near starved, but I prayed the young devil would get killed and the Yankee soldiers would come and free us. But one day, it wasn't the Yankee soldiers that came but a bunch of men that looked like they had rided straight out of hell and at their head the Latimer devil hisself. I just stood there screamin' and screamin' till he pulled out a knife and cut out my tongue. I had never knowed such pain. Then they shot Betty right in front of my eyes, and they strung up old Clay and cut off his man parts.

Nan stopped for a moment, reluctant to read on any further. "This is appalling. I can see why it riled you, but how did it hearten you?"

"Because she didn't give up. She hardened her heart and waited for revenge on the bastard. Skip the next part. It's more hard reading about how he kept her, used her. Then the sea voyage with all its dreadful hardships. She was chained in the hold for most of it. Go to the page headed 'Vengeance is mine sayeth the Lord.' It brings you to the part about her life here and maybe solves at least one mystery."

It was always so cold here in this big house in this small country. One good thing was that the young devil let me move around outside. Never seemed to think I'd try to escape, and he was right, I'd nowhere to run to. I went out at night when no one was around. Often down to that crossroads and its old tree. Somethin' drew me to it. There was times I thought of the old ways and how maybe here I would meet the Dark Man. A bit of me knew this was where it would all end. I couldn't keep on livin' with that man. He was still doin' vile things to me I don' want to tell here, and there was them things him and his new friends did. They was tryin' to conjure up the dark man hisself, I think, but he was killin' gals and g'tting rid of their bodies in the sea. He made me help so I'd be bound to him and his awful crimes and have even less reason to try to get away. But I bided my time. One night, I knew he was havin' an evil meetin' in the round room with some of them other devils and whores. I put Jimsonweed in their drinks. When I heard the screamin' and crashin', I ran down to the old preacher's house with a note askin' him to come up 'cause I was scared. His own boy was one of them there though there was no light of God in that man. So the old boy come up fast. We found one of the whores at the foot of the stairs with her neck broke, and in that room was like hell had visited. The preacher's boy was stone-cold dead, and the look on his face told me the Jimson had given him horrible visions. The devil and one of his rich White friends were out cold, and the other White boy was up against the wall shakin' and cryin' and makin' no sense. I could smell the shit comin' off him. I'm sorry to say the devil and his friend came round, and I was shoved out of the room. I could hear their voices though, kind of desperate and urgent.

Nan was conscious of Sol watching her reading with a sad, concerned expression. "This reference to Jimsonweed? What is that?"

Sol said, "I googled it. Apparently, it's a plant that if taken can deliver intense spiritual visions but also can cause paranoid delusions and fatalities."

Nan skipped toward the end of the journal, but the last pages were missing. She looked questioningly at Sol. "There are a couple of pages that had come loose from the main journal, and there appeared to be some water damage. They're still with some of Dr. Grant's associates. She reassured me that when they've worked out what was in them, they'll restore them to the original document."

Nan sat silently for what seemed like hours but could only have been a few minutes. Sol just sat and watched her patiently, a look of compassion on her face. After all, she had read the journal too and must have sensed the effect that the girl's harrowing account would have on the reader.

Eventually, she said, "That poor girl."

Sol took Nan's gloved hand. "Dr. Grant said it looks likely that this will solve the mystery of the remains that were dug up at the Big Hoose."

"And that's not the only mystery it solves. For so many years, the stories that have circulated round the happenings at the house only seemed to shroud them in more confusion, attribute them to some kind of supernatural agency."

"And really it was all too human. Told you, the psychology of these things is fascinating. Latimer was an old-fashioned psychopath who surrounded himself with like-minded degenerates. What Harriet did was the result of years of abuse. An all too familiar story, I'm sorry to say."

Nan pushed the small book away and removed the gloves. As a detective, she was gratified by the revelations in the journal, but as a woman, she was deeply saddened by them. Sol embraced her wordlessly as she stood up, sensitive to her bleak mood. They stood for a moment before Nan said, "I wish I could find a diary with a written confession that solves the current case."

Sol looked into her face. "At least this underlines what I was saying about the séance. No supernatural influences there either, which tells us someone there was revealing something about themselves.

That's something to go on." Then seeing Nan still looked crestfallen, she said, "I ain't afraid of no ghosts."

Nan smiled weakly, and Sol said, "That's better," and kissed her lightly on the mouth. "You able to stick around? I don't have any more lectures today. I could show you the pokey accommodation that's all we lecturers can afford in this town."

"Sorry, I have to do a night shift tonight. Surveillance job."

"That's okay. Some other time. You have a suspect?"

"I'm not sure. I'll tell you more about it when we know more."

As she left Sol's office, Nan felt some of the dark clouds above her beginning to dissipate at the promise that there would be "some other time."

CHAPTER 23

Bumps in the Night

As if the prospect of spending a fruitless night watching McKissock's garage wasn't depressing enough, Nan found her mood sinking further when she realized she had been paired with Sergeant Eastman whose opening shot was "Had a curry earlier, so you might want to keep the window down."

The officers whose watch they were relieving had told them that nobody had gone out or come in since they were watching the premises. There was a light on in the room above the garage.

Eastman said, "Settle in for a long fucking boring night. Go easy on the water. I'm no holding your legs at the side of the car while you take a pish."

After a couple of hours of Eastman's reminiscences about policing the mean streets of Glasgow, he began to doze. She was grateful for the silence, so though they both ought to have been remaining alert, she let him sleep. Despite the tedium, she was wide awake. Her brain was full of images from Harriet Jackson's journal.

She had gone to speak to the DI about it but found that Dr. Grant had informed him about its existence already. Nevertheless, when she related some of the details, he looked suitably appalled. Nan sensed that part of him was also secretly relieved that the evidence indicated that the remains were those of the dead major.

The single light in the house remained on, and she wondered how late the residents normally stayed up. From what Angus had told them about his father's habits, it was entirely possible he had simply fallen into a drunken sleep while watching television, and it was typical of men of Angus's age to be glued to some electronic device into the early hours.

She glanced at her watch, 3:00 a.m. Another four hours of what was increasingly looking like a pointless vigil. Eastman was beginning to snore with his mouth open. She silently cursed him for mentioning her intake of water because she was beginning to feel a niggle in her bladder. Besides, her legs were beginning to feel cramped, and the dull ache in her knee and elbow was changing to sharp little needles of pain.

She opened the door carefully in an attempt not to wake the snoring sergeant and stood for a moment in the chill night air, stretching her legs and arms to get her circulation going. If she did have to pee, there was no obvious place to go that she could see. She could hardly go into any of the surrounding gardens, and the last thing she wanted was for Eastman to wake and come looking for her only to find her squatting behind someone's fence with her pants round her knees. She could imagine him gleefully telling that to all and sundry at the station.

Before she could speculate further on the horrors of that scenario, she thought she heard a faint sound in the night like the tinkle of breaking glass. Perhaps a cat had knocked over a milk bottle on someone's doorstep, she thought, though the sound did seem to have come from the vicinity of the garage. She waited silently, trying to detect further noises, but the only sound was the soughing of the wind in the nearby bushes.

Then she was sure she could make out a shape in the shadows of the garage. Just when she thought her eyes must be deceiving her, the shape began to move, and a flicker of light moved to the front door of the house. She went to the passenger side of the police vehicle and rapped urgently on the window. Eastman jerked awake with a small cry. He was disoriented for a moment before he sprang out to join her. He looked somewhat embarrassed as he wiped the drool from the side of his mouth.

"Sorry, must have dozed off for a second there. What's up?"

"I thought I saw someone with a torch down there by the garage moving toward the front door. I'm sure I heard glass breaking."

"Let's have a wee look." He reached into the car to retrieve two torches.

"No, let's wait a few minutes. We don't want to go charging in there if it's a false alarm."

They stood for a while straining eyes and ears till Eastman said, "To hell wi' this for a game of sodjers, let's get closer."

He moved quickly down the hill, so Nan had no choice but to go after him. When they reached the garage, Nan indicated that they should circle the building in different directions. She went around the workshop side till she came to a small side window. In her torch's beam, she could see pieces of glass shining on the ground and noticed that one of the panes on the workshop window was broken. She tried to peer inside, but it was too dark.

She met Eastman back in front of the building. "Window broken at the side."

"Legitimate grounds for suspicion and for us to enter the building." In the torchlight, she could see his conspiratorial wink though she was uncertain whether this was sufficient grounds for them to break cover. Before she could urge caution, he was at the front door.

As he tentatively began to open it, the handle was suddenly wrenched from his grasp. A burly figure barreled into him, knocking him to the ground, and ran off up the street.

Nan went to Eastman and helped him to his feet. "You okay?"

"Aye, a bit winded. Bastard took me by surprise."

"You get after him. I'll check the house."

Whoever had been in the house had disappeared into the night, but Eastman took off in the direction he had gone in a limping run. Nan entered the dark hallway, shining her torch along the wall till she spotted a light switch. Flicking it on had no discernible effect on the dimness of the hall. Nan could see the bulb was covered by an old dusty-looking fabric lampshade of a style that must have gone out in the '80s.

It roughly matched the faded carpet on the stairs that went to the upper level of the house. Beyond the staircase, two doors led off from the hall on the right, and there was one in the corner on the left that she surmised must be an entrance to the garage workshop. The sharp odor of petrol or oil hung in the air.

She tried the first door on the right. The room she entered was illuminated only by the flickering light of the television that was tuned to an all-night news channel, but she could see how untidy it was. A discarded pizza carton and a number of empty beer cans lay on the floor by the settee, on which a man was slumped, snoring loudly. A half-empty bottle of Teacher's Whisky was on the coffee table at his elbow, and when she went over to him, she saw that a glass lay in his lap. The whiskey that remained in it had surprisingly not spilled though it perched precariously between his legs.

"Mr. McKissock? Police. We think you've had a break-in. Mr. McKissock." He grunted briefly but was otherwise unresponsive. Nan gave up and decided to look upstairs for his son. At the top of the stairs, there were three doors. The one facing her was ajar and was obviously a bathroom. She took the door on the left, reckoning that this must be the room above the workshop where they had seen a light on.

The bedroom was empty. It contained a neatly made single bed, a small wardrobe and chest of drawers, and a computer desk on which was a small monitor and games console. The screen displayed a paused image of a battlefield. Nan went out onto the landing and called Angus's name, but there was no reply. The tension of the last few minutes had lent an urgency to her earlier toilet dilemma, so she quickly used the bathroom.

When she reentered the bedroom, she thought she could smell smoke, and the temperature in the room seemed to have risen. She remained stock-still with her senses alert, prickling with anxiety. She was certain the smell of smoke was getting stronger. Before she could move to investigate, her attention was drawn to the chest of drawers.

DI Bruce often spoke of what he called "Copper's Nose," the connotations of which were both positive and negative. On the one hand, it referred to the instinctive natural curiosity that was an essential tool for a detective. On the other, it carried the implication that it could lead its possessor to ignore caution and expose themselves to danger.

Nan was conscious of Bruce's words now as she pulled open drawers. The top two drawers contained only neatly folded T-shirts and underwear. Common sense was telling her to get out. After all, if she did find something incriminating, it would be inadmissible as evidence, and she realized with a shiver of fear that the room was filling up with smoke.

She was about to abandon her search when she pulled open the third drawer down. It also contained underwear but not the male boxers of the other drawer. Instead, Nan found a colorful mixture of female panties. There were knickers of several styles, colors, and materials from ordinary white and pastel-colored cotton pants to diaphanous black lace briefs and skimpy thongs.

Before she could take in the implications of her discovery, she was suddenly aware that she was struggling to breathe as the acrid smoke thickened in the room. She tried to yell out, "Fire!" but the smoke caught the back of her throat and caused her to have a retching coughing fit. She headed for the stairs. The downstairs hall was full of smoke. When she was halfway down the stairs, she could just make out that the smoke seemed to be billowing in from the door at the end of the hall that she had assumed led to the garage.

She had just pulled her jacket up around her nose and mouth when the front door opened, and Eastman's startled pale face appeared. She stumbled down the remaining stairs to meet him just as flames began to lick out from the door to the garage. She had done enough courses on fire safety to realize that the fire had been exacerbated by the draught created by Eastman's entrance.

He pulled out a handkerchief and put it up to his face, mumbling, "Let's get the fuck out of here."

With halting breaths, Nan told him that McKissock was in the living room. Above the handkerchief, she could see his eyes widening with fearful realization, and after a moment's hesitation, he followed her through the thickening smoke, both of them trying to keep low and hug the wall.

The smoke was just beginning to swirl into the living room so they could make out the recumbent oblivious figure on the sofa. Eastman went to McKissock and shook him, then none too gently slapped his face. The man grunted awake dazedly. "Get up. We have to get out of here, and I don't fancy carrying you, you fat bastard."

Nan went and helped him to get McKissock to his feet, and with one of them at either side of him, they got him into a lurching stagger. When he saw the flames and the smoke in the hall, a look of sheer terror crossed his face.

"Keep low and stick to..." Nan had uncovered her mouth to issue the instruction, but she recognized she would be overcome by the smoke if she breathed it in.

Eastman shouted through his handkerchief, "Try to hold your breath!"

After what seemed like an age, they reached the front door and reeled out, all three of them falling to their knees outside, coughing and gasping in the cool night air. McKissock vomited noisily onto the ground. Eastman took out his mobile and called for the fire brigade, then said, "Thank fuck this cunt didnae breathe out. His breath would strip paint. His head would probably have went up in a fireball."

McKissock said, "Angus, where's Angus?"

Eastman looked at Nan questioningly. She said, "There was no sign of him upstairs." Then as realization dawned, she got to her feet, almost whispering, "The garage." She moved painfully to the front of the building, fearing that at any minute, her knee would give way beneath her.

Eastman called out, "Nan, wait for the fire service to get here," but she ignored him as she examined the large rusting padlock on the front door of the garage.

As she tugged at it impotently, Eastman appeared at her side. "Out the way." He still carried his heavy torch and began to rain blows with it rhythmically on the padlock. Just when Nan began to think his efforts were futile and she was considering what might prove a suicidal dash back into the house, the lock gave way, the body of it clanging to the ground, leaving the shackle hanging.

She reached past Eastman and wrenched the door open. The inside of the garage was filled with thick smoke. She could make out the shapes of two cars with their bonnets open, and behind them, flames seemed to be rushing up the back wall and the entrance to the body of the house. She pulled her jacket, which now reeked of smoke, back up to her face and plunged inside.

She ignored Eastman, who was yelling at her, "Nan, don't be mental! Wait for the fire brigade. He might no' even be in there."

She could hear sirens in the distance, but she continued past the cars, examining the floor through watering eyes. She was about to turn back when she thought she could make out a figure slumped on the floor by the broken window. Flames were devouring the back wall of the garage as she reached the unconscious body of Angus McKissock.

Her fear lent her the strength to reach under his armpits and begin to haul him across the floor, but she quickly realized that adrenaline wouldn't sustain her attempt to drag him to the door in time, and she was beginning to fade and feel light-headed.

Then Eastman was by her side, handkerchief pressed to his face. He pushed her away brusquely, shouting, "Get out, you fucking crazy bitch!" as he manhandled Angus to the entrance.

They had only just pulled him clear when the fire engine came into the forecourt in a wave of sound and flashing lights. After a wrenching fit of coughing, during which she thought she might bring up a lung, Nan leaned across the unmoving body of Angus.

She gulped in deep draughts of night air before placing her lips over Angus's mouth and breathing into it. Eastman had recovered sufficiently to come over ready to apply pressure to his chest, but they felt strong hands on their shoulders. Two firefighters lifted Angus and ushered Nan and Eastman farther away from the fire that continued to consume the building despite the efforts of their colleagues who were releasing a deluge of water onto it.

They had gone several hundred yards up the hill away from the garage when more blue lights and sirens indicated the arrival of two ambulances. Four paramedics appeared on the scene, two of them administering to the motionless young mechanic and the others asking Nan and Eastman rapid fire questions about their condition.

Nan suddenly remembered they had left Angus's father near the house, but just as she was about to alert their rescuers, he appeared half stumbling, half carried by another member of the fire rescue services. When he saw his son, he gave a pathetic cry and fell to his knees, reaching one hand toward him.

The next few minutes seemed to pass in a blur for Nan. Her chest ached almost more than her leg and arm, and her eyes continued to sting and run. She was vaguely aware of Angus being lifted onto a stretcher, an oxygen mask strapped to his face, and carried onto one of the waiting ambulances. The paramedics helped his father into the same ambulance, which sped off in a confusion of lights and noise.

Nan and a protesting Eastman were ushered into the other ambulance. Nan noticed that several lights had come on in the neighboring houses, and a few of the residents had gathered outside in their night clothes. They were taken to the Queen Victoria Hospital, which was the nearest one with an A&E department. Nan was examined by a harassed-looking young woman in scrubs who introduced herself as Dr. Kindness. Nan almost giggled, thinking this must be some kind of joke, but the woman's serious eyes and the dark rings beneath them testified to a long shift during which humor was no doubt in short supply.

The doctor recommended that Nan be kept in overnight since she had inhaled some smoke, but she was anxious to get back to her own bed and reassured her she felt fine. Indeed her lungs did feel clearer after she had hacked up some disgusting-looking black phlegm in the back of the ambulance. The young doctor said sternly it was against her advice but agreed reluctantly and informed Nan of warning signs she should look out for.

On her way out, she passed a cubicle whose curtains were pulled back to reveal Eastman sitting on a chair by the side of a trolley. His soot-smudged shirt was open to the waist, and his face was blackened by smoke.

Nan hadn't looked at herself in a mirror, but her clothes were similarly blackened, and she suspected her face must resemble his. She thought the two of them must look like a couple of Dick Van Dyke's sidekicks in *Mary Poppins*, and suddenly she was laughing uncontrollably. The thought that her tears must be making tracks down her filthy face made her laugh even harder for some reason.

Eastman simply watched her, looking faintly worried and bemused. With an effort, she pulled herself together, aware that she was on the brink of hysteria. She went to Eastman and startled him by kissing his dirty cheek. "Thanks for *you know*."

He smiled briefly, his lips looking redder in his blackened face. "I just did what any lionhearted hero wi' gigantic balls of steel would have done."

Nan left him before her emotions overwhelmed her and made her way to the front entrance of the hospital. The faint light of dawn was appearing on the horizon as she went out. Two women in the uniforms of domestic staff were on their way in probably to begin their shift.

They looked at Nan curiously and then disapprovingly as she shouted "fuck" loudly when she remembered the car was still back near McKissock's garage.

CHAPTER 24

Debriefing

Nan was woken around noon the next day by a hacking cough which left her breathless. After the taxi had dropped her off, she had bundled her stinking clothes into the laundry basket and stood under a scalding hot shower, washing and rinsing her hair several times and scrubbing her skin till it was red. Even so, as she woke, she thought she could still smell the faint traces of smoke on her body.

After another shower, during which she was overtaken by a further fit of coughing, she dragged herself into the kitchen where she staved off her feeling of nausea by drinking a strong coffee and eating two slices of dry toast. Her body ached. Even the roots of her hair felt uncomfortable. She felt like falling back into bed, but she forced herself to get dressed and put on some makeup to cover her pallor.

She was too anxious to know about the condition of Angus McKissock and his father not to go into work. Besides, she wanted to run what she had discovered in Angus's bedroom by DI Bruce to test its significance as well as to get his advice on the best way to proceed.

Her arrival at the station drew curious glances, but she hurried quickly to find the DI before someone decided to ask how she was. Not only did she not feel like getting into the events of the previous night, but also she was still feeling emotionally fragile and was uncertain how she would react if anyone should show concern for her.

Fortunately, Bruce was his usual blunt self. "Nan, what the fuck are you doing here? You ought to be still in hospital or at least at home recovering. We went to the hospital in the early hours of the morning, but you'd already gone. Sergeant Eastman gave us a state-ment. What the fuck did you think you were playing at going into the house?"

Nan ignored his question. "I feel okay, sir."

"You don't look it."

"I needed to find out what was happening. How are Angus McKissock and his dad?"

"They're recovering. McKissock was discharged from hospital this morning. They've kept the son in because he'd inhaled a good deal of smoke, and he had suffered a mild concussion."

"Concussion?"

"Someone hit him over the head. As you no doubt suspected, the fire service's initial findings point to arson. Somebody poured accelerant through the broken garage widow. It appears not to have worked, or at least not worked quickly enough, so obviously the per-petrator decided to make sure by entering the garage through the house. Presumably, it was the person that you and Eastman just missed. There were signs of two probable sites where the fire started, under the broken window and at a pile of old tires that were up against the back wall."

"Shit, a disappearance, a murder, assaults, and now arson. What the hell is going on in the Law? Things just keep getting murkier. You think Angus might have discovered the culprit and that's why he was struck?"

"Maybe. I'm going to the hospital later to interview him."

"Can I come?"

"I'm not sure that's such a good idea."

"With respect, sir, I'd like to follow this through." As he hesi-tated, Nan told him about what she had discovered in the drawer in Angus's bedroom.

"For fuck's sake, Nan, what were you thinking? You're about to be burned to a crisp, and you start searching through this man's drawers, illegally searching at that."

"I get that, sir, but is there any way we can use this? At the very least, it's suspicious considering Janine Gunning's underwear was missing and someone assaulted Beth March and removed her knickers."

Bruce put a hand to his forehead as if his thoughts were causing him pain. After a long pause, he said, "All right. We interview Angus McKissock, but we have to tread carefully. We can't simply confront him with this because: a, he'd probably just clam up, and b, his lawyer would be all over this in a heartbeat."

"I know I crossed a line, sir."

"You certainly did, Sergeant. You failed to follow correct procedure and were reckless and irresponsible." His stern expression softened. "However, you were also very brave, and you probably saved two men's lives."

*****

When they arrived at the entrance to the Victoria Hospital, Bruce stopped her and said, "Remember, officially, we're investigating a case of arson and not some fetish that may or may not be relevant to our inquiries."

"Got it, sir." A man with no legs in a wheelchair eyed them curiously as he sat smoking blatantly under a No Smoking sign. The DI said, "Christ, does security not police these things?"

"Good advert for the perils of nicotine addiction though, sir." She thought that Bruce looked uncomfortable for a moment.

Angus McKissock was in a ward on his own. When they entered, a nurse was checking his blood pressure and temperature. He looked freshly scrubbed though his eyes were bloodshot, and Nan thought she could detect a wheeze in his breath that almost set her own cough off again. There was a dressing on the back of his head.

When the nurse left, Nan took out her notebook and pen. Bruce said, "How are you, Angus?"

"'A' the better for havin' a visit from the constabulary." Then as if he was weary, he dropped the sarcastic tone and said, "I'm fine. They're sayin' I'll probably be discharged the day." He looked at Nan. "They told me about what you did so thanks and that. You and your mate saved me and the old man so, you know…" His face reddened as he struggled to articulate his gratitude.

"Glad you're going to be okay. What do you remember about last night?"

"I was in my room playing a computer game. Dad was downstairs in his usual comatose state in front of the box. I'd been down earlier to turn the sound down on it. He often slept there half the night with it on."

"Did you go into the garage?" Nan asked, which drew a warning look from Bruce. She realized there might be an implied accusation in the question that he might have somehow been responsible for the fire himself.

However, he seemed unaware of it and went on, "No' then, no, but I'd only just been upstairs a few minutes, and I thought I heard a noise coming from there. My room's just above it as you know."

"So you went to investigate?" Bruce prompted.

"No' right away. I didnae want to pause my game again. I was pretty absorbed in it. But then I thought I heard somebody outside. Even though I was a bit pissed off, I thought I'd better check. We've got some nice motors now, and to tell the truth, we havenae exactly beefed up the security at the garage." He looked anxious for a moment. "Shite, I hope the old fool has kept the insurance up to date."

Bruce tried to pull him back on track. "What did you find when you went to check?"

"I went into the garage through the house. I never switched the lights on like, and at first, I never noticed anythin'. But then I thought I smelled somethin' chemical, no' the usual engine oil and that. Then I saw the window was broken. I moved farther in to have a look, and that's when the lights went out. I felt this god-awful pain in my head, and that's the last thing I remember till I came round in here wi' an oxygen mask strapped to my face."

Nan asked, "Did you hear anything before you were struck?"

"No' a thing. Whoever it was must have had their baffies on."

"Can you think of any reason why somebody might have done this?"

Nan thought she saw a furtive look crossing Angus's face for a moment before he muttered, "No."

Bruce said impatiently, "Angus, this is a serious crime. We're not just looking at arson here but attempted murder as well."

"I telt you, I havenae a clue." His irate reaction set off a spasm of coughing. Nan set her pen down on the unit next to his bed and poured him a cup of water from the plastic jug there. After he had gulped some down, he gasped, "Thanks. That fucking cough makes me feel like my head's comin' off."

Bruce rose reluctantly. "When you feel up to it, we'd like you to come into the station to make a formal statement. In the meantime, if anything else comes back to you." Bruce handed him his card, and they left.

They went along a hospital corridor that was busy with bustling nurses and patients, some of whom were pushing portable trolleys attached to bags with unspeakable-looking liquids in them. Bruce said, "I'm getting seriously bad vibes from that young man. I'd bet my pension there's something he's not telling us. And not just because of what you *noticed* in his bedroom. We'll get him down the station and interview him under caution. He can have a lawyer there."

When they were back at the hospital entrance, Nan said, "Damn, I've left my pen up there."

"Leave it. You can get another one."

"But it's my good pen. It's a Waterman."

"Hurry up then. I'll wait by the car." He gave her an odd look. Nan couldn't decide if it was because he suspected she had engineered a moment with McKissock on his own or whether he suspected she knew he would light up a cigarette at the first opportunity.

When she returned to Angus's room, she saw he hadn't moved. He was lying, prone and sullen, staring at the blank pale green wall at the bottom of his bed. His eyes flickered toward her when she entered, but he said nothing. "Left my pen. Sorry to disturb you again."

She retrieved the pen and stood for a moment at the side of his bed till he turned his head toward her suspiciously. "What now?"

"Angus, I didn't want to bring this up when the detective inspector was here, but last night, I saw something in your room."

"What the fuck? You were snoopin' around in my bedroom?"

"I was looking for you. I couldn't rouse your father, and besides I needed to use the loo."

"You had fuck all right to be goin' through the house. You didnae have a warrant."

"My colleague and I had seen suspicious activity which gave us justifiable cause to investigate. Let's face it, if we hadn't, you and your dad would be dead."

He hesitated for a moment before continuing to glower at her. "But it didnae give you the right to go through my stuff. I'm gettin' in touch wi' a lawyer." His anger set him off coughing, but he pushed away the plastic cup of water she proffered.

"I didn't rummage through your belongings as you suggest. One of the drawers in your bedroom chest was open, and I happened to see what was inside."

Nan hoped he wouldn't detect her lie, but he snarled. "No way. That drawer was never left open." He must have realized that he had more or less admitted to having something in his drawer that he would prefer to keep secret because he slumped back against his pillow, and facing away from her toward the window, he muttered, "I'm sayin' nothin' else till I see a lawyer."

"Do you really want it to come out that you have a collection of female underwear?"

He turned furious eyes on her once more. "Are you tryin' to blackmail me?"

"Oh, come on, Angus. You must see how this looks. Janine Gunning's underwear was missing. Then there was the incident with Beth March. Are you saying that's a coincidence?"

There was a long silence during which a number of emotions passed across his face: anger, frustration, and finally fear. He seemed to shrink into his bed, and for a moment, he looked at Nan like a small boy who wants to pull the covers over his head to hide from a storm.

"Look, I had nothin' to do wi' Janine's murder. You have to believe me. And I would never do anythin' to Beth."

"What about the knickers in your drawer?"

Nan almost felt sorry for him as he flushed with shame and couldn't meet her eye. In a small voice, he said, "I'm no' proud of myself but the…the underwear, it's just a harmless fetish. I dinnae hurt anyone. I mean I'd never attack a woman and take off her—"

"How do you *acquire* them then?"

He looked close to tears as he said, "Off washin' lines mostly. And I go to the launderette wi' me and my dad's washin' once a week, and sometimes I'll see a basket there wi' *women's things* in it, and I'll take a couple of pairs."

He hung his head for a moment before looking up at her imploringly. "This…this doesn't need to come out does it? I mean my dad and my mates would…I mean I dinnae wear them or do *dirty things* wi' them or nothin'. I just like to have them."

"I'll be straight with you, Angus. We can't use this in evidence, but you must realize this makes you a prime suspect, and the police are going to pick over your story in minute detail."

He put a hand up to his eyes as if it pained him to look at her. "I'm no' a murderer."

As Nan was leaving, a thought occurred to her. "Did anyone else know about your *secret*?"

With his hand still up at his face, he murmured, "No."

Back at the car park, she found DI Bruce pacing, cigarette in hand. Two more stubs were scattered at his feet.

He eyed her suspiciously. "Took you a while to get your pen. You didn't?"

She shook her head. Clearly dissatisfied, he got into the car. She was unsure how to process what Angus had told her and now wasn't the time to discuss it with her boss. Of one thing she was certain though, Angus McKissock wasn't telling her the whole story.

CHAPTER 25

Dirty Money

When they got back to the station, they discovered that DCI Carpenter had called a team briefing for early that afternoon. As they filtered into the incident room, Nan noticed there was none of the usual banter. The team was tense, fearing that their efforts had brought them no closer to a solution to Janine Gunning's killing, and they were no doubt expecting a rocket from the DCI.

A couple of them muttered, "Good job, Sarge," or "Nice one," to her, and one or two of them shook her hand or patted her shoulder. Nan ought to have felt gratified by her colleagues' acknowledgment of her courage, but she was too much on edge. What was she to make of Angus's confession about his weird sexual habit? Was he telling the truth or merely trying to cover up an even bigger guilty secret?

If Carpenter was feeling the strain of the investigation, it didn't show. She was immaculately turned out in a beige jacket and skirt, and her hair looked freshly blow-dried. "You'll all have heard about the fire last night at a premises that we were keeping under surveillance. First, may I commend the bravery of the police officers who rescued two men from the house and garage." There was a moment of spontaneous applause, which made Nan blush.

When it had died down, the DCI fixed Nan with a steely gaze and said pointedly, "However, I must stress that there is no excuse for my officers to place their own lives on the line with such a blatant disregard for procedure." There were a few discontented rumblings from her audience. Nan thought the DCI had just released a cloud-burst on her parade.

"It's fair to say that the said surveillance had produced no tangi-ble results up to that point though I believe Angus McKissock remains a person of considerable interest in our inquiries?" She looked to DI Bruce as if for confirmation, and he nodded.

"We have had one major breakthrough in our investigation into the financial dealings of several businesses in the area, however. As I speak, a team are sifting through evidence of a widespread money laundering operation for the Tweedie gang involving among others the McKissock garage, the Cross Inn, and Rand properties. Bizarrely, the list also includes the local undertakers. The fraud team have brought Walter Dixon in for questioning. There's strong evidence that he might be the link between the locals and our friends across the river. Anyway, in the light of this, yesterday's fire seems a coinci-dence too far."

DI Bruce raised a hand. "You think McKissock got cold feet, ma'am, and the arson was an example to the others not to jump ship?"

"I wouldn't like to speculate at this stage, but unfortunate things have a habit of happening to associates of the Tweedies who fall out with them. We'll know more when we round up all the suspects and confront them with the evidence in their accounts."

Nan's head spun with a host of worries and questions. If the DCI was right about the widespread nature of the money-laundering scheme, it would be devastating for the Law and its inhabitants. And how, if at all, was this connected to the murder and assaults? Janine Gunning's mother was some kind of relation to Walter Dixon. Was there something they were missing? Was it even relevant?

As if Carpenter had read her mind, she said, "Of course, signif-icant as this is, I fail at present to see how this advances our murder inquiries. However, if there is a connection, we have to find it. I'll be liaising with the fraud investigators, and I'll keep you all in the loop. Meanwhile, we'll continue to put pressure on the current suspects." She turned to Bruce. "For example, I want the McKissocks brought in as soon as they've recovered enough to answer questions."

As the meeting broke up and everyone exited hurriedly, Nan thought that for a moment, DCI Carpenter's professional facade appeared to slip when she was no longer the centre of attention. Her posture was less upright, and her look was that of someone who has wandered into an unfamiliar neighborhood and suddenly finds themselves lost.

Nan couldn't blame her. There was something unreal about what was happening in Upper and Lower Law. It resembled those fictitious sleepy rural villages in TV detective fiction that seemed to harbor crime suspects beneath every thatched roof.

A wave of depression washed over her, which probably had something to do with the aftermath of her previous night's ordeal, and yet seemed to run deeper, seeping into her bone marrow. She was struck by the thought that there was something rotten at the core of this town, which teemed with crooked business dealings, perversion, violence, and misogyny.

This led her to recall the accounts of inhumanity in Harriet Jackson's journal. Was there a blight at the roots of human nature that produced spoiled fruit in an unending cycle? She had been accustomed to encountering the worst excesses of human behavior when she worked in the city, but in such a small town as the Law, it seemed more concentrated somehow. Clearly, though the tentacles of the beast at the heart of that same city were reaching over here.

She sat at her desk later, staring at her computer screen where the words seemed to go in and out of focus. There was something nagging her about her confrontation with Angus McKissock. She couldn't help feeling that he had lied when she'd asked him if anyone else knew about his guilty fetish, and her instinct told her it was somehow vital to find out the truth.

DI Bruce appeared at her elbow, jolting her from her reverie. "The DCI's asked us to contact our colleagues in Edinburgh to pull in Graham Neeson and the guy who was with him when he paid a little visit to McKissock and Sark recently. The second man has been identified as Benny Slavek. He runs a boxing gym in Sighthill and has a lucrative sideline in beating people up from time to time for the Tweedies. They've to check these two charmers' whereabouts last night and in the early hours."

"Probably a waste of time, sir. In my experience, these thugs are adept at covering their own arses."

"Aye, well, we have to go through the motions." He looked so hopeless momentarily that Nan felt sorry for him. She felt she ought to hold out some hope for him even if it was akin to throwing a man drowning in high seas a slippery rope.

"I still think Angus McKissock might give us more."

"You think he's our killer?"

"Frankly, I'm not sure, but if he isn't, he might be the key to finding out who is."

"Get on to the hospital again. Find out when he's being discharged, and we'll bring him in. I'm not sure where he'll go to ground now the house and garage have been destroyed. I hear his old man's holed up in the Cross Inn."

Nan had just lifted the receiver to dial the hospital when Elsie Telfer appeared, waving a sheet of paper. "Thought you might be interested in this. We've just had a report from a Mr. Andrew March that two shotguns are missing from his gun safe, one single and one double-barreled."

For a moment, Nan and DI Bruce looked nonplussed. Then recognition dawned on Nan. "March, that's Beth March's estranged father. Remember, sir, he works at the Big Hoose as a groundsman and gamekeeper."

Telfer piped up, "That's right, Sergeant. He told us he kept them in room at the Big Hoose."

"What the fuck is going on now?" He looked at the female PC apologetically. "Sorry, PC Telfer."

"Quite all right, sir."

"Let's take this one, Nan. It's time to pay another visit to the Lakes."

Nan had no time to reflect that it was acceptable apparently for the DI to swear in front of her but not another female officer before she was trailing in his wake as he grabbed his coat and hurried out.

CHAPTER 26

Guns

Colin Sark stood outside the closed doors of the Cross Inn. He was flustered. He had spent the afternoon fending off inquiries from irate regulars who wanted to know why the bar wasn't opening at the usual time. He had made up a story about a suspected vomiting bug that had hit the staff that was why the inn had been left undermanned, but from the skeptical looks he received from the punters, he knew he wasn't convincing anybody.

The truth was he was at a loss. After Angus's dad had shown up with his bombshell about the garage burning down and asking for temporary accommodation at the inn, they had received a visit from the police who removed his father's laptop and cashbooks. His parents had had a furious row, and now his dad and McKissock were sitting at the bar, sinking drams as if they were trying to get rid of the pub's whiskey stocks before they were impounded.

He knew he was being selfish when his parents' livelihood and possibly their marriage were at stake, but he couldn't help fearing that if his dad and McKissock were involved in anything illegal, it would jeopardize his chances of getting into the police. Though the day was bright, he huddled against the wall under his own personal cloud of gloom.

Jennifer Lake appeared around the corner arm in arm with Letty Vance and Beth March. "Hey, Clipper, cheer up. It may never happen." She eyed the pub's closed doors. "Are you shut? What's going on?"

Colin began to tell them his rehearsed story about stomach bugs and short staffing when he was interrupted by the appearance of Darren Boyd's Citroën Saxo. A morose looking Angus McKissock was in the passenger seat. The exhaust roared as Darren revved the car so that he had to shout, "What's the problem? Why's the pub no' open?"

As Jennifer noticed Angus, she said, "We heard about the fire at the garage. Should you not be in hospital? Fuck, Darren, will you stop revving that piece of junk."

Darren cut the engine and said, "I've just picked him up from there. And now he's in serious need of some liquid refreshment."

Letty said, "Well he's out of luck here."

Colin couldn't be bothered repeating his prepared statement, so he merely said, "Sorry, guys, but I cannae see us openin' the day."

"That's a' we fucking need," said Darren exasperatedly. "Queen of the Forth?"

"There's no way I'm going into that shithole," said Jennifer.

"Me neither," agreed Letty.

"Look, why doesn't everyone come back to mine? We can have a few drinks in the basement."

Darren immediately cheered up. "That sounds like a plan, Jen."

"I've nowhere else to go," muttered Angus.

Colin thought of telling him his old man was inside attempting to drink the bar dry, but Angus looked so broken as he sat hunched forward in the car that he didn't have the heart.

"Meet you up there." Darren started the engine, and they roared off in a cloud of choking exhaust fumes.

"Come on, girls."

Beth, who had been silent and subdued up till then, said, "I think I'll just head home, Jen, if that's all right with you."

"Don't be daft, Beth. Your mum was expecting you to be out at the pub, so you may as well enjoy the freedom. There are a couple of movies on Netflix we can watch."

"Aye, come on, Beth," said Letty.

Before Beth could object, the other two girls had grabbed an arm each and started marching her down the street. At the corner,

Jennifer turned and shouted, "Hey, Clipper, you've got the day off obviously, so why not join us?"

Colin could barely suppress the grin that was beginning to break over his hitherto depressed countenance. An invitation to the Big Hoose and a chance to spend some time with the Law Society, maybe this was an opportunity to gain admittance to the group at last.

On the walk up to the Big Hoose, Colin found himself alongside Beth as the others seemed to be in a competition to see who could walk the quickest. She asked him shyly if he had told them the real reason why the inn was closed. She looked at him sideways, and perhaps it was the innocuous look in her blue eyes that made him blurt out a confession about the police visit.

"You shouldn't worry, Colin. There might be a perfectly innocent explanation."

"And what about the fire at Angus's?"

"God, how I hate this place." Her vehemence took him by surprise. "All these small-minded people with their petty little lives. They have nothing better to do than stick their ugly noses into everyone else's business. You can bet they've already made up their minds that your dad and Angus's dad are up to their eyes in something criminal. They practically come in their pants at the hint of anything mildly scandalous."

Colin had never heard Beth talking like this, but he remembered the circumstances of her father's abandonment of her and her mother, so he could understand her bitterness. They had reached the crossroads and were passing the shadow of the Dule tree.

"I still get the creeps when I pass here. Remember Letty's story? And of course, this is where they found poor Janine's *body*."

Colin noticed a visible shudder running through her. He thought of putting a comforting arm around her, but he was afraid that she might misinterpret the gesture.

"What do you think, Colin? You must overhear things all the time in the pub. Any clues?"

"No' really."

"Come on, you must have heard something that aroused your suspicions."

"I wouldnae pay attention to half the shite the punters in the inn come out with."

They had entered the Big Hoose's long drive and were passing between the trees that loomed rather menacingly on both sides. Many of them arched so far over the path that daylight struggled to penetrate through. The last thing Colin felt like discussing was a murder that had been committed near here, but Beth was undaunted by his elusive and monosyllabic replies.

"You think one of your customers might have done it?"

Colin shrugged his shoulders. "No, but I suppose it's possible it's one of the regulars. We're no' exactly a sophisticated venue where the literati discuss philosophy and the latest developments in the worlds of science and art."

"That'll be the Queen of the Forth."

Colin was relieved that Beth was attempting to lighten the conversation, and he laughed. "Aye, maybe our punters are a step up from some of the Neanderthals that drink in there right enough."

However, almost instantly, she was serious again. "It's scary to think of some maniac still at large in the Law. I mean, the way she was violated and that."

Colin was lost for a reply. He was sensitive to the fact that Beth had suffered some kind of assault though he didn't know the details. It perturbed him to think it might have had a sexual element to it.

"I confess all the black magic rumors spook me too. They say that stuff was written on Janine. And when we had that séance, I seriously freaked out."

Colin looked at her questioningly. The snooping, inquisitive part of him was eager to hear more details about what had taken place that night, but a nagging voice in his head was warning him not to pursue it.

"No wonder you're looking at me so oddly. Sorry, Colin. I hope my gloom and doom isn't making you regret coming along with us."

He could only mutter unconvincingly, "Of course not."

To his surprise, she grabbed his hand and said, "Come on, let's catch up with Jennifer and Letty."

He was relieved when she propelled him into a half run but struggled to shake off his feeling of unease as, panting, they rejoined the girls.

There were several cars parked at the front of the entrance to the Big Hoose. Colin recognized Campbell Lake's Volvo and Darren's Saxo. The proximity of the latter to the politician's gleaming car made it appear even more shabby and beaten up.

As they mounted the stairs to the house, Jennifer said, "Weird. I wonder why the front door's wide open."

She led them into the entrance hall, glancing around agitatedly. She turned to the others and said, "You guys head down into the basement. You know where the drinks and snacks are kept. I'll be down in a minute when I've checked in with the parentals."

"Dinnae need to ask me twice," said Darren as he bounded toward the stairs. "Come on, Angus. Time you got your miserable gob round a can of lager."

Angus slouched after him, and after a quizzical look at Jennifer, the two girls followed. Something about Jennifer's demeanor made Colin hang back. She went to a room to the right and listened for a moment outside its closed doors.

"Jennifer, I—"

Jennifer held a finger to her lips and whispered, "Shush."

Feeling like a schoolboy who has been reprimanded for talking in class, Colin waited behind her. Suddenly, she threw open the double doors. At first, Colin had difficulty interpreting the scene before him. There were four people in the room. Campbell Lake and his wife were sitting on the edge of a chaise longue together.

His face was drained of color, and beads of sweat stood out on his upper lip and forehead. His wife, on the other hand, looked poised and erect with a faintly amused expression on her face. Colin thought she might be presiding over a weekly meeting of her book club.

The only thing that appeared to disturb her sangfroid was a middle-aged woman who was spread-eagled up against a wall near her. She was so still it looked as if she was waiting for someone to come and draw round her outline on the wall. Between her legs, a yellow puddle had formed on the highly polished wooden floor, and the regal-looking Mrs. Lake kept giving her distasteful glances as it trickled toward an expensive-looking red rug with an elaborate pattern.

The reason for the tableau quickly became clear as Colin observed the man standing before them in a crumpled-looking suit. It was not the man's wild eyes that arrested his attention but the heavy looking shotgun that he was pointing shakily toward Campbell Lake.

As he took in the scene slowly, Colin suddenly felt the clammy hand of fear gripping his own heart as almost in slow motion, the gun swiveled toward him and Jennifer. "Come in and close the door," the man ordered in a strangled voice.

Jennifer seemed frozen to the spot, so Colin gently put a hand on her back and made her take reluctant steps into the room as he closed the doors quietly behind them. He heard a stifled whimper from the woman who was up against the wall.

"Beside them, where I can see you." The man waved the shotgun to indicate that the two young people should stand behind the couple on the chaise.

Campbell Lake cleared his throat before croaking, "Please, Liam, don't harm my daughter."

The man suddenly roared, "And what about my daughter, you bastard?" His sudden anger made Lake flinch and elicited a moan from the terrified woman.

Lake's wife simply looked at the man impatiently and disdainfully as if he had appeared on her doorstep uninvited, trying to sell her double glazing.

Lake once more found his voice though it emerged high and quivering. "What's this about, Liam? I had nothing to do with your girl's disappearance. I was as upset as anyone else."

Colin was barely taking this in as he stared mesmerized into the dark barrels of the gun. It dawned on him through the fog of his fear that this was Liam Chalmers, Carol's father. He never frequented the Cross Inn, but Colin had a vague recollection of seeing him in the streets of Lower Law, handing out fliers at election time.

"What about this then?" The man pulled out a piece of paper from the pocket of his jacket, an action that made the gun dip alarmingly as he tried to hold it in one hand. Colin imagined that the gun could go off at any moment, and he could feel Jennifer trembling next to him. When he managed to focus on the paper in Chalmers's hand, he thought it looked like the ransom notes that kidnappers always sent in films. The random letters on it appeared to have been cut out of different publications.

In a voice that shook with tension, Lake said, "What…what does that say?"

"I found this by one of the trees in my back garden. Someone had considerately placed it under the stock of this gun to stop it blowing away." Without even looking at the note, he recited, "Ask Campbell Lake what happened to Carol. I know he did it."

"Liam, listen for a moment. Can't you see this doesn't make any sense? Think, man. Why would anyone leave an anonymous note next to a loaded shotgun? Someone's trying to set me up." Lake started to rise but faltered when Chalmers pointedly leveled the gun at him, and he almost fell back into his seat.

It looked to Colin as if Chalmers was wavering for a moment. After all, wasn't he a lawyer, someone used to presenting cases in a logical and precise way? He must see that Lake had identified a weakness in this whole scenario. However, Chalmers went on, "What did you do to her, you bastard? I always suspected you were involved. You're always sniffing round women, taking advantage. Carol liked you and you…"

He seemed to flounder for a moment, and Colin watched the gun nervously as it waved unsteadily. Sensing weakness, Lake spoke urgently, "I know my behavior around women hasn't always been *politically correct perhaps*, but I swear I would never have harmed a hair on Carol's head. You've worked with me, Liam. You know how easy it is for someone in my position to make enemies. This all smacks of somebody trying to get back at me for something, real or imagined, that I've done to them, and they're using you and…and your grief to do it."

Chalmers gripped the gun more firmly as he continued to point it at Lake. "This is par for the course for you, Lake. Thinking you can use that smooth tongue of yours to talk your way out of anything, but it isn't going to work this time."

Unexpectedly, Lake's wife interjected, "Oh, for heaven's sake, you tiresome little man. If you're certain my husband is responsible for your daughter's disappearance, shoot him and get on with it instead of all of this shilly-shallying. But take him outside to do it. This room contains some very valuable furniture and fittings, and I don't want them ruined."

Colin was both impressed by her composure and shocked at her apparent indifference to her husband's fate. Chalmers, too, appeared stunned by her outburst. Before he could react, the doors swung open to reveal DI Bruce and Sergeant Wilson. Chalmers swung the gun round to confront them and then seemed to change his mind and returned to pointing it at the group at the chaise.

It seemed to Colin that the police officers had taken in the situation at a glance. Bruce spoke first, "I won't pretend to know what's going on here, but I'd be grateful if you would put that gun down immediately, Mr. Chalmers, sir, before this gets out of hand."

Eloise Lake snorted at this, apparently amused by it. The following silence seemed interminable to Colin. In it, his senses were highly charged. He could see the way Chalmers's eyes swiveled between the Lakes and the police. As Lake turned carefully to look at his daughter, Colin could see a bead of sweat running down his chin from his lip. The air smelled of a mixture of sweat and perfume. A clock chimed musically somewhere in the house, and outside the window, he could hear the scrunch of tires on gravel.

Eventually, Bruce broke the silence. "Mr. Chalmers, Liam, please put that down and let's talk about this before someone gets seriously hurt."

Colin saw a current of emotions passing across the lawyer's face: rage, grief, fear, indecision. For a moment, he looked almost deranged, and Colin was afraid he might be capable of discharging the shotgun.

"Ask Lake what he knows about my daughter." Chalmers's voice was almost a whisper.

"Inspector, this is absurd. He's had some kind of anonymous message implicating me in his daughter's disappearance and—"

"Shut up." Colin thought the man's order was accompanied by a visible tightening of his finger on the trigger.

Sergeant Wilson spoke up, "Mr. Chalmers, we have reason to believe that the weapon you are holding is one of two guns that were stolen recently from the locked safe of the gamekeeper here. Can you tell us how you came to be in possession of it?" She sounded official and in control, and Colin sensed Chalmers hesitating.

"I-I found it with the note."

"You found it with the note?" DI Bruce sounded incredulous, and once again, Colin could see a glimmer of doubt on the face of the man wielding the gun. Bruce went on, "You're a logical man, Liam. May I call you Liam? Surely you can see something stinks in all this. Hand over the weapon, and we can discuss this sensibly. I promise you, if there's anything in this anonymous note, we'll investigate it thoroughly."

"Like your thorough investigations into my daughter's disappearance? After all this time, I still don't know. I still don't know where my little girl is." Tears began to run unchecked down his face.

Sergeant Wilson began to limp toward him. The DI said warningly, "Nan," but she continued to move implacably toward Chalmers.

He turned the gun on her and called out in a voice thick with tears, "Don't come any closer. My quarrel's with Lake. I don't want to have to shoot you."

Colin could barely watch as the sergeant moved so close to Chalmers that the barrels of the gun were resting against her chest. "I know you don't, Liam. You don't want to shoot anyone." She reached out her hand gingerly and grasped the gun. Colin had once come across a rabbit that had just been caught in a trap near the Cross. The reaction of Chalmers as he relinquished the gun and slumped to the ground reminded Colin of the tortured sound it emitted and the helpless anguish in its eyes.

DI Bruce moved quickly. He took the gun carefully from his sergeant and examined it before handing it back to her and handcuffing the unresisting man on the ground. Colin couldn't help feeling sorry for Chalmers despite the danger he had presented. He looked as if the last vestiges of his human spirit had been drained from him, leaving an empty shell.

He heard the DI muttering under his breath, "Haven't you displayed enough heroics over the last couple of days?"

He heard her reply more clearly, "I noticed the red dot above the trigger wasn't showing, so I knew he still had the safety on."

Jennifer placed her hand on her father's shoulder, and he grasped it as if she had saved him from drowning. Colin placed a tentative arm around her shoulders and was relieved when he wasn't rebuffed.

Her mother said coolly, "Well, I trust that's enough excitement for one day. I don't know about anyone else, but I could do with a good strong cup of tea." She turned to the woman who still had her back up against the wall as if she was standing on the ledge of a skyscraper building.

"Brenda, perhaps you could..." Then observing the catatonic look on her face, she said, "Or perhaps not." If Colin thought she was demonstrating some sympathy for the poor woman, he was quickly disillusioned when she went on peevishly, "For God's sake, pull yourself together, Brenda, and go and get yourself cleaned up."

Colin thought the woman looked as if someone had slapped her face as she jerked into motion. She appeared to see the pool of water at her feet for the first time and looked shamefaced.

Mrs. Lake, with her usual warm sensitivity, said, "And yes, send Brewer in to clean up your mess before my Persian rug is ruined."

For Colin, the next few minutes passed in a blur of noise and activity as more police arrived in a wave of blue lights and sirens and burst into the room.

After a quickly murmured consultation with DI Bruce, two of them grabbed the handcuffed and broken Chalmers, hauled him unceremoniously to his feet, and led him out. Bruce removed a pair of nitrile gloves from his coat pocket, retrieved the note Chalmers had been clutching which had fallen to the floor, and placed it in an evidence bag. A uniformed officer took the shotgun from Sergeant

Wilson. He handled it with practiced ease as he examined it. "Not loaded, Sarge."

Colin was fascinated by the reactions of the others on overhearing this. The DI and the sergeant exchanged a look that had more of despair in it than relief.

Mrs. Lake looked exasperated and gave her husband a withering stare before muttering, "You mean to tell me all of this...this..." She seemed to be lost for adequate words as she rose imperiously and began to sweep from the room.

DI Bruce called after her, "We'd appreciate it if you would wait, Mrs. Lake. My officers will need to take statements." She continued out of the room but raised a hand behind her in reluctant acknowledgment.

Lake himself seemed to hang his head even further and clutched his daughter's hand more firmly. She looked up as her friends appeared at the entrance to the room, obviously having been alerted by the noises of police activity. Darren and Letty were in the lead with Angus and Beth hanging back tentatively behind them. Inevitably, Darren was the first to voice the fearful curiosity of the others. "What the fuck is happenin', Jen?"

Sergeant Wilson intercepted the group before they could go to their friend. "There's been an incident here, and we'd appreciate it if you all would wait in another room till an officer has spoken to you all."

Letty called out, "Are you all right, Jennifer?"

Jennifer only nodded and attempted to smile reassuringly though she was betrayed by the tears standing out on her eyelashes. It seemed to Colin she had lost something of her aristocratic poise.

Two uniformed officers appeared to round up the young friends, but before they left, a stocky bearded man appeared at the door. He was dressed for the outdoors in a padded body warmer over a twill shirt, heavy-looking corduroy trousers, and scuffed and muddy work boots. He seemed to be shaken when he encountered Beth March, and there was no mistaking the naked hatred in her eyes as she looked at him.

As the group of friends left, he stood on the threshold, looking flustered and out of place.

Sergeant Wilson said, "You must be Mr. March."

That explains Beth's reaction, thought Colin. He wondered how often she encountered her estranged father and they reenacted this same scene. After all, the Law was a notoriously small and insular environment where if someone sneezed in the street, four other people would say, "Bless you."

Jennifer spoke up at his side, "Do you mind if we join our friends, Inspector?"

"No, we'll get round to you in due course. Perhaps you ought to join your wife too, Mr. Lake. There are a couple of things we need to talk to you about."

The MSP jerked up as if someone had thrown cold water over him when he was asleep. "Right, right. What will happen to Liam? Mr. Chalmers?"

When neither the DI nor the Sergeant answered, his daughter gripped his elbow to guide him from the room. Colin followed awkwardly behind, feeling more than ever like the unwelcome guest everyone had forgotten to invite to dinner but who had shown up anyway.

Colin and Jennifer were ushered into another of the many rooms that led off from the vast hall. This one looked to Colin like a particularly well-appointed reference room in a library. The shelves around the walls were lined with old-looking volumes, and there was a Chesterfield and a couple of comfortable-looking leather armchairs in the centre of the room. Yet another impressive-looking antique desk sat in the bay window.

The others looked up expectantly and somewhat guiltily Colin thought when they entered. Angus was sitting in one of the leather chairs with his feet flung over the arm, unheeding of any marks his filthy trainers might make. Darren was fidgeting over at the window, and Letty and Beth were side by side on the settee. The latter came over immediately and put a proprietorial arm on Colin and led him over to the settee, which made him feel unaccountably embarrassed, and he was conscious it left Jennifer marooned on her own little island in the middle of the room.

Letty seemed to sense her isolation and went over to her and wrapped her up in a hug. "God, poor you and Sarky. What an ordeal. I mean we have guns at the farm, but nobody's ever pointed one at me."

This seemed to break the silence, and suddenly everyone seemed to be talking at once, making comments and asking questions that Colin only partly registered, and he only nodded and gave perfunctory responses to them.

Darren had more practical matters on his mind. "Hey, do you think they'd let us grab some bevy? Fuck knows how long we'll be stuck here and anyway, Jen and Sarky have had a shock."

"You mean you came here for a drink, Darren, and you're damned if some lunatic brandishing a gun is going to get in the way," said Letty. She was trying for a light tone, but to Colin, there was something untypically cruel in her assessment of Mr. Chalmers, and though the banter continued, there seemed to be an underlying edge to it.

A current of unease ran through the group. It was as if they were in a courtroom waiting to be called to give evidence, and all were fearful that they might incriminate themselves in some way and that their naked guilt would be exposed to the world.

CHAPTER 27

The Centre of the Web

As soon as the door closed on Campbell Lake, DI Bruce indicated the gun that the PC was still holding. "Is this one of the guns that you reported as stolen, Mr. March?"

As he went over to examine it, the PC drew it back, but Bruce nodded that he should allow March to handle it. "Aye, that's wan o' them. See that deep scratch in the stock? Where's the ither yin?"

"That has yet to be discovered, sir. Could you tell us again how you came to notice them missing?"

"I aye keep them under lock and key in the gun safe here at the Big Hoose. Mr. Lake lets me use a room here in the basement for a' my stuff. It's kept locked as well, and of course, the security at the Big Hoose fulfills a' the demands of the license. We're havin' bother wi' rabbits the now on the estate, so I went to fetch a gun. I was surprised the room was unlocked, and then I saw the safe lyin' open as well and two of the guns gone."

"Who else has keys to the safe?" Nan interjected.

"Just me," March replied, rather too quickly, Nan thought.

"Where are they?"

March reached into the pocket of his body warmer and produced a set of keys.

"And you're sure there are no other copies?"

"Aye, it's a strict condition of the licenses that I ken where a' the keys are at all times."

His hesitation and the fact that his eyes slid away from hers alerted Nan to the probability that he was lying as was the fact that he quickly changed the subject. "How did that man come to hae it? Was it him that stole it?"

"He says he found it in his garden, Mr. March."

March scoffed, "Huh, a likely story."

"Could you go with Constable?"

"Dalglish, sir."

"Constable Dalglish, could you take Mr. March to the room where the gun safe is kept and get his statement? And call in forensics to dust the room for fingerprints. Oh, and then you'd better get that down to the station."

When the two men had left, Nan said, "If there isn't another set of keys for that gun safe that our friend there has *mislaid*, I'll eat my warrant card."

"You could understand why he'd be cagey about something like that. He'd risk losing his gun license and probably, by extension, his job."

Nan sighed. "I'm beginning to think there's a web of lies around this whole investigation, and somebody is deliberately weaving it."

The DI seemed to be voicing his frustration aloud when he said, "Why would someone steal a gun and plant it with a note in the Chalmerses' garden? It doesn't make any sense unless that same person is convinced that Lake really is responsible for the disappearance of Carol Chalmers and was using her father to take revenge."

"I can't help feeling whoever is pulling his strings is trying to pull ours too. How many blind cul-de-sacs has this investigation led us down?"

"And you think someone is deliberately leading us down them?"

"It's as if we no sooner start to draw lines and make connections, then somebody comes along behind us and drags a dirty eraser over them so they're obscured."

The DI began to pace back and forward between the door and the desk. "Okay, let's set aside the fire at McKissock's garage and the attacks there along with the threats to Len Sark. I'm convinced they're all part of this money-laundering case and a distraction to the murder inquiries. That brings us to the people we keep coming back to and circling around."

"And they're all in this house as we speak."

"Time to have another pass at them. And leave Angus McKissock till last. I want him to stew a bit longer. One way or another, I think he's in this up to his neck."

*****

They brought Jennifer Lake in first, followed by Colin Sark. They were still shaken clearly by their encounter with Liam Chalmers and were unable to add much to what Nan and Bruce had garnered already about the incident though Jennifer had recovered sufficiently, Nan noticed, to run a brush through her hair and apply fresh lipstick. Colin kept glancing at her in a way that told Nan that he had fallen under her spell as much as her other admirers.

Mr. and Mrs. Lake were next. He was carrying a glass of what looked like a hefty measure of whiskey or brandy that swilled around as his hand shook. Eloise Lake looked as if she had just come back from a bracing walk in the grounds, and her monosyllabic responses to their questions made it quite clear that she couldn't wait to have the police gone from her house. She gave her husband disapproving looks every time he raised the glass to his lips.

If he had looked scared to death before, DI Bruce's request that he come down to the station later on another urgent matter drained even more of the color from his face.

When they had left, Bruce said, "Okay, let's wheel in the lot that were in the basement though apart from McKissock, I don't see what more they can add."

Nan said, "I'm not so sure. I can't help feeling that the relationships within that group might hold the key to all this."

"Fair enough. You can pursue that when the opportunity presents itself."

Beth March seemed taciturn and laconic and only became more animated when the DI asked her what she knew about her father's arrangements for his guns and if she knew where he kept the keys to the gun safe. Her eyes flashed angrily as she said, "Me and Mum have had nothin' to do with that bastard since he walked out on us, and even when he was around, he never told us much about his work. Frankly, I wish he had been sacked. If he showed such disregard for his family, how much commitment did he have for his job! Maybe they'll get rid of him now since he's been so careless."

Nan found this rather illogical but could understand the girl's feelings about her father were still raw, so changing the subject, she asked how relations were between her and Angus since her earlier suspicions.

"I've been a bit cool with him to be honest. I feel a bit guilty because of the fire and everythin', but I just cannae bring myself to trust him."

Darren Boyd simply confirmed that he had been with the others in the basement when they heard the commotion upstairs. Nan asked him if he had noticed any recent tensions in the group. "Beth's been a bit off with Angus lately, and when I try to ask her about it, she just clams up. Angus seems a bit preoccupied as well as if he's carryin' a big weight aboot wi' him."

They were interrupted by Beth March knocking on the door and poking her head round. "Sorry to barge in, Officers, but would it be okay for me to go home? Colin's agreed to walk back wi' me."

Nan thought that must be a wrench for the young man to tear himself away from Jennifer Lake.

The DI nodded. "All right, but we'll probably need to talk to you later."

Darren chipped in, "I'd give you a lift, Beth, but I've had a couple of beers. Was goin' to ask Jen if her old man would let me leave my car here."

As he left, Letty Vance was shown in. She, too, had known nothing about the events taking place upstairs till they heard the arrival of the police. Nan said, "You seem to be a bit on edge, Letty."

"Do you wonder after everything that's happened in the Law lately? The murder, the attacks, what happened at the séance, the fire. Now somebody threatening folk wi' a gun. It creeps me out. I think

I've never stopped being spooked since that night walkin' home from the Cross."

"Have you had any more thoughts about who you thought might have been following you?"

"No, but after what happened to Janine, I think I was right to be scared."

Bruce nodded sympathetically. "You and the others have been friends for a while. If you don't mind me saying, you all seem so different."

"You mean I'm the daughter of a pig farmer and Jen's part of the local gentry."

The vehemence of her response suggested to Nan that they had hit a nerve, so she attempted to placate her. "We don't just mean your backgrounds, Letty. You all seem very different characters."

Letty's face was flushed as if she was aware she had overreacted. "We all seemed to get on in school, and it's just gone on from there. We've stuck together even though I'm sure we get on each other's nerves at times, more so recently."

"Why's that?"

"Just…just everybody's reactions to what's happened. To Darren, everything's a joke, and Jennifer seems to float above it all. And that stupid séance was her idea. Angus just seems to rub Beth up the wrong way. They had a right row the night they were both attacked."

Both Nan's and Bruce's ears pricked up at this. The latter asked, "Do you know what it was about?"

"I don't know what started it, but when we were outside the pub, I heard her calling him a perverted creep, and he called her…"

Nan said, "Go on."

"He called her a fucking frigid closet lesbian."

"Why would he say that?"

Letty shrugged. "They had a bit of a thing going years ago, and it petered out. They were off with one another for a while after that till everything settled down again. Also…"

There was a pregnant pause while Letty looked down into her lap. Nan sensed the DI's tension. Neither of them wanted to challenge her hesitancy in case she shut down.

"The thing is, you know when you're young and you're not sure about *stuff*, you tend to experiment a bit." She was silent once more.

Nan ventured, "Sexually you mean?"

Letty's face was ablaze as she said in a voice so quiet they had to lean in to hear her, "Me and Beth had one of these *experiments*. It never went that far, and I think we were both a bit sheepish afterward. We never really talk about it now."

Nan immediately felt sorry for the girl and rose and went to her. "Thank you for being so candid, Letty. You have nothing to be ashamed about."

"The thing is, I'm not, but I suspect Beth is. She's really sensitive about what people think about her."

After Nan had shown her out, Bruce said, "You might be right about the relationships in that group. Plenty of underlying tension there. Do you think Letty might have been responsible for the attacks on Beth and Angus?"

"You mean she leapt to the defense of the girl she had a crush on that night and attacked Angus? Then what? Went after Beth and was rejected, so she attacked her and stole her underwear?"

"Stanger things have happened."

"If Beth knew her attacker, why didn't she say anything?"

The DI said, "Shame. Loyalty?"

"I just don't see it, sir. But something about this is nagging me."

"Let's wheel Angus McKissock in and get his take on all this."

The young mechanic was twitchy and seemed to want to squeeze himself into as small a place as possible when they asked him to sit down. He was immediately on the offensive. "I telt you I didnae want to speak to you again without my lawyer bein' present."

"Come on, Angus, you've been watching too many crime shows. We're just questioning you with the others about tonight. It's routine."

"So are you sayin' I'm no' a murder suspect anymore?" When neither Nan nor Bruce replied, he said, "Thought as much."

Nan tried to be conciliatory. "Listen, Angus, we just want to know what you heard tonight."

After a surly silence, he at last told them he hadn't heard much till the arrival of the police, which tied in with the statements of the others.

Bruce interjected, "The night you were both attacked, did you have a row with Beth March?"

Nan was fearful that the boldness of the DI's question might have the effect of pushing Angus back into his hostile shell, but instead he said, "Who told you that?" Then realization seemed to dawn. "Letty, she has a habit of sneakin' around in the background, listenin' to conversations she shouldnae."

Bruce pressed on, "But this wasn't a conversation, was it, Angus? It was a heated argument, and straight after it, she was attacked."

"Have you lot forgotten I was attacked as well?"

Nan asked as gently as she could, "Why did you call her a lesbian?"

His eyes flitted around the room as if he was looking for an escape route. "Because…because, look, I was just angry and lookin' for any insult that might hit home."

"But why that specifically?"

After a long pause, during which Nan thought she had lost him, he replied, "Typical male ego bullshit. Beth and me, we got together a few year ago, and it didnae work out, particularly when it came to *the sex stuff*."

Nan waited, hoping that Bruce wouldn't push him. She could sense Angus wanted to explain.

"You ken when a lassie doesnae really fancy a guy, you put it down to the fact she must be a lesbian. Stupid fuckin' male pride or face savin' or whatever."

"And there was nothing more to it than that?" Nan prompted.

"I thought once I saw…Beth and Letty havin' this intense like conversation outside the Cross Inn. Their heads were thegither, and they were…"

"Go on."

"I thought they were holdin' hands. Look, she called me some things that night an' all."

Nan and Bruce exchanged glances. She could tell they were both eager to bring up the insults that Beth had hurled at him that night but reluctant to do so in case he retreated behind a wall of silence and threats to bring in a solicitor.

At last, Nan said, "Angus, remember, I asked you in the hospital if there was anyone else who knew about *the collection* in your bedroom?"

For a moment, he looked at her with such desperate pleading that she felt she had overstepped the mark, and she suddenly felt sorry for him. He looked as vulnerable as if she had asked him to undress in front of her.

He mumbled, "I know how this must look, and a'right, maybe I am a pathetic pervert. But that doesnae mean I attack lassies, and I could never kill anybody. And whatever's goin' doon wi' my dad I ken nothin' about it."

Bruce intervened cautiously. "Sergeant Wilson asked you a simple question, Angus. Did anyone else know?"

Again, the young man looked hunted, and Nan could see he might be contemplating bolting from the room. She thought fleetingly and absurdly he must resemble one of the rabbits that were apparently plaguing the Big Hoose's estate that March had sought out his shotguns to cull.

All at once, the electric tension seemed to drain from his body as though someone had pulled a plug. He shrank back in dejection and defeat. "Darren. I told him one night when I was drunk and he was stoned."

Nan and Bruce studiously avoided looking at one another. "How did he react?" Nan ventured.

Angus laughed mirthlessly. "It's Darren. How do you think he reacted? Treated the whole thing like a big joke. Called me a dirty wanker. Then he asked if he could see them 'cause he'd maybe recognize them if they belonged to one of the local lassies he'd shagged. To tell the truth, I was terrified he'd tell the others, but he never mentioned it again. As I say, he was pretty stoned that night, so maybe he didnae remember it."

"And he never tried to use it against you? Blackmail you with it perhaps?" Angus looked aghast at Bruce as if he had just suggested his friend was responsible for all the criminal activity in the Law.

"Darren? You have to be kiddin' me. He might be a bit dodgy at times, but he'd never do in a mate."

Nan imagined Bruce was thinking the same thing as her—that this was yet another dead end—but as Angus rose to go, she exclaimed, "And you're certain he never told anyone else and that nobody else knew?"

He froze for a moment, glanced at the door, and sat back down. "I'm no' sure of this, but I think Beth March might have known."

This time, Nan and Bruce scarcely attempted to disguise their interest and surprise. "Beth March knew?"

"I'm no' sure. But a while ago, she came up to my bedroom a couple of times when I thought there was a chance we might *you know*, and one time, I left her sittin' on the bed while I went to the toilet. When I came back, she was standin' over by the chest of drawers, lookin' kind of guilty as if I had caught her snoopin' through my stuff. Then she said she had to get back for her mum and disappeared as if her arse was on fire. When she left, I noticed the drawers werenae shut properly and a couple of bits of...of underwear were shut in one of them."

Nan crossed to him impatiently. "Did she mention anything afterward?"

"No, but then no' long after, she said the two of us werenae workin' and we needed to move on."

"And you think that was the reason?"

"Who knows? Maybe she was disgusted. Maybe she felt guilty for sneakin' around in my room. But honestly, I think she just wasnae that interested in guys."

"All right, Angus, you can go. For now."

His relief was palpable as he rose hurriedly, but at the door, he turned and said, "I havenae dropped Darren and Beth in anythin', have I? Only, as I said, I'm convinced Darren didnae remember me tellin' him about my...about me. And I might have been mistaken about Beth."

Nan decided he needed some reassurance. "The truth never harmed anyone, Angus." Even as she spoke, she realized how wrong this platitude was. If everyone told the unvarnished truth, they might do a great deal of damage to people around them; and if they told the truth about themselves, they might well find that they were standing naked and shivering in the cold blast of the derision and contempt of others. Wasn't it fear of the repercussions of the truth that had prevented her from coming out to her parents?

"What are you thinking, Nan?" DI Bruce's words shook her out of her introspection.

"I still don't like Darren for any of this."

"Because he comes across as a harmless joker, or is it feminine instinct?"

Nan bit back an angry retort. The DI was under pressure, and he wouldn't usually attempt to undermine her judgment or indeed be guilty of such casual sexism.

Bruce must have sensed her resentment because he held up an apologetic hand. "What about the March girl?"

"We've always assumed the murder of Janine Gunning must have been the work of a man because of the way it was perpetrated. But what if it wasn't? What if we shift perspective for a minute? Here's a young woman who's at great pains to hide her true self from her friends. Is good at it even. But what's she like when the mask slips? You saw how she looked at her father. That was pure hatred and malevolence."

"Hang on a minute, Nan. He left her and her mother in the lurch. What do you expect?"

"Granted. But I'm trying to claw my way through this web to get to the spider at the centre of it. Whoever it is, they're capable of spinning lots of webs, of deception and duplicity on a big scale."

"And you think that might be Beth March?"

"She keeps coming up. And it's not just feminine instinct." She cut off his apology and went on, "As you said yourself, she doesn't take kindly to any kind of rejection. The incident tonight was linked to her, if indirectly. It's possible that her father did have another set of keys to the gun safe that he's loath to admit he may have mislaid.

Who else might have had access to his keys in the past? It would be a neat way to shift suspicion onto Campbell Lake. Lead us down another blind alley. She no doubt resented the fact that Lake had kept her father on after his betrayal of her and her mother. Maybe she thought she'd kill two birds with one stone by making sure March lost his job."

Nan noticed Bruce's skeptical look. She knew that by airing her tentative suspicions before him like this, he thought she probably was clutching at gossamer-thin strands that were barely there.

"You make her sound like some kind of psychopath."

"Yes." Unperturbed, she pressed on, "How come Angus McKissock keeps cropping up as a suspect? That story she told about the smell of his aftershave...what if it was just that *a story*? And she conveniently falls down a flight of stairs with Angus close behind. That night he was attacked, maybe it was her striking out at him after he'd called her out on her sexuality. If she did know about his collection of female underwear, she might well have faked her own assault, and the removal of her knickers was another subterfuge to point the finger at him. Another pair for his store. Throughout all of this, there's been obfuscation and confusion. We've been led up so many garden paths we're not even sure where the gardens are any more."

"I've always been working from the premise that there's more than a strong possibility that whoever killed Janine Gunning was also responsible for the disappearance of Carol Chalmers. You think Beth March is capable of that?"

"I don't know. And that's just it. How much do we actually know about her? I suspect that all through her life, she's flown below the radar. She's been the quiet, mousy one in the corner. We know she may be capable of subterfuge. Going out with Angus McKissock, keeping quiet about her relationship with Letty Vance, all to disguise her real sexuality."

"Maybe she's not sure about it herself, and it's a huge leap from there to carrying out a brutal murder."

The cold water of the DI's words threatened to extinguish Nan's speculations, but she continued with more confidence than she felt. "Maybe rejection is the key after all. Rejected by her own father.

Feeling rejected by friends like Angus and Letty. Scared of rejection by her other friends—the whole small-minded community of the Law perhaps if they found out what she saw as her guilty secret. What if she had turned her attentions to Carol in the past or Janine? How would she have reacted if they had rejected her too? And the one strong foundation of her life, her mother, is crumbling daily before her eyes as her illness takes its toll."

"A lot of perhaps and maybes, there but okay, let's get her back in and see if we can unsettle her enough to get a glimpse of the real Beth."

*****

When they went out into the hall, it was empty. Jennifer appeared from upstairs heading for the basement, conveying what looked like a tray of snacks. "Sorry, Officers, but all this excitement has made me ravenous. If I had your jobs, I'd be the size of a house probably."

"We were looking for Beth March, Jennifer."

"Oh, she left with Clipper about ten minutes ago. Tried to persuade them to stay, but she wasn't having any of it. She was behaving a bit weirdly."

Nan asked, "In what way?"

"Really jumpy and distracted. I got the impression that Clipper would have liked to stay, but when he suggested to her that if they stayed, it might take their minds off things, she looked at him as if she wanted to kill him."

CHAPTER 28

Nosy Bastard 2

B eth stamped off down the drive of the Big Hoose so quickly that Colin had to hurry to catch up with her. "Beth, sorry if I was being a bit insensitive back there. What with your dad showing up like that and everything, probably the last thing you felt like doing was socializing with the others."

She slowed down and muttered, "Sorry to drag you away."

Colin couldn't decide if this was a genuine apology or a sarcastic reproach. They walked on together in silence. She seemed skittish, and her eyes kept drifting toward the heavily wooded areas surrounding them. At last, Colin said, "Look, I get it that you've been through a lot in the past while, but try not to let it get to you. God knows we've all got our problems jut now. I'm scared my dad is going to be in trouble with the police. We might lose the inn."

She snapped, "And that's more important than murder and assault and arson and all the other shit that's been happening here."

Colin was stung. "No, of course not, but..." She quickened her pace again. "Listen, Beth, the police will get to the bottom of this eventually. They always do. In the meantime—"

She stopped abruptly. "Sorry, I forgot your admiration for the boys in blue. You're keen to join them, aren't you?"

"Who told you that?"

She ignored him. "You've got some of the right attributes, an inquiring mind. I've noticed the way you hang around on the periphery, eavesdropping on conversations. Always on the outside looking in, eh, Colin?"

He was angry suddenly. "And what about you? Do you think you fit in here? You've always been a bit, well, odd. Even more so lately, I've noticed."

She stopped abruptly, her face reddening. "You think I want to fit in here, in this stinking town with its pathetic citizens sniffing round each other's arseholes like dogs. Every one of them reeks of failure and corruption. Most of them will never climb higher than their poor downtrodden women's mounts of Venus."

"They're not all like that. What about your friends?"

"They're no better. Darren, permanently half stoned, a bottom-feeder on the drugs scene. Angus with his filthy fingernails and no ambition. Letty will live her life among the pigs till her father dies and she takes over the farm. Even Jennifer, beautiful and rich, a bit of a goddess, but let's face it, a spectacular underachiever."

Colin could scarcely conceal his shock at her vitriol. "I've never heard you talking like this before, Beth."

"No, you wouldn't have because nobody ever listens properly to me. I'm trapped here as much as the others. Sometimes I scream at my reflection in the mirror. When I can bring myself to look into it, that is."

"I know you have a hard time with your mother and everything."

She turned on him. Her eyes were like chips of blue marble. "My mother is the only worthwhile thing in my *existence*—I'd hesitate to call it life. And she's not going to be in it for much longer." There was no trace of grief or self-pity in her demeanor. She might as well have been wearing a mask of ice.

Suddenly, she was smiling at him, and her voice was at once challenging and provocative. Her demeanor changed so quickly it was as if a storm cloud had passed over, leaving a sky that was disturbingly attractive yet still threatening. "And is the boy detective with his inquiring mind close to solving the case?"

Her behavior wrong-footed Colin, and he urged, "Let's just get you home, eh? You're not yourself."

233

"I saw it in your face the moment I slipped up earlier. You looked confused. I knew it was just a matter of time before you put two and two together."

"Beth, I haven't the faintest idea what you're talking about."

She began to shift from foot to foot. "Oh, dear, I should have gone before we left the Big Hoose. I'll just go in the bushes here. Wait for me. And no peeking."

She gave him an impudent grin before disappearing behind a row of tall poplars whose branches swayed in a rising wind. For a long moment, that was the only sound that broke the silence. It was dusk under the canopy of trees, and Colin felt uneasy though he couldn't understand why. Certainly, he was perplexed by Beth's odd behavior. He reflected that perhaps the events of the earlier part of the day were catching up with him.

And then for the second time in a few hours, he found himself staring down the barrel of a gun as Beth emerged from the trees carrying what looked to Colin's untrained eye like a long single-barreled rifle. Despite her slight build, the girl held the weapon steadily, sighting down the barrel as if she knew how to handle it.

He could only stammer, "Beth, what's going on?"

Her laugh was high pitched and discordant in the sighing wind. "There you are, Colin. We've solved the mystery of what happened to my father's other gun." Then she laughed again. To Colin, it sounded like the laughter of the madhouse.

"Let's walk on, shall we, Detective?" She indicated the path with a small movement of the rifle. "And don't try anything. It is loaded, and one of the useful things Daddy imparted to his beloved daughter before he fucked off was how to handle guns."

With leaden steps, Colin began to move in front of her down the path, fearing that at any moment, he would hear an explosion and feel the hot agony of a bullet penetrating his spine.

"Faster." He tried to turn to look at her but stumbled. "Keep those inquisitive eyes of yours in front."

"Please, Beth, let's just stop and talk about this sensibly." He hated the way his voice sounded, high pitched and wavering.

"Please, Beth," she mocked. "Don't play the innocent wee boy, Colin. You spotted it when I got careless on the way up here."

"I swear I didn't notice anything."

"When I was talking about Janine's death, the moment I mentioned the stuff written on her body, I knew I'd given too much away. And you knew it too."

"You have to believe me, Beth. I never thought anything about it. You give me too much credit for my observational skills. My dad's always reminding me I'll never be Endeavour Morse." Colin was surprised by his own attempt at humor given his precarious predicament.

"Just shut up and keep walking, Colin." The weariness and deadness in her voice sent a painful chill through his bowels. "I never intended to kill them. You have to believe that."

Colin wanted to stop up his ears. He feared that she might as well be spelling out his death sentence.

"And you're wrong about the police. They couldn't find their arses in the dark with both hands. I've had them stumbling through the woods for years, dangling clues under their noses, pointing them in different directions. They only ever saw me as a victim, not a suspect."

"Beth, you're not well. We need to talk to them. Get you help."

Again, her response was that chilling laugh. "If I'm as mad as you're suggesting, how come I've got away with it for so long? I'd worshipped Carol Chalmers from afar for years at school. When I finally plucked up the courage to approach her, she looked at me as if I was a piece of shit she'd picked up on her immaculately polished shoes."

Colin realized they would soon be at the crossroads. He looked around feverishly, calculating his chances of making it into the woods before she could fire. Despairingly, he realized she was too close behind him. He would never make it.

"I kept her for a while in one of my dad's outhouses. Of course, I soon realized I had to dispose of her. I told you the bastard taught me some useful skills. I've watched him skinning and gutting all sorts of wild life, big and small. And remember, Letty once told us her father's pigs would eat literally anything. She was right about that."

Her girlish giggle made Colin want to drop to his knees and throw up, but somehow he managed to hold himself upright, fearing that if he stopped, he would feel the cold barrel of the rifle pressed against the back of his skull.

"Janine was an accident. Christ, I still don't know how I wasn't caught that night. Taking out the rust heap of a van that Daddy dearest left rotting in our yard. It didn't have any insurance or anything. And I was pissed. Should have been done for drunk driving." She sniggered eerily. "I've no idea what possessed me to come up here. And there was Janine.

"But you must admit, I had the police chasing their tails again. What was the significance of the noose they wondered and they must have spent hours looking at ritualistic markings and symbols. You see, Colin, everyone underestimates me. I'm no bodybuilder, but years of gymnastic training has made me strong. Handy for strangling an overweight tart or rolling down a staircase without hurting yourself."

Colin realized she was talking about the events at the séance. "You wanted everyone to think you were pushed?"

"Poor Angus. He was such an easy fall guy, pardon my pun." Again, that insane giggle. "I admit I lost my rag the night we fell out in the pub. I followed him. I knew as soon as I hit him, I'd have to come up with a cover story, so I faked my own attack. You know, the disgusting little pervert has a collection of girls' panties in his room. I had the brilliant idea that my attacker had stolen my knickers. Another bit of trickery that had the police looking in the wrong direction. I intended at first to try to plant them in Angus's room but realized it was too risky, so I made it look like my attacker had panicked and abandoned the pants. When the police got to know about his little hobby, I knew he would be implicated.

"I planted the note and the gun at the Chalmerses' place. If everything had gone to plan today, that pompous bag of shit Lake would have had his guts blasted all over the antique furnishings and my father would be out on his ear, would even be up on charges for negligence. The stupid prick 'mislaid' his other set of keys months ago."

Despite his abject terror, Colin found himself saying angrily, "And what about poor Carol's father? Hadn't you done him enough damage?"

"Oh, he'd have got off, diminished responsibility, the effects of grief and all that."

They had now reached the crossroads, and the Dule tree stood menacingly in their path like a harbinger of death. "How can you be so fucking callous?"

"I had to learn how. Up against the tree."

Colin hesitated, but she pushed the gun barrel hard into his chest. He was forced to back off till he felt the trunk of the tree at his back.

"What are you going to do, Beth?"

"I'm not going to do anything. You're going to end it all yourself. Appropriate place for it, don't you think? Lots of deaths here over the years, including some suicides."

Colin could feel a tide of panic rising in his chest. He had to keep talking, try to make her see the insanity of the situation. "Think, Beth. Why would I do that? It doesn't make any sense."

"They'll find a note in your room, just like the one they found in the garden of the Chalmers. Only I won't use the cutout letters, of course. I'll print it on some of the inn's stationery. I'll even use one of their pens. It will spell out your confession to the murders and attacks. How you just couldn't live with the guilt anymore."

"They'll never believe it."

"It will keep them guessing for a while though. You have to admit it's plausible. A young barman, a bit of an outsider, bit of a voyeur. Goes a bit too far with a couple of girls he fancies. Shuts them up. I'm surprised the police didn't take more interest in you before. Anyway, who knows what goes through a deranged mind?"

Despite the frenzied beating of his heart and his increasingly strangled breathing, Colin could barely prevent himself from pointing out the ironic truth of that.

"Now sit."

Colin slid down tentatively to a sitting position, his back still against the tree. He couldn't take his eyes off the black hole of the gun barrel.

"Don't worry, Colin. It'll be quick. And you'll be found pretty quickly too, I imagine. They might even hear the shot up at the Big Hoose. Open wide." She pushed the gun toward his face.

"Please, Beth, don't do this." Again Colin was ashamed of the pathetic pleading note in his voice. "They'll never believe I did this."

"They'll find you here. Your arms are just long enough to prop up the gun and pull the trigger. Open your mouth."

"No."

"It'll be easier than having me putting it under your chin. More efficient."

"Please, Beth, no." As he spoke, she suddenly thrust the barrel of the gun into his mouth. He felt it grating against his teeth and could taste metal and oil. It made him want to gag.

Beth's voice seemed to come from far away. "A little suicide, the case is closed, and I'm in the clear."

So this was it. All his dreams and all his plans for the future ended here. He'd join the lost souls of Carol and Janine. All the others perhaps who had been executed here, his name just as reviled as theirs had been once. He closed his eyes, which were streaming with tears.

A man's voice echoed from the edge of the trees. "Put the gun down, Beth."

Colin felt two of his front teeth chipping as the barrel was violently and painfully removed from his mouth. When he opened his eyes, he saw the figure of DI Bruce standing a few yards away.

Beth had swung the rifle round to point at him. "You don't understand, Officer, he tried to attack me. He's the one you want. I was just keeping him here till you got here."

"Put the gun down. It's over. I heard enough."

Though Beth continued to hold the gun steady, her eyes flickered uncertainly, and then her shoulders slumped. The detective inspector moved slowly toward her. She snapped back to attention and aimed the gun at him. "Stay where you are."

"It's all over, Beth."

She looked at the gun in her hand, then gazed up at the branches of the tree as if they held the solution to her predicament. For a moment, she looked like a vulnerable and lost little girl, and Colin almost felt sorry for her.

She whispered, "Over. Yes." Awkwardly, she swung the gun round till the barrel was under her chin.

"Don't, Beth. There's been enough death." Colin was surprised that the words had come from his bruised mouth. She was struggling clearly to reach the trigger, but her arms were too short.

Suddenly, a body appeared out of nowhere and cannoned into her. Beth landed on the ground with a sickening thud, and the gun flew out of her grasp. Before she could recover her breath, Sergeant Wilson was on top of her, removing handcuffs from her belt. DI Bruce moved quickly to secure the gun and help his junior officer subdue the wriggling girl.

Both the women's skirts had ridden up over their thighs, and Colin reflected ruefully that in another place and at another time, he might have enjoyed the sight, but he was so sickened and chastened by his ordeal that he thought he might never take an interest in the female sex again.

CHAPTER 29

Loose Ends and Loose Leaves

I t was just Nan's luck that the first person she met as she entered the station the next day was Gerry Eastman. "Well, well, if it's no' the heroine of the hour. Hear you've solved the case and faced down two gun-wielding nutters in the process."

She tried to ignore him, but he continued to walk along beside her. She could scarcely evade him by speeding up since every step sent flames of pain up her leg. Her arm ached more than ever too. She had jarred something when she tackled Beth March, and even the strong painkillers she had swallowed since had failed to give her relief.

"Wouldnae be surprised if you got some kind o' commendation oot o' this. I'm anglin' for one myself after my life-saving exploits in the line o' duty."

Despite the fact that the man's demeanor set her teeth on edge, she mumbled grudgingly, "You deserve one, Gerry."

"Thanks, doll. Seriously though, you must have a sphincter like a steel trap. We havenae been idle here by the way. We've got our arsonist."

Nan stopped abruptly, causing a PC who was coming up behind them carrying a pile of files to swerve round them. "The Tweedie gang?"

"Kind of. Ken, the young Eastern European mechanic McKissock had no' long taken on? Well, he turns out to be one Havel Slavek."

For a moment, Nan failed to recognize the name, and then she remembered the connection to the two heavies that had visited Sark and McKissock.

Eastman noticed her dawning recognition. "That's correct. Turns out he's a cousin of thug number two, Mr. Ten Counts, a.k.a. Benny Slavek, that has the gym. Course he claims he doesnae know who paid him to cosh young McKissock and torch the garage."

"So unless he talks, we've nothin to link it to the Tweedies?"

"And he'll no' talk. Cannae say I blame him. If I was in his shoes, I'd prefer my balls to be danglin' between my legs, too, rather than wearin' them as a pair of earrings."

Nan felt a wave of weariness suddenly. Finding out the truth ought to be satisfying, to give some sort of closure. But she felt weighed down by the evil that was still out there and that hung around these cases like fetid gas.

She forced herself to walk on with Eastman still chattering animatedly by her side. "Expect we'll be movin' out once the DCI's done the necessary and made sure she gets her face all over the news, claiming the credit. Cannae say I'll be sorry to leave this shithole town with all its weirdo cunts. Then I think I'll ask to be transferred back west. It'll be back to the fresh green pastures of my old beat with its crack addled whoors, child molesters, and guys who'll chib one another for wearin' the wrong football colors. Elysian Fields, indeed."

Nan smiled painfully. She was surprised that the garrulous and potty-mouthed sergeant knew the classical reference. He seemed to read her mind.

"Aye, classical education, hen. Did a bit of Greek and Latin mainly to avoid fucking woodwork and metalwork and techy drawing at which I knew I'd be shite."

When they reached the office, Nan tried to brush off the congratulations of the team with a modest smile. DI Bruce rose from his desk to greet her. "Christ, you look terrible. You should have called in sick."

"Thanks, boss. Makes me feel so much better. I couldn't not be here. Get anything more from Beth March?"

"She's clammed up. Just sits there staring into space. She's so quiet and still it's almost as if she's catatonic. Refuses to eat or drink anything. Carpenter's ordered a psychiatric evaluation."

"So where do we go from there?"

"We have enough to charge her for the two murders given Colin Sark's statement and what we heard at the crossroads."

"I can hardly believe it. A young girl like that. Caring for a sick mother. She wouldn't have been on my prime list of suspects."

"Can't judge a book by its cover and other clichés like that."

Nan was arrested by the sudden vision of the ailing woman she'd met at the March house, huddled fearfully in her wheelchair. "God, what'll happen to her poor mother?"

Bruce unexpectedly reached out and touched her shoulder. He said gently, "Come on. The DCI's got a briefing in five."

The incident room was packed and noisy with the excitement that accompanies the sense of a case nearing its conclusion. Nan smiled along with her colleagues, but inside, she felt only a wintry bleakness in her spirit.

In contrast to how she felt, it seemed as if DCI Carpenter was glowing with triumph. She was immaculately turned out in a perfectly tailored black suit and matching patent pumps. Her skin looked perfect, and her hair was even more sleek than usual. When the room quietened down, she said, "First of all, a huge well done to everyone involved in bringing in the perpetrator of these horrible crimes."

There was some muted applause. The experienced officers in the room knew there was still a way to go before justice was served.

"Not only have we solved a year's old disappearance, but we now have firm evidence against the murderer of Janine Gunning. On top of that, we've uncovered a major money-laundering operation taking place here in the Law. Arrest warrants for a number of individuals have been issued in connection with this. They include a local property developer and the owners of the garage and the inn." She paused for dramatic effect before adding, "One of the warrants issued was for the MSP for the constituency."

There were murmurs from some of the officers present. Nan couldn't decide whether they were voicing their shock or their satisfaction.

Eastman raised his hand. "Any chance of linking this to those bastards, the Tweedies? Excuse my language, ma'am."

"I have every confidence that we will follow the strings back to the main puppeteers and also to their part in the arson attack on the garage."

As the meeting broke up, Nan sensed the change in mood among the DCI's audience. Hardened police officers knew from bitter experience that Carpenter's confidence undoubtedly was misplaced and cynically recognized that really bad people continued to go about their business untroubled by thoughts of a heavy hand falling on their shoulder in the street or of their door being battered down in the early hours of the morning.

She hovered at her desk uncertainly. Bruce came over. He seemed even more disconsolate than she did. "I know we did our job, Nan, but it doesn't give me any satisfaction."

"Nor me," she admitted.

"I remember we studied *Macbeth* at school. There's a line in it where he says, 'We have scotch'd the snake not killed it.'"

"But it's not just the thought that those evil bastards across the river are still able to carry on their operations, untouched by us. We've been the equivalent of a storm to this town, leaving terrible destruction and damage in our wake. I can't help thinking of how Beth's mother is feeling now or Colin Sark and Angus McKissock, Jennifer Lake and her family."

She realized she had left out the bereaved families of the murder victims deliberately. His anguish was written on his face, and she had no desire to exacerbate it.

But he swallowed painfully and said, "We've brought no consolation to Janine's and Carol's families either if it comes to it. I mean, how I am I going to tell Carol's father and mother how their daughter's body was disposed of? When Colin Sark gave us the details, I had to rush to the toilet. I was so sick I thought I'd bring up my spleen." He smiled ruefully, but Nan thought his eyes were moist. "The tough old police detective, eh?"

"You've lived with the case for a long time, sir."

"And now I think I'll always have to live with it." He gazed out of the window at the rain clouds that seemed to have sat over the Law for days. "Anyway, enough doom and gloom. Why don't you take yourself off home? There's nothing to be done till the professionals have spoken to her. Even then, I'm not sure I want to hear how the petty slights and disappointments, the opinions of others, the way she felt victimized, real or imagined, brought her to such acts of, well, wickedness."

Just at that moment, Nan's mobile pinged with a message. It was from Sol. Despite her despondency, she felt a jolt of expectation. "Excuse me, sir, I'd better answer this."

"See you later in the pub? Not the Cross Inn, obviously, but—"

"Yes, sir, I'd like that."

The message from Sol read:

> Got some time today? Have something to
> show you. I'm free around lunchtime.

As she left the building, she messaged Sol that she would come to her office. She met Colin Sark and Jennifer Lake on their way in. She had no wish to engage with them to find out if they were there for further questioning about the murders or if they were there in connection with their fathers.

Nevertheless, she went over and said how sorry she was about the way things had turned out. She added, "And if you're still thinking about a police career and you need a reference, Colin, I'd be happy to provide one. You showed a lot of guts yesterday."

He shuffled his feet and looked embarrassed before muttering, "Thank you."

She was quite gratified by the way Jennifer gave him an admiring look and then grasped his hand. Perhaps something good might come out of all this, after all.

*****

A watery sun looked over the university buildings in St Andrews as Nan approached. Sol met her in the foyer. She kissed her on the cheek and took her arm to guide her to her office, oblivious to the curious looks of the reception staff and one or two of the students. "Got a transcript of the last part of the diary. Dr. Grant assured me that once they've been cleaned up—don't ask me how they do that— they'll restore them to the original document."

When they reached her office, Sol said, "Coffee?"

"Thanks. I could do with the caffeine hit."

As Sol operated her complicated-looking machine, she said, "Rough night?"

"You could say that." As she sipped her coffee, Nan filled her in on the events of the previous day, conscious that she was minimizing the danger she had placed herself in. Sol listened without interrupting, her eyes widening at the account of the standoffs with the guns, and she could not restrain herself from gasping in shock at the revelation of Beth March's culpability. When Nan finished, she must have looked as desolate as she felt because Sol came to her, laid her cup on her desk, and embraced her silently.

After a moment when Nan felt how easily she could lose herself in the other woman's comfort, she broke apart and said, "Anyway, you were going to show me the rest of the diary."

Sol opened her desk drawer and took out a couple of typewritten sheets. "Don't know how you'll feel, but to me, there was something more visceral somehow about reading Harriet's account in her own handwriting. It still makes grim reading though."

Nan sat to read the sheets. She knew instantly what Sol meant though the words still wormed their way into her heart.

The last straw come tonight when them men come from the town spittin' fire and smashin' things. Even the devil hisself must have knowed it was all up for him. He had his rifle, and he handed me a pistol. He'd never done nothin' like that before. He must have been desperate. Like he thought I would help him after everythin' he'd done. I put two bullets in his gut. He looked surprised, but he must have seen the naked hate on my face. It took him a while to die. Then they were in the house. I shot one of them in the head, and he went down in the hall, but the other one rushed me and tried to drag me into a room. I'd seen that look too many times in a man's face not to know what he had in his mind but somethin' made me strong that night. I was bigger nor him, and I fought him all the way. He couldn't hold me or get the gun. I shot him in his man parts first, then put a bullet in both his knees.

Maybe if someone finds this and reads it, they think I'm a bad woman, but I wanted them men to suffer just like me and so many of mine done. I hauled the devil's body outside when I heard others come into the house. I put him and a shovel into the old barrow and took him out into the dark away from the house. Took me a while to get him into the ground, but nobody came near, and it was black dark. I sneaked back in the house to get a candle so I could finish the writing of this. I didn't meet nobody though I heard noises out front. Now I'm goin' to bury this too. And then I have a date with that old tree. I'm tired to my bones of this life but at least

I've laid that devil to rest. I knows I done wrong in the eyes of God, no matter what that man and his friends done. No matter about Betty and Clay. No matter about them poor dead girls. I knows there's a darkness in the heart of men but it's in the hearts of women too. I found the darkness in my own heart that for sure. If you found this, try not to judge me too hard. I'll be judged by a higher power anyways.

> May God forgive my sins,
> Harriet Jackson

Nan was startled when she felt Sol's hand on her shoulder. "Penny for them."

"Sorry, it's just her story is so relentlessly bleak."

Sol lowered her head apologetically. "I should have shown you that later, especially after all you've been through."

Nan clutched her hand. "No, you did right to show me it. Her courage and her pain has a resonance across all these years."

"And her strength."

Nan smiled sadly. "Yes, and her strength. And the bit about the darkness in the hearts of men *and* women is only too apt in the circumstances."

"Fortunately, there are strong women like you around to confront it."

"Thanks, Sol, but it doesn't seem to make much difference in the scheme of things."

"Don't sell yourself short, girl. Come on. I'm done for the day, and you could use a drink."

"I have my car and—"

"Leave it at mine."

Nan felt herself coloring under the frankness of Sol's gaze.

When they got outside, the wind had risen and was driving rain across the gray pavements and buildings of the town. Nan raised her face up to it as if it might wash her clean. Sol was holding her arm and must have noticed Nan was leaning heavily on her for support. "Looks like someone needs some more spiritual healing."

As they drove toward Sol's house, Nan noticed the leaden waves of the Forth crashing onto the shore, indifferent to the small lives and deaths of those who watched them over the years.

ABOUT THE AUTHOR

B ruce Adam lives in Fife in Scotland. He was a lecturer in drama and English for many years and continues to have an eclectic involvement in theater—writing plays, performing, directing, and adjudicating drama festivals. *The Dule Tree* is his second novel.

Milton Keynes UK
Ingram Content Group UK Ltd.
UKHW022105120524
442525UK00001B/37